PRAISE FC

"Meserve's narrative has a . . . logue throughout. Kate's relatable qualities of self-reliance with vulnerability drive this gratifying mystery-romance about finding the good guys—and knowing when to recognize them."

—*Publishers Weekly*

"In her debut novel, Meserve writes a . . . solid feel-good romance sparked with mystery."

—*Kirkus Reviews*

"If you are a Nicholas Sparks or Richard Paul Evans fan, I'm betting you will like author Meserve's book *Good Sam.* Uplifting, heart wrenching, and a two-hankie read, this story is a winner."

—Cheryl Stout, Amazon top reviewer and Vine Voice

"This story had everything from suspense to drama. And the heartfelt ending had us smiling for days."

—*First for Women* magazine

PRAISE FOR *PERFECTLY GOOD CRIME*

"A first-rate and undaunted protagonist easily carries this brisk tale. Kate is intuitive and professional, but it's her steadfast compassion that makes her truly remarkable."

—*Kirkus Reviews*

"Dete Meserve delivers a novel that is simultaneously mysterious, fascinating, and inspiring."

—BuzzFeed.com

"A feel-good mystery . . . an enjoyable escape."

—BookLife Prize in Fiction

"Books that are changing the world."

—2016 Living Now Book Award, gold medal in inspirational fiction

"In a story saturated with unexpected twists and shocking motives, Kate Bradley follows clues—and her heart—to discover that some crimes have powerfully good intentions."

—*Sunset* magazine

PRAISE FOR *THE SPACE BETWEEN*

"Chiseled prose gleefully weaves the protagonist through bombshells . . . A labyrinth of plot and character motivations makes for a thoroughly enjoyable novel."

—*Kirkus Reviews*

"*The Space Between* is a fast-paced novel that combines the best elements of suspense and romance. In this story of a broken marriage, Dete Meserve uses the mysteries of the universe to keep you on the edge of your seat as she weaves a tale that winds its way through the past and present to bring about a truly satisfying conclusion. Highly recommended."

—*USA Today* bestselling author Bette Lee Crosby

"From tragedy to triumph, Dete Meserve's new novel took me on a roller-coaster ride I'll not soon forget. Coupling the mysteries of the night sky with an unthinkable domestic situation, this tale is stunning and unlike any I've read. *The Space Between* is a must must must read!"

—Heather Burch, bestselling author of *In the Light of the Garden*

"As captivating and complex as the night skies that feature in *The Space Between*, this is a thrilling read. A precipitous shift in perceived reality causes everything past and present to be suspect. Meserve skillfully crafts all the elements of a superbly suspenseful page-turner."

—Patricia Sands, bestselling author of the Love in Provence series

"Dete Meserve's *The Space Between* has it all. It is a story written with a knowledge of space, realistic characters you want to root for, romance, and a mystery with a satisfying ending. I predict that after you read the book, you'll gaze at the stars and think of them in a new way."

—Judith Keim, bestselling author of the Fat Fridays Group series

"Woven with the stars, this is an incredible story of love, betrayal, and the infinite power of hope. Suspenseful to almost the last page; I couldn't put it down."

—Andrea Hurst, author of *Always with You*

"Dete Meserve's *The Space Between* hits all of the sweet spots: a smart and engaging female lead, an intriguing mystery, and elements of danger and suspense sure to keep readers turning pages long past bedtime. If you're a fan of Nicholas Sparks or Kerry Lonsdale, grab this book!"

—Kes Trester, author of *A Dangerous Year*

"With the starry heavens as a backdrop, Meserve spins a fast-paced story about astronomer Sarah Mayfield, as she questions everything she believes to be true in the space between the heartache of her rocky marriage and the mystery surrounding her husband's disappearance. This is Meserve's best work yet, a romance wrapped in suspense that will keep readers guessing until the very end."

—Christine Nolfi, bestselling author of *Sweet Lake* and *The Comfort of Secrets*

PERFECTLY GOOD CRIME

ALSO BY DETE MESERVE

Good Sam

The Space Between

PERFECTLY GOOD CRIME

A KATE BRADLEY MYSTERY

DETE MESERVE

LAKE UNION
PUBLISHING

This is a work of fiction. Names, characters, organizations, places, events, and incidents are either products of the author's imagination or are used fictitiously. Any resemblance to actual persons, living or dead, or actual events is purely coincidental.

Published by Lake Union Publishing, Seattle

www.apub.com

ISBN-13: 9781542003698
ISBN-10: 1542003695

Cover design by Caroline Teagle Johnson

Printed in the United States of America

Dedicated to Good Sams everywhere, who, through actions big and small, bring light and hope into the world

CHAPTER ONE

My heels dug into the muddy ground as I clambered up the hill. Cries for help mingled with the drone of helicopters overhead, filling the early-evening air. I had no idea what I would see at the top of that hill, but I suspected it would give me nightmares for a long time to come.

The sharp smell of burning metal and diesel fuel choked my lungs. I ducked under the yellow police caution tape that stretched across the hill and separated the train tracks above from the sleepy Glendale, California, street below.

"Step back behind the tape," someone shouted at me. Damn. In the dim light, I could see the voice belonged to a Los Angeles County sheriff's deputy, clad in a tan uniform shirt and dark-green trousers.

"I'm with Channel Eleven," I answered calmly, even though I knew it wouldn't get me access. Every other news outlet had been sequestered at the bottom of the hill, where ambulances and fire trucks bathed the scene with red-and-white flashing lights.

"No media allowed up there. It's not safe," he said, shining a flashlight in my face. I motioned for Josh, the cameraman who had been running behind me, to head back down the hill, but I didn't move. This officer was the one thing standing between me and an exclusive report from the scene of one of the biggest train disasters in Los Angeles history.

"Any way you can give me two minutes up there?" I said, steam rising from my mouth in the cool mountain air. "I covered the last Metrolink crash, and we'll—"

"Officer." A paramedic raced up, interrupting me. "It's gridlock by the ambulances. We need help to get through with our stretchers."

The officer started running down the hill with the paramedic. Then he stopped and pointed at me. "Get back behind the tape."

I waited until he disappeared into the inky-blue darkness, and then I darted up the hill. Flames and smoke poured out of the twisted wreckage of the train. There were bodies lying all over the ground, lit by the harsh blue-white light coming from the medevac helicopters overhead. Metal and debris were scattered in chunks along the hilltop as though a giant had ripped the train apart in a rage.

Everywhere I turned, rescue personnel were removing victims from the blazing wreckage. Los Angeles County Fire Department search dogs scoured the train cars for victims. A man in a neck brace was being hoisted up to a hovering helicopter.

A few feet away I spotted a woman's shoe. A spiral notebook. A briefcase.

It was a scene so raw my first instinct was to look away. To give the victims their dignity. But the wreck was massive, and there was nowhere else to look.

"Kate, they want us live in three minutes!" Josh shouted at me as he rushed up the hill.

"I'll be ready," I said calmly, but there was no way I was calm or ready.

A wave of nausea engulfed me. I had covered natural disasters, murders, and tragedy for eight years on TV news, but nothing had prepared me for this level of devastation. I couldn't shake the feeling that I should be doing something to help—anything—rather than preparing for a news report.

Running out of a curtain of smoke, a group of paramedics carried a small girl on a stretcher down the hill. Through the haze I saw Eric standing with a group of other firefighters, all in yellow turnout gear as they prepared to ascend a ladder to get inside the toppled train car.

"Eric," I called out to him, but my voice was drowned out by the deafening noise around me. Still, he glanced in my direction, and I ran toward him.

His face was smudged with dirt and sweat. "You shouldn't be here," he said, his voice raspy with emotion. "The fire is out of control. There are dead bodies on top of survivors. This is something you don't want to see."

I wanted to assure him I was okay, so I reached out to touch his free hand. But my hand only grazed his fingertips as he and his team headed up the ladder.

After my exclusive live coverage from the scene, my follow-up report was slated for the opening slot in the all-important eleven o'clock newscast.

Or so I thought.

"We're going to lead with Susan's report," my assignment editor, David Dyal, said in my earpiece. "Then come to your story about ninety seconds into the cast."

I opened my mouth to reply, but no words came out. Susan Andrews covered celebrity news—celebrity crimes, celebrity trials. Celebrity meltdowns. What story could she possibly have that would trump exclusive on-the-scene coverage of one of the most devastating train accidents in LA history?

"What's she covering?" I asked.

"Burglary at an estate in Bel Air."

There was no way a burglary could go ahead of a train disaster in the news lineup. In the city of LA, over fifty burglaries took place every day—more than eighteen thousand per year—and few ever made the TV news. Unlike robberies, which involved some kind of violence or threat during the theft, burglaries didn't play well on TV. You couldn't show the stuff that had been stolen, and frankly, burglary stories were boring to viewers unless they knew the victim. Which had to mean that a celebrity was involved.

"Which celebrity?" I asked.

"No one famous. But the thieves stole over two million dollars in cash and luxury goods."

A two-million-dollar heist. I didn't like being second to any story that entertainment reporter Susan Andrews covered, and certainly not second to a burglary story. But a two-million-dollar heist was unheard of, even in Los Angeles, and I was intrigued. For a microsecond. "I cross police lines and put my own safety at risk to cover the biggest train disaster in the city's history, and you're telling me—"

"I'm telling you we're leading with the burglary story."

~

My assignment editor, David Dyal, was in sugar rehab. His doctor had told him to lose a few pounds, get his cholesterol in check, and lower his blood pressure, so the first thing he quit was his six-a-day habit of Dr Pepper. He replaced it with a juice he made fresh each morning using kale, spinach, and some other dark leafy greens I'd never heard of. The stuff made the lunchroom smell like a compost heap.

Worse, it was making him cranky.

"Not now, Kate," he said when I stepped into his office the next morning. His face was ash white instead of its usual ruddy complexion, and he was typing rapidly on his laptop.

I had hoped for at least a nod of appreciation for last night's exclusive reporting from the train-disaster scene. But given David's aversion to compliments—he thought any form of praise made reporters "soft"—I was more likely to win the lottery.

"I don't understand why we led with the burglary story last night instead of the train disaster. It makes us look like we aren't serious about reporting the important news stories."

"Point registered," he said without looking up from his laptop.

"How can we expect to be number one in the market if we don't lead with the biggest train disaster in LA history?"

"I heard you, Kate."

I didn't move. I knew if I waited there in his doorway long enough, he'd have to look up eventually. One . . . two . . . three . . .

He took off his reading glasses and placed them on his desk. "If it makes you feel better, we were all conflicted about it. But we determined that a two-million-dollar heist of a billionaire's home would attract a bigger lead-in audience than the train derailment."

"People lost their lives in that train wreck. The right thing to do was lead with a story about eight dead and a hundred and fifteen injured, not a fluff story about a billionaire's estate being robbed."

He sighed. "This is the news *business*, Kate. Sometimes doing the right thing isn't the best thing for attracting an audience. You know that."

Even though I didn't like hearing it, he was right. Three months after covering the story about Good Sam, the man who anonymously left $100,000 in cash on doorsteps throughout Los Angeles, I was struggling to find purpose in many of the stories that dominated our newscasts. I'd covered several high-profile stories for the network since then: the Suitcase Murder, about the dead body of a man found stuffed in a suitcase in the Verdugo Wash; the accidental shooting of a former city council member during a chaotic hostage situation in West Hollywood; and the gunman who shot seven students on the campus of LA Valley College. Judging from Channel Eleven's jump from fourth to second in the ratings, those stories were attracting viewers. But even as I covered them, I wondered, Were they really news? What did viewers gain from knowing about these murders and tragedies? Were we simply selling fear and sensationalism?

David rolled up a sleeve of his blue plaid shirt, a sure sign that a lecture was coming. "That's one of your problems, Kate. You think the world is black and white. But there aren't good decisions or bad ones. Good guys or bad guys. That's not the way things work. Most of the time we're muddling around in murky shades of gray."

"*One* of my problems?"

"That, and you're stubborn."

"I'm not stubborn," I said, realizing his mini-analysis of me was distracting me from what I'd come here to do. "I know that if we want to be number one, we should be opening our casts with the train-derailment story."

"Heard you loud and clear, Kate. Now why don't you get back out there and cover that story instead of talking to me about it?"

As I headed back to the newsroom, I knew David was wrong. Maybe his perspective was warped from too many years in the executive chair. But in a reporter's world, things were black and white. The drive-by shooting victim was either dead or alive. Terrorist attacks were bad. Landing a rover on Mars was good.

Back in the reporters' bullpen, I found Josh and our associate producer, Hannah, peering intently at Hannah's computer. "That's got to be a typo," Josh was saying, pointing at a photo on the screen. "That house can't be sixty thousand square feet. They must mean six thousand. Right?"

"Actually, no," Hannah said. "It has a ballroom, three elevators, a paddle tennis court, a closet the size of a boutique store, a guardhouse—"

"One of you shopping for a new home?" I asked.

"Not one like this." Hannah pointed to the screen. "This is the estate that was robbed last night. Château du Soleil in Bel Air. Susan's story."

I frowned. Even Hannah and Josh had fallen under this fluff story's spell.

"It's got a squash court. What the heck is that?" Josh asked.

"It's a racket game you play, and afterward you sit around drinking liqueurs while discussing the S&P 500," Hannah said. She was barely twenty-two years old, but her far-apart blue eyes gave her a kind of other-century look that made her seem much older.

"Damn, what kind of guy lives in those kinds of digs?" Josh asked.

"A Silicon Valley entrepreneur," Hannah said. "The guy spent north of sixty million dollars building his dream château, then got robbed within a year of moving in."

"Okay, story time is over." I pointed at my watch. "Josh, we're replacing Ken and Christopher at the derailment site. Time to get back to reporting on some *real* news."

~

After another fourteen hours reporting from the train-derailment site, I awoke the next morning feeling like I'd been in a desert sandstorm. My eyes were gummed up, and my skin was parched and tight from the smoke-filled air. I'd been so exhausted that I'd forgotten to remove my contacts and had fallen asleep on top of my duvet, still dressed in the navy-blue slacks and tan blouse I'd worn to the scene.

Once the fire was contained, reporters had been allowed within several feet of the train-wreck site. But even hours with unfettered access didn't make the coverage any less dramatic. This one single tragedy shattered dozens of families' lives. I was crushed by the stories of lives lost and the many people who sustained life-altering injuries. Even talking with the lucky survivors, some of whom escaped with little more than a scratch, didn't make the reporting easier.

But this was why I had signed up for the job of covering tragedy, conflict, and disaster on local news. Not because I actually liked those things—I rarely watched them on TV if I wasn't reporting on them—but because I hoped I could be the one to show the silver lining. The helpers, the first responders to the scene, the people who would make the situation better. And for once, this story had plenty of that. Throughout the night, there were many moments of astonishing heroism on display as Eric and the Los Angeles County Fire Department's Urban Search and Rescue team, along with other firefighters, paramedics, and rescuers, worked to free victims from the wreckage.

Josh had not fared so well. Eventually the smell and the bodies became too much for him. At one point, he dumped his camera in the grass and retched into a large trash container.

"How do you do it?" he asked later, gulping from a huge bottle of water. "Do you have some kind of tragedy gene that helps you deal with all this?"

I didn't have an answer. I once worked with a TV news helicopter pilot who had claimed that his abusive childhood had been excellent training for reporting on the chaos of LA riots, earthquakes, and violence. He did his best work under tremendous stress, he said, because that was the environment he grew up in. My childhood was abuse-free and secure, so I couldn't point to anything that had made reporting on tragedy easier for me than for other reporters.

"No tragedy gene," I said. "I only know that if we stay in it and don't quit—no matter how hard it gets—we can show stories that give viewers hope. What we do matters."

I didn't know if my pep talk helped Josh any, but we did manage to labor through several more hours on that windy hilltop. But I hadn't escaped that long night of reporting unscathed. I sat up in bed and looked in the mirror above my dresser. My face was pale with fatigue, my light-brown hair had turned into a frizzy mass, and there were dark, puffy circles beneath my eyes. My clothes reeked of smoke, and I doubted even an expensive dry cleaner could ever get the acrid smell out of them. I frowned at my low-heel pumps, their leather scarred and pitted from the mud and gravel by the train rails.

I was headed to the shower when I heard the doorbell ring. As I opened the door, Eric presented me with a venti-size cup of Starbucks coffee.

"You have a key," I murmured, kissing him.

"I'm still getting used to that."

His sandy-brown hair was damp from a shower, and he had changed from fire gear into jeans and a snug white T-shirt.

"You okay?"

He pulled me close, and I drank in the clean smell of soap. "It was rough, but we finally got everyone out. What we've been through hasn't fully hit me yet. You took a big risk the other night getting so close to the fire."

"That's what we do, right? We both have to get close to the fire to do our jobs."

"Some of us are prepared with state-of-the-art equipment and fire protection," he said, brushing a lock of hair from my face. "While others of us go into the fire wearing heels—"

"They were actually sensible, practical shoes," I countered.

"And holding a microphone." His voice softened. "I was worried about you."

I took a sip of the warm coffee. "I'm getting used to that about you. That worrying thing you do. I was fine. And watching you and your team pulling everyone out of the wreckage made the whole ordeal worthwhile. It made me . . . proud."

"It's what we train for," he said quietly.

I shook my head. "It's more than just training."

He nuzzled my cheek. "That's what I love about you. You see something more in me. Something I don't see. Yet you're sure it's there."

I kissed him. "It's there. Here's what I said in my report." I used my reporter's voice for show. "For nearly twenty-four hours, the brave men and women of the Los Angeles County Fire Department's Urban Search and Rescue team, headed by dashing—okay, I didn't say dashing—Captain Eric Hayes, demonstrated incredible perseverance and self-sacrifice, working tirelessly to extinguish the burning wreckage and saving countless lives."

He smiled. "And we all know that if you say it on TV news, of course it's true."

I swatted him playfully. "It's true about *you.* Why can't you see you're a hero?"

"Maybe I need more convincing." His mouth was warm and firm on mine, and I felt myself melt into him at the tenderness of a kiss that seemed to last forever. Still, I had the feeling something was wrong.

"I'm leaving later this morning," he said, breaking off the kiss. His expression sobered. "We're being sent to South Carolina for Hurricane Juanita."

"I thought Hurricane Juanita wasn't supposed to hit land."

"The forecast changed early this morning. She's spinning out and turning into a Category Four hurricane that will hit landfall in South Carolina within forty-eight hours. They're activating search and rescue teams up and down the East Coast and about a dozen from California and Colorado. This is big, Kate."

He had once told me he and the search and rescue task force he captained had been called to work on other disasters, like Hurricane Sandy, but I always figured that was something in the past. Not something that would take him away now.

"There's always a chance you won't actually be deployed, right?"

He shook his head. "Our team has some of the most experienced swift-water rescuers in the country. If they're right about how much rain is coming, they're going to need us."

Worry crept into my veins. It was an unfamiliar feeling, because I'm not one to worry much. But after nearly drowning twice earlier in the year, I knew firsthand the enormous destructive power of water.

Even Eric, with all his training and his highly experienced team and sophisticated equipment, might not be a match for an extreme hurricane like Juanita.

"I'll be fine," he said.

I detected a brief flicker of fear in his eyes, but then it disappeared, and in its place was a look so warm it knocked the breath out of me.

"I'll miss you," he whispered.

His light-brown eyes roamed over my face, setting me aglow. I had never been wanted by anyone like this before and wondered if this was how everyone felt when they were in love. He cupped my face in his hands and kissed me again, deeper and more possessively, and I knew he was worried too.

CHAPTER TWO

The morning's assignment meeting, held in the Fish Bowl—a glass-walled conference room in the back of the newsroom—had turned into a rant fest. Megyn Carlson, who covered entertainment news with Susan Andrews but rarely spoke in the assignment meetings, was turning crimson as reporter Russ Hartman raged on about the story she'd pitched on the *Renovation Heaven* house being rehabbed in Silver Lake.

"No offense to Megyn, but how is that news?" he said loudly. "That's just a promotion for the *Renovation Heaven* TV series that will premiere on this network later this week. Seriously? We've got a cyclone whipping up trouble on the East Coast and FEMA sending eighteen LA search and rescue specialists to the scene, and we're reporting on the new stainless steel appliances and granite countertops the Gibbs family is installing."

My phone vibrated, alerting me to a text.

Are you on the El Mirasol story?

The text came from Los Angeles police detective Jake Newton. We'd met covering the gruesome murder of a flight attendant whose severed head was found in the Hollywood Hills a few years ago. The other stories I worked on with him weren't always as graphic or sensational, but Jake was a secret inside source of information on high-profile homicides, stabbings, and, once, a bank robbery in Gardena involving a fake bomb.

Don't know what that is, I typed back.

A $3 million heist. Malibu. You must cover. Call me.

Covering train disaster, I wrote.

Seconds later, his text pinged back: *This is bigger. Much.*

I swallowed hard. Jake never exaggerated. As a police detective, he was, not surprisingly, a facts-and-details guy. If he said the El Mirasol story was bigger than the train derailment, he probably wasn't feeding me hype.

Really don't cover burglaries. You know that.

I glanced at the whiteboard. David had written "Train-Derailment Cleanup," but the story had moved from the column labeled "Breaking News" to "Follow-Up." Now that all the victims had been removed from the crash site, the story had definitely slowed down.

Jake's text flashed up: *High-tech, sophisticated heist. Reporters swarming. Working on exclusive access for you. If you want.*

Exclusive access on a high-profile crime outmatched just about any news story. Especially a follow-up story about efforts to clean up the crash site, a story even a novice reporter could cover. Could I get myself assigned to El Mirasol?

David had scotched the Hartman rant and was droning on about the mayor's Great Streets initiative, trying to find an angle on the story and a reporter to cover it. The story felt like a snoozer, and nearly all the reporters in the room were looking at their phones or scanning the newspapers on the table, hoping David wouldn't assign it to them.

"I'll take on Great Streets," Russ said finally, which was a smart move, because after his outburst, David was likely to stick him with a string of mind-numbing stories that would end up on the Channel Eleven News website, but not on air.

The room was silent for a second, so I leaped at the opportunity to speak. "I just got a lead on the El Mirasol heist."

"I'm already on that story," Susan Andrews shot back, raising a Pilates-toned, spray-tanned arm in the air.

"Since when do you cover a crime story?" Russ asked, rolling his eyes. He was still riled up from his *Renovation Heaven* rant and maybe a little too eager to pick a fight.

"El Mirasol is owned by music mogul David Geffen," she said.

"*Used* to be owned by David Geffen," Hannah piped up, reading from her laptop. "Its new owner is Richard Ingram, founder and CEO of Enterprise Products. An oil producer."

Susan pursed her lips. Clearly she didn't recognize the name or the company.

"Feels like a breaking-news story—a crime—more than entertainment . . . so I can take it on," I said, but not too eagerly. If Susan felt I wanted the story too much, I was pretty sure she'd latch on to it as though it had Peabody Award potential.

David shot me a smug smile. "You want to give up reporting on the worst train derailment in LA history for a 'fluff' story?" He was baiting me, enjoying watching me squirm after the lecture I'd given about covering serious news. He stretched his arms over his head. "Welcome to the dark side, Kate."

"I'll take on the train derailment," Conan Phillips volunteered. Conan had come to Channel Eleven after being a reporter in Phoenix, Arizona. He had classic reporter good looks—a year-round tan, thick brown hair with a hint of gray at the temples—and had established a trademark light-blue polo, which he wore on every Channel Eleven live shot. He was one of our best at on-air ad-libbing and at explaining complicated stories, and I had no doubt he'd do a great job with the derailment story. Maybe too good a job.

"All yours, Conan. Kate, you're on El Mirasol."

As I headed out of the assignment meeting, I wondered if I had just made a major career mistake. Had I taken myself off the biggest disaster story of the year in favor of a burglary story?

Got you exclusive access, Jake texted me.

On it, I typed back.

~

I had no idea such places existed. El Mirasol was a twelve-thousand-square-foot mansion with a two-story hand-carved limestone entryway and a hand-laid *pietra dura* mosaic made from antique marble. *Pietra dura*, I learned from a small plaque on the entryway wall, was an art that flourished in Florence four hundred years ago and was used primarily in tabletops and small wall panels. This mosaic covered the entire one-thousand-square-foot entryway.

The entryway wasn't the main attraction, however. The part of the estate that literally made my jaw drop was the natatorium, an indoor pool with a frieze over the door crafted out of more than a million sea-shells. Twenty-foot-tall ceilings and gilded chandeliers soared above the glittering blue pool tiled in Murano glass. The room made the Pacific Ocean and the pristine Malibu beach, a few steps away, look ordinary.

Considering that most of the stories I covered were about murders and disasters, my beat rarely brought me to extravagant homes like this. Even as the daughter of a US senator and someone who reluctantly attended many political events in wealthy donors' homes, I'd never seen such luxury and meticulous perfection. The estate was like a palace by the ocean.

"It's the most high-tech, highly organized burglary we've ever seen," Jake said.

With his thick brown hair and handsome good looks, people often assumed Detective Jake Newton was a lightweight in the brains department. He used that to his advantage, surprising suspects—and often his bosses—with his sharp instincts and almost encyclopedic recall of crime scene details. At thirty-three, he had already risen quickly within the ranks of the LAPD and worked on a busy slate of investigations, yet he always made time to clue me in on the most newsworthy ones.

"The place is secured like Fort Knox," he continued as we left the natatorium and stepped onto a floating walkway of travertine slabs that connected the pool house with what appeared to be a greenhouse. "Motion sensors, cameras, alarms on every door and window." He pointed out several cameras perched on the rooftop. "The thieves got past the expensive security system and, without disturbing anything or anyone, walked out of here with over three million dollars' worth of stuff."

"Did the cameras see anything?"

"They went black for exactly nineteen minutes, forty seconds. Security guys monitoring them thought something was wrong with the signal transmission. By the time they sent a patrol to investigate, the heist was already over."

"Any suspects?"

He shook his head. "We're looking into a gang called the Chicago Connection. But this isn't their handiwork. This is meticulous, carefully thought out. Perfect."

I stared at him. "You always say there's no such thing as a perfect crime."

He loosened his tie. "This might be as perfect a crime as I've ever seen." He opened the door to the greenhouse, and a whoosh of warm, moist air rushed at us. We stepped inside to see thousands of orchids lining two tiers of shelving that stretched from one end of the greenhouse to the other. "We're hoping some of the stolen stuff ends up on the black market, where we can trace it back to its source. But what they took is highly untraceable, easily sold without suspicion."

"What did they take?"

"Some was cash—a few hundred thousand—the owners kept in a safe. Plus they took about a dozen high-end watches that cost anywhere from twenty thousand to two hundred thousand."

"Each? What kind of watch costs two hundred thousand dollars?"

"A lot. Rolex, Patek Philippe. We think this heist is linked to yesterday's burglary at Château du Soleil in Bel Air." He peered at an exotic yellow-and-dark-purple flower. "Same kind of stuff stolen, same stealth-like approach. No fingerprints and no evidence."

"How did they disable the security systems?"

He shook his head. "No clues yet. These weren't smash-and-grabs where the thieves cut the phone lines or smashed the security black box. The systems don't appear to have been tampered with."

"Then it must be an inside job. Someone on the household staff who knew the security codes."

He smiled. "Like I've said before, you'd make a good detective. Now that there are two robberies, we're looking for someone who'd have security access codes for both homes. So far, that's a dead end."

"What can I tell viewers?"

"Same as always."

The rules with Jake were simple: no cameras, no quotes, and I couldn't use any information that would lead directly or indirectly back to him. In exchange, I shared with him any intel I gathered from eyewitnesses or other interviews on the story.

He touched his hand to my arm. "You want to grab lunch after you're finished? I've been here since four this morning, and I'm starving."

I hesitated. We'd never socialized away from working on a story together, but there was something about the way he asked, a little too nervously, that made me think there was more to it. "Don't you need to stay here?"

"This one is so high profile there are at least a half dozen other detectives on the scene. Besides, Geoffrey's Malibu is only five minutes from here. We'll be back in under an hour."

"It's a bad idea to be seen together in public. People might make the connection that you're my inside source."

"Geoffrey's is the last place anyone in the department would head for lunch. Too upscale. And no one there will even give us a second look. We're safe."

That made me nervous. Up until now, Jake and I had avoided situations where we might be seen together. This lunch seemed fraught with the possibility of discovery.

He grinned. "It'll be fine."

"Okay," I said finally. "See you in about an hour."

My report opened the noon cast. It was complete with exclusive details about how the thieves had evaded a top-of-the-line security system, stealing high-end watches and cash and leaving behind zero evidence. But as I watched it on playback, my spirits sank. Yes, I had inside information that no other station had. Yes, the visuals were outstanding, and my performance was polished and concise. But in one shot I appeared to be smiling as I listed off the items that had been stolen. I sounded like a sports reporter reveling in the excitement of the game.

A journalist's number one priority was to remain objective, so the idea that I might be biased about this story disturbed me. A few years ago I'd covered a story about a family in Inglewood whose Christmas presents, along with their dog, were stolen at gunpoint. When I saw how the home had been ransacked, with only the torn wrapping paper left behind, my anger over the senseless situation seeped into my report. The story sparked so much interest that dozens of people delivered gifts to the family the next day.

It had been natural to feel sympathy for the robbery victims in Inglewood, but clearly I was having a hard time mustering a similar feeling here. Instead of sympathy for the billionaire victim, there was a different emotion—one that surprised me. I actually felt a twinge of admiration for the people behind this carefully planned maneuver. *What was wrong with me?*

In every other story, I had always wanted to see the criminals caught and justice served. But I appreciated the criminals' ability here to vault past high-end security systems and walk away with $3 million without damaging anything or leaving behind any evidence. I actually liked that they got away with it. Was it because the victim was a billionaire who could afford to lose $3 million? Was I allowing stereotypes of pampered CEOs and greedy Wall Street investment bankers to color my impression of this crime?

My lack of objectivity troubled me, and that unsettled feeling stayed with me as I headed to Geoffrey's Malibu for lunch with Jake. Call it reporter's intuition, but the way he'd made the invitation and his willingness to be seen with me in public made me think this was more than a collegial lunch. But Jake had given me inside police department information on some of the biggest stories on my beat, and turning down his invitation wouldn't be a smart move. Not if I expected that exclusive access to continue.

By the time I drove along the Pacific Coast Highway to Geoffrey's Malibu, the early-morning haze had burned off, and the ocean glittered in the sunlight. I found Jake sitting at a table on the patio with a picture-perfect view of the sun-drenched beach. Instead of taking in the view, he had his head down, his phone pressed to his ear. He was listening intently, his jaw clenched. "Got to run, but we'll figure this mess out later." He tossed the phone on the table and waved at me to have a seat.

"Everything okay?" I asked.

He shook his head and drained the last of his cocktail. "Can't get anything done. The department is in chaos with all the swatting going on."

Swatting involved calling 911 and reporting a serious but fake emergency in the hopes of unleashing police or a SWAT team on an unsuspecting person.

"I cover the crime beat every day. How come I rarely hear about swatting incidents?"

He took off his aviator shades and folded them next to his phone. "We don't want the pranksters to get more notoriety. Even if we send an entire SWAT team over to a celebrity compound for a fake hostage situation, the media won't hear about it if it turns out to be a prank."

The waiter, a twentysomething guy who had the kind of camera-ready looks that made me think *aspiring actor*, handed me an inch-thick wine list. I never drank during working hours, and not for any reason except blatant vanity. I couldn't afford the calories. Women reporters had come a long way, but those with expanding waistlines mostly didn't get their contracts renewed. So I ordered some spring water, and Jake ordered a scotch and soda. I had the feeling he was still on duty and wasn't supposed to be drinking, but I wasn't going to call him on it.

Jake leaned on his elbows and lowered his voice. "Swatting was used as a planned diversion during the El Mirasol robbery. During the time the thieves were on the property, we received two calls about a gunman on Beyoncé's Malibu property. We sent a dozen police officers to her home, but of course there was no gunman. That left us with little manpower when we got the report on the El Mirasol burglary a few minutes later."

"Why can't you guys trace the swatters?"

"It's tough. Sometimes they use services for the deaf that allow them to type their message and have it spoken by an operator. They also have other technology available to hide their numbers. Apps and such."

"There are apps to make anonymous prank calls?" I said with a laugh, then picked up my phone and pretended to search for one. "I'm going to download one right now."

I looked up from my phone and found Jake looking at me. His serious expression was gone, and a big grin swept across his face. "This is why I've always liked you, Kate. You report on tragic stuff, yet you are still funny and *normal*."

He looked at me expectantly, but I didn't know what he was hoping I would say in reply. "Thanks. Not always sure about the normal part, though."

"I guess it's no secret that I've had a . . . thing for you since—well, for a while now." He stopped talking. I wasn't sure if I should fill the silence or if he was planning to say more.

"From your expression, I'm guessing you didn't know." He swallowed hard. "Well, this is awkward . . ."

"No, I'm—"

"I thought I'd been giving out all the signals."

Thankfully, the waiter arrived with our drinks, and Jake immediately gulped down half of his scotch and soda.

From the look in his blue eyes, I knew he was hoping for a different answer, but I had to be honest with him. "I'm flattered, but . . . I'm seeing someone."

"It's not that fire captain Hayes, is it? You're going to make me insanely jealous if you ended up falling for one of those rescue guys."

I nodded. "His name is Eric Hayes. One of those rescue guys."

He sat back in his chair and ran his hands through his hair. "You know, I saw you interview him a few months back. You were covering the story about his rescue of the boy caught in Malibu Canyon white water. I kinda wondered if something was going on between you two but hoped I was wrong. It was the first time I ever saw you flustered on air."

"I wouldn't say I was flustered on air. Ever, actually."

"Maybe if I'd rescued a boy from rushing water and swung from a helicopter performing CPR, you'd have chosen me instead?"

I smiled. "Jake, I really like working with you and—"

"No, I get it," he said, then drained the rest of his drink.

"I hope this doesn't change anything between us . . ."

"No. We're good. Nothing's changed."

From the look on his face, I knew this was going to change everything.

CHAPTER THREE

My report on the El Mirasol burglary opened every newscast for the rest of the day on Channel Eleven. But it wasn't my reporting or the exclusive inside information Jake had given me that was making it the top news story. Viewers were lured in by Josh's shots of the stately greenhouse, the natatorium, the tennis courts, and the rampant luxury.

TV news viewers weren't used to so much eye candy. Most of the time, crimes weren't committed in these übersanctuaries. Audience members were more accustomed to seeing crime scenes in gritty neighborhoods, not in mansions with greenhouses and eighteenth-century chandeliers.

My Twitter feed heated up as viewers started responding to my tweets about the El Mirasol and Château du Soleil burglaries. One viewer with 250,000 followers retweeted my story with the comment, "Why do the superrich have to give their homes such pretentious names?" But the post that fueled the most response was from one viewer who tweeted, "60,000 square feet? Those rich people deserve to be robbed." That got hundreds of retweets and responses, like one from Andrea London that read, "I'm sick of hearing about the poor, poor billionaires," or GavinLA, who wrote, "How am I supposed to have sympathy for someone who has 25 bathrooms?"

As I sat at my desk in the newsroom the next morning scrolling through all the tweets and replies, I realized I had been wrong about this being a fluff story. LA was a nonstop news town where anything could—and did—happen. But even here, where people could easily suffer from sensational-story overload, the news of someone targeting megaestates and robbing them of millions had viewers riveted.

Hannah interrupted my thoughts. "Another burglary." With her oversize slate-gray glasses and her hair pulled up in a messy bun, she could easily have passed for a hipster librarian. "Thieves got away with five million dollars' worth of stuff this time."

"How do you know?"

"Soundtrack of my life. The police scanner. This estate is in Rolling Hills. La Villa de la Paz."

"Why *do* these people give their homes such exotic names?"

"These are estates, not homes. And one way to differentiate them from your ordinary ten- or twenty-million-dollar home is to give them a name or a brand. Did you know that the owners of El Mirasol actually hired a branding company to develop the name?"

I wasn't surprised she knew something like that. We'd hired her as a full-time associate producer after a stint as our intern because she had a strong intuition for news. But what we didn't know then was that she could locate impossible-to-find information on the internet by searching what was called the deep web, the part of the internet that wasn't indexed by standard search engines. Using a search engine, she said, was like dragging a net across the surface of the ocean; a great deal might be caught in the net, but there was a lot of buried information that standard search engines couldn't see or retrieve. By searching the deep web, Hannah often found information other producers and reporters didn't have.

"Problem is," she said, "Susan's already on the La Villa de la Paz story."

I frowned. "Since when is Susan taking on breaking news?"

"Since she sniffed a ratings winner. Everyone's into this story. CNN had an expert on saying the Russian mafia might be behind it because it would take an organization that big to pull this off. Do you think you can get another exclusive inside-the-grounds report on this one?"

"It's gotten . . . complicated."

She rolled a pen between her hands. "Everyone's warned me not to ask about your source, because they say you won't ever tell who it is. They say that not even David knows."

I nodded. "They're right. If my source was found out, it could severely compromise his position. It's better for everyone if you don't know who he is either." I stood. "I'm going to get David to assign this story to me. Can you dig up some facts about La Villa de la Paz and email them to me?"

I headed to David's office and found Susan already in there. Dressed in a sapphire sheath dress with a chunky antique-glass necklace, she looked like she was headed to a dinner party even though it was ten in the morning.

"Even most celebrities don't have homes like La Villa de la Paz," Susan was saying. "A top celebrity might own an estate that costs five, ten, maybe twenty million. Oprah or Ryan Seacrest might have more expensive homes, but they're the exception. The current owner bought La Villa de la Paz for fifty-three million."

"The owners are in a wealth stratosphere that's beyond even the biggest-name celebrities," I added, making my case that this was a news story, not an entertainment piece.

"You can't imagine the extravagance. The Turkish spa alone cost over five million dollars to build," Susan said.

David clasped his hands together. "I think you both should work on this story."

"Together?" Susan said, as though he had just suggested we become partners on *Dancing with the Stars*.

"Team coverage," he said.

I'd done plenty of team coverage before but not with the entertainment reporters. Maybe it was snobbery, but I didn't consider entertainment a real news beat, so working on a story with the entertainment reporters didn't happen often. Actually, it never happened.

"Susan, nab an interview with the owner," David said. "Kate, get to the scene and see what's going on."

"This story is going to be big, and you know why?" Susan asked. "Because people suspect the superrich are enjoying the highest rewards without really deserving them. From the way viewers are responding to this story, I think they enjoy seeing some of the überrich taken down a little."

"This is the news we're doing," I said quietly. "Not entertainment. We need to treat this like any heist or high-stakes burglary we've ever covered. We have to remain objective. No matter what we think viewers want."

David rolled up his sleeves. "Kate's right. This story gives viewers a look inside the exclusive world of the leisure class, but let's not assume that everyone wants to 'take them down.' For many of our viewers, the wealthy have a hallowed, revered status—they represent the ideal that anyone can become rich if they work hard enough."

While Susan worked on getting an interview with the owner of La Villa de la Paz, Josh and I raced to Rolling Hills, situated on the crest of Southern California's Palos Verdes Peninsula. Neither of us had ever covered a crime in this exclusive part of the California coast, so Josh, who had a homing pigeon's sense of direction, actually had to use a GPS app on his phone to find the place.

Meanwhile, our social media producer, Amy Guzman, sent me a text pleading for more tweets about the heists, saying they were generating record retweets and favorites. The station was using the story in its promos, playing up the extravagant items, the opulence, and the lavish lifestyles.

The day had turned into such a heavy news day that there was utter chaos in the control room as they struggled to put a schedule together. That morning the head of the Department of Water and Power had resigned because of a scandal involving $30 million in ratepayers' money that had been handed over to an unknown nonprofit organization. At lunchtime, the mayor had been a passenger in a police SUV that had struck a female pedestrian in a downtown crosswalk. Meanwhile, thirteen sheriff's deputies had shown up at the home of a famous pop singer to investigate an egg-throwing melee that had caused $25,000 in damages. Still, my heist story was going to open the next newscast.

Reporters were allowed to stand inside the courtyard of the estate but not on the grounds. A cool breeze blew sweet yet unfamiliar scents from the Moorish gardens and orchards sequestered behind tall iron gates. Even from our limited vantage point, we had 180-degree views of the entire LA Basin, from the Pacific Ocean below to the San Gabriel Mountains and the sandy beaches of Santa Monica to the north.

It baffled me to think that there were many homes this extravagant in LA—not to mention throughout the rest of the world. And I was sure viewers would be surprised to learn that so many enjoyed such over-the-top wealth that thieves could easily steal millions of dollars in cash and high-end goods in under twenty minutes.

My phone rang, and I grabbed for it in my purse, hoping it would be Jake. Or Eric. Instead, the name Hale Bradley flashed up on the screen.

"Dad," I said, apparently too loudly, because a nearby reporter from Channel Nine, who was recording her stand-up, flashed me a crabby look.

"Katie, I'm coming to LA on Friday," he said.

I walked down the driveway, away from the reporters' camp. "What for?"

My dad was a bit of a capital creature, which meant he spent weeks in DC and only came home to California for brief stints before he was called back for hearings, fund-raisers, and other work. But in the months before midterm elections, I could count on him being home a lot more as campaign fund-raising reached a fever pitch.

"I'm attending a few fund-raising events. With control of the Senate at stake, this year is a game changer for the party."

"Should I get in touch with Lisa to get on your calendar? Maybe lunch? Dinner?"

"All of those are already spoken for this trip—sorry. So I'm going to ask you to do two things for me while I'm there. First, I want you to go to a few of these fund-raisers with me."

"Dad," I groaned.

"Yes, I know how much you *love* political fund-raisers," he said with a laugh. "But it's the only way I'm going to see you. Plus, you must meet the candidate we're backing for governor. She can be a valuable resource for you as a reporter."

"Thanks." Meeting the possible future governor of California would be a plus for my career, but I was more interested in meeting the politician who would fix the potholes on my commute to work.

"Which brings me to my second request. I was talking with Andrew Wright, executive vice president at American News Channel, and he'd like to talk to you about some opportunities there. He's going to be in LA later this week as well. I'd like you to meet with him."

This had to be my dad's fourth or fifth attempt to get me a political reporting gig. From his vantage point, the Bradley family political dynasty was incomplete if his only child continued to report on breaking news and didn't enter the political arena at some point. I'd told him plenty of times I wasn't interested in covering politics, but as the majority leader of the Senate, my dad was used to getting what he wanted.

"I've already told you I'm not interested in leaving LA."

"This is the second time he's asked to meet you. What kind of leader am I if I can't arrange a simple meeting between a top journalism executive and my own daughter? Do your old man a favor on this one."

I sighed. "As long as it's clear that I'm not looking to jump into political reporting—"

"Wonderful. Lisa will set it up. See you Friday."

I headed back up the driveway. "Police just announced that they *aren't* going to make a statement. Neither are the owners," Josh said when I reached the top. "Strange, right?"

I nodded. "And if they're not talking, what's the story angle? All we know is that this is yet another multimillion-dollar heist."

I watched several other reporters record their stories in front of the estate. The reality of television news is that sometimes all we have is a "money shot," only a few shards of information, but to make our deadlines, we have to make it look and sound like so much more.

Searching my email, I found the one from Hannah outlining the information on La Villa de la Paz. The house read like a fairy-tale castle on steroids, but it wasn't giving me a way into the story or anything new to say.

I walked to the end of the driveway and looked over the rugged coastline hugging the Pacific Ocean, trying to find my lead. What could I say about such an extravagant view and place that didn't sound clichéd? I turned to look down the hill at the uniform red-roofed mansions, each with its own jewel-like turquoise pool shimmering in the golden sunlight. But when I lifted my gaze a little, I saw downtown LA, the cluster of skyscrapers appearing like tiny spires in the smog, but nonetheless recognizable even from this distance.

That's where I found my lead. A few minutes later, I recorded my report.

"Less than twenty miles from downtown Los Angeles, where forty percent of residents in adjacent areas are living below the poverty line," I said, "is the gated city of Rolling Hills, California, nestled on the peak of the Palos Verdes Peninsula. This month, the average price of a home on the market here is over eight million dollars. Rolling Hills' best-kept secret is a fifty-thousand-square-foot estate named La Villa de la Paz, meaning Town of Peace. Earlier today, that peace was disturbed as thieves stole more than five million dollars' worth of luxury goods in under twenty minutes. But while the hacienda looks impressive from the street, what's not visible are five subterranean levels accessible only by a labyrinth of elevators, passageways, and secret stairs. Once below, you'll find a tennis court built to US Open standards, a Turkish bath, a chapel, and an English library, plus thirteen bedrooms and twenty-five bathrooms. It even comes with its own geothermal energy system—"

My phone began ringing, ruining the take. I pulled it from my purse. Jake Newton.

"Hey," I said, careful not to say his name.

"I can get you five, maybe six minutes here in the Villa," he said hurriedly. "There's a back entrance down the hill. No cameras. Hurry." He hung up.

I quickly filled in Josh about what was ahead; then we drove down the hill until we spotted a multicar garage secured behind another set of ornate iron gates. Josh dropped me off several dozen yards farther down the hill so I could walk up without being seen getting out of the news van. I raced up the steep hill, and by the time I got to the back entrance, Jake was waiting for me.

"We have five minutes," he whispered and whisked me inside.

We stepped through the gate and into a large fountained motor court that led into a six-car garage occupied by a cardinal-red Bentley.

"Wow," I said under my breath.

"And that's the one they left behind. Because it's worth a mere one hundred seventy-five thousand. The other five cars stolen were worth much more."

"The thieves stole five other cars? How?"

I scribbled notes as he spoke. "The keys were inside the house. That's why the haul here was so big. At least five million. They stole five luxury cars, including an Aston Martin Vanquish, which costs around three hundred thousand, a Mercedes-AMG, a Ferrari FF, a Maserati Ghibli, and a Porsche Carrera. That's well over a million dollars in cars alone. We suspect they took them straight to the port."

"To be sold where?"

"China is the fastest-growing country for billionaires. Many of them obsess over luxury cars. The thieves will be able to sell these cars within hours."

He hurried me out of the garage into a large marble-lined foyer and then pressed a button on the wall to summon the elevator.

"What makes this heist so spectacular is that the estate has sophisticated surveillance cameras and breach sensors. The system was set up by one of the world's foremost security experts, a guy named Bruce Rennert, who served in the Israel Defense Forces and designed surveillance at maximum security military prisons. Bruce can't figure out how they were able to breach his system."

A mahogany-paneled elevator arrived. We both got in, Jake pressed 3, and the elevator began its descent. "How did they do it?"

"Same as before. The security system went down. Bruce has already confirmed that no wires were cut and the system's black box wasn't compromised. And get this. The thieves didn't enter a security code to turn off the system. At 11:17 last night the system went down. Then came back on at 11:30."

"The thieves turned the security system back on as they left? Without a security code? How? Could the people who installed these security systems be behind it?"

He shook his head. "We're already on that. The estates have different security companies, with no common thread between them."

When the elevator doors opened, my breath caught in my throat. In front of us was a Moroccan-style Turkish bath with a cobalt-blue lap pool decorated in twenty-four-karat-gold tiles and fountains. It was more lavish than any hotel spa I'd ever seen, even those I'd only dreamed about while looking at photos on the internet.

"This is where the thieves got their biggest haul. The owners put a safe in the sauna—the last place where you'd expect to find a safe—but the thieves made a beeline for it, broke in, and stole over a million in cash, watches, and jewelry there alone."

"It's like they knew exactly what they were looking for and where to find it."

He nodded.

I spotted two cameras overlooking the pool area. "There are cameras everywhere," I said, worried we were being watched.

"The techs have taken them off-line while they test the system." He glanced at his watch. "We're good for about another three minutes. But here are the rules, Kate. Don't mention that you've seen the crime scene. We're under strict orders from the chief not to show or talk about the crime scene. A full cone of silence."

I scanned the room. "Why? What's here that could compromise the investigation?"

He ignored my question, guiding me back to the elevator. "This is the last access I can get you on this story. You've got to be especially protective of my identity."

"I shouldn't be here," I said. "I'm putting you at serious risk."

"You're worth it, Kate."

His words hung in the air. His blue eyes met mine, imploring me not to look away. "Someone is spending a lot of time and money to orchestrate these burglaries, and it may not be for the reasons we all suspect."

"What do you mean?"

He drew a deep breath. The expression on his face was more anxious than I had ever seen before.

"What aren't you telling me?"

He didn't answer. Instead, he walked over to the elevator and pressed the button. "The cameras go online in two minutes. Get in the elevator and press 1. When the doors open again, walk out the door. We never had this meeting."

"There *is* something. What is it?"

He touched my arm. "You need to get going."

The elevator arrived, and I stepped inside. As the doors began to close, he added, "Remember what I told you about the Hidden Mickey."

CHAPTER FOUR

The Hidden Mickey is a silhouette of Mickey Mouse, concealed in plain sight by park designers in dozens of rides, murals, light poles, manhole covers, and plantings throughout the Disney theme parks. Guests might look at something dozens of times until they finally recognize the Hidden Mickey within it.

When Jake and I were working on the investigation into the murder of the flight attendant whose severed head was found in the Hollywood Hills, he'd told me that many cases had a "Hidden Mickey," a piece of evidence hiding in plain sight. Once it was found, the whole case would crack open. In that grisly case, once police found the Hidden Mickey—some shards of glass and a half-smoked cigarette inadvertently left at the crime scene—they had a solid suspect.

Now he was saying that there was a Hidden Mickey in these heists. Had they found some piece of evidence that cracked the case wide open? Was that why the police chief had clamped down on all communication with the media?

Josh and I went back to the main entrance and reshot my report. While I laid out the exclusive information Jake had given me about what had been stolen, I didn't mention anything about the crime scene.

In the news van, Josh and I assembled the report. After we finished the edit, Josh went to pack up the camera equipment, and I switched the monitor to the network news feed. The images of Hurricane Juanita's huge path of destruction flickered across the screen—flooded neighborhoods, downed power lines, homes gutted and flattened into rubble, cars crushed under debris, and storm-torn buildings.

I turned up the sound. "Hurricane Juanita pummeled the East Coast with strong winds as high as seventy-five miles an hour, bringing widespread flooding, fires, and power blackouts," the anchor was saying.

I checked my phone again for a text or a call from Eric. Still nothing. I had texted him several times since he left, hoping he'd respond, even if it was with a simple emoji. Now the cold ache of missing him rattled through me.

In the three months we'd been seeing each other, we'd been in touch every day. I always felt a buzz of excitement when his text flashed up on my phone or I heard his voice on the other end of the line. I pulled up a photo of him that I kept on my phone. Dressed in uniform, he was sitting at a table, resting his chin in his left hand, smiling a boyish grin at me. Like I was the only woman in the world.

"At least three rescuers are trapped at this hour in an under-construction school building in Wilmington as high winds from Hurricane Juanita batter the South Carolina coast," the anchor said. "Urban Search and Rescue team members saved two people trapped inside Argyle High School, then went back in to search for more victims when the roof collapsed on them."

My mouth went dry as I imagined the worst. Could Eric and his team be the rescuers trapped in the building?

"High winds and blinding rains have hampered efforts to rescue the firefighters," she continued.

My apparent fearlessness, David Dyal said, was what made me one of the best at breaking news. But as I watched the storm images flash across the screen, that facade crumbled.

I called Eric's phone, but the call went straight to voice mail. I managed a smile when I heard his warm voice on the outgoing message: "Hey, it's Eric. Leave a message."

My next call was to Hannah. "Rescuers are trapped at Argyle High School in Wilmington," I said, but my tone was high pitched, on the edge of panic. I steadied my voice. "Can you find out if any of them are from the LA County Fire Department?"

~

The sales guys at Channel Eleven rarely talked to the reporters. Maybe it was because their offices were in a different wing of the building, separated by the lobby and a warren of hallways that led to the newsroom. But it was also because there was supposed to be a clear separation between what the news department reported and what the advertisers would like us to talk about.

There was one exception to this rule at Channel Eleven: the station was owned by a major Hollywood movie studio, so the lines between delivering the news and promoting the studio's latest movie releases and television shows were constantly blurred. But otherwise, the guys selling airtime rarely interacted with the reporters and anchors. So when one of the sales executives approached me as I walked into the newsroom that afternoon, I had no idea who he was.

He extended his hand. "Kate? I'm Marc Beck. National sales." He was dressed in a navy-blue suit and a crisply ironed white oxford. His precision-trimmed hair was slicked back in a style reminiscent of Gordon Gekko without the cigar.

He offered me a stick of gum, but I declined. "Thought you'd like to know that Frank Tepper is quite the Channel Eleven News junkie and a big fan of yours."

"Frank Tepper?"

"CEO of Tepper International. They're the single largest owner of companies that put security systems in homes and businesses. He loves the heist stories. Says they're very entertaining and have already begun to boost business for him."

"I don't need to know what Frank Tepper likes about the news."

"Hey, I only wanted you to know. He's a big fan of yours, that's all."

"Are you new here, Marc?"

"Been here three months, actually. Came from the New York station."

"Let me explain something. Reporters don't have fans. We're not celebrities. We have viewers. We don't cater to advertisers, even if they call themselves our fans."

He looked at me as if I had just fallen off the turnip truck. "If it helps you sleep at night, you keep thinking that way, Kate. Because the truth is a lot uglier than that. Why do you think that you report on breaking news? The tragedy, the robberies, and the disasters? You think that's what viewers want? That's what viewers are demanding?" He looked around to see if anyone could hear him and then lowered his voice. "Crap. It's because that's what the advertisers want. They want to sell cars, appliances, and other products that make people feel safe and secure after they've seen all the crime and mayhem you've just reported on."

I shook my head. "Damn, I thought I was cynical. But you—"

He shrugged. "I only speak the truth. Great meeting you, Kate."

Marc Beck had gotten under my skin. I didn't cross police lines and secure exclusive access to sometimes-dangerous crime scenes to satisfy advertisers' needs to sell products to frightened viewers. I did it because they were important stories. But it made me wonder. Were crime stories and tragedy really what viewers wanted, or were viewers searching for something more?

Worrying about Eric added to my gloom. I careened between worst-case scenarios and sound reasoning that it was highly unlikely he was one of the trapped firefighters. But the news reports' relentless images of destruction, flooding, and pounding rain made the worst-case scenario feel more likely. Meanwhile, Hannah had texted me that the identities of the trapped firefighters had still not been released.

Communication from the scene is scarce, she wrote. *Team here monitoring for updates.*

I tried to look calm as I returned to the newsroom only to find Susan pacing behind my desk, talking on her cell phone. She was frowning, which wasn't an expression I'd seen on her face often.

"Okay, then, thank you for trying," she said and hung up. "Struck out. No luck getting an interview with the La Villa de la Paz owner. I tried her assistant, talked to her corporate PR firm. I even had a friend of mine who knows an executive at her company reach out to her. She's refused to be interviewed. How'd you do?"

"Police aren't talking. Billionaires aren't talking. Which leaves us in the dark. But someone is spending a lot of money and time to orchestrate these burglaries. Maybe not for the reasons we suspect. Besides ordinary greed, what other reasons could they have to do it?"

She looked at me as though I'd asked her how to calculate the length of a hypotenuse. No wonder. Most of the celebrity stories she covered didn't ever require her to consider suspects, motives, or evidence.

"I was thinking we should interview a few celebrities," she said. "To find out if they're worried about becoming heist targets."

I shook my head. "That's hyping the story. What we need is to uncover *why* they are orchestrating these heists. Why these estates? This isn't an entertainment story."

I felt a little guilty for being so direct, but the heist story *was* my beat, while celebrity news, gossip, and scandals were hers. Seriously, part of her job was monitoring Ashton Kutcher's and Hugh Jackman's Twitter feeds. This wasn't even remotely an entertainment story.

Except that it was. With all the spectacle of the items stolen and the high-end estates, some of the reports felt a little like the *CSI* version of *Lifestyles of the Rich and Famous*. Even advertisers were coming aboard for the "entertainment" value of the story. If I had any hope of holding on to my reputation as a reporter, it was time to dig deeper.

Shrouded behind a stand of tall palm trees, Matt Wexler's home looked like any number of stately homes on Rimpau Boulevard in Hancock Park, an affluent neighborhood in Central LA built in the 1920s around a private golf course. Mark was the creator of a 1990s hit sitcom, one of the many about a dysfunctional but loving family. A few years back, he'd hosted a $32,000-per-person fund-raiser attended by the president. Today, attendees could pay the relatively paltry sum of $2,500 to meet the candidate my dad was backing for governor of California and hear a brief speech by the Speaker of the House.

This was the first of three fund-raisers my dad had summoned me to attend. Most of the fund-raisers were for a specific candidate running for political office in the state—governor, congressman, US senator—but occasionally we attended larger events to raise funds for the political party my dad belonged to.

Earlier in the day, he had texted instructions. Or, I should say, his assistant had—my dad definitely didn't send text messages. The instructions were simple: *Be on time and remember you're not a reporter tonight.*

I couldn't pretend I wasn't a reporter, and my dad knew it. People who watched TV news in LA, especially politicians, often recognized me. Even if they weren't sure which station I reported for, they knew my name. And they definitely knew I was Hale Bradley's daughter. But what my dad meant was for me not to ask questions like a reporter.

He wanted me to listen intently and contribute to the conversations but back off from asking questions. Even gentle confrontation could unsettle donors and politicians in a setting like this.

When I arrived, a uniformed valet in a black vest checked my name off a list and took my keys, whisking my silver Acura off to some side street while a gleaming white Lamborghini and a Bentley were prominently displayed in the brick-lined driveway circle.

Bathed in blue-gold lights and studded with palm tree–inspired chandeliers, the heated tent in Wexler's sprawling yard had been transformed into a high-end tropical paradise, complete with a luxurious aquarium filled with a rainbow of tropical fish. I recognized a few of the faces—an action-movie star, a pro athlete, and a few politicians—but otherwise I didn't know anyone in the room. Except my dad.

"There you are," he said, embracing me in a brief hug. His dark hair, graying at the temples, gave him the look of a distinguished statesman, but he appeared far younger than his sixty-two years. Maybe it was his line-free skin, which was perpetually tanned even though he avoided the California sun. But it was also his strong, sloping shoulders, bolstered by years as a runner, that gave him an active appearance that some of his fellow senators lacked.

He introduced me to a tall man in his early forties with a thick head of wavy hair that reached to his collar. He was dressed in a black pin-striped suit, and an expensive watch peeked out from his suit sleeve.

"Stephen, this is my daughter, Kate. Stephen Bening."

Stephen shook my hand with a grip that was stiff and formal. He had a commanding presence about him, which made me think he was a senator or a congressman. But his shaggy hair and ten-day beard made it clear he was some kind of tech guru or entertainment executive.

He looked familiar, but at first I couldn't place him. Then I realized he was the Silicon Valley entrepreneur whose Château du Soleil was the first estate robbed in the heists.

"I've seen you on the news," he said.

I glanced at my father before answering. "Yes, on Channel Eleven."

"Stephen is hosting the fund-raiser for Congressman Blair on Sunday," my dad said, changing the subject. "Kate will be attending with me."

This was the part of these fund-raising events I dreaded. From my experience, most of the evening would be dominated by polite introductions, pointless chitchat, and subtle bragging, occasionally punctuated by an interesting but always brief discussion about a noncontroversial subject.

My dad lowered his voice. "I'm sorry to hear about the incident at your home," he said to Stephen.

Stephen shifted his weight to the other leg and looked down at his drink. "Everything should be back in order by Sunday."

"Incident?" I asked, even though I knew exactly what my father was referring to.

"If you'd rather not—" my dad started.

"I'm not talking publicly about it," he said, looking straight at me. "But my home was robbed in the recent heists."

"By a very sophisticated group of thieves," I said. "Are there any suspects?"

He shot me a frosty smile. "It would be my luck to meet the only reporter invited to tonight's event." There was no mistaking the irritation in his tone.

My dad smiled nervously at me. No doubt Stephen was a big fish in my father's world, and I could feel my dad silently urging me not to ask any more questions.

"I'm not here as a reporter," I said, touching my father's arm. "I'm here to spend time with my father."

"Good, then," Stephen said. "Completely off the record? I think the police know more than they're saying. They've refused to share the results of their investigation with me. The other victim—Richard

Ingram—told me he's experiencing the same wall of silence. And . . . there have been other irregularities."

I couldn't help myself. "Like?"

"Katie, no more questions," my dad chided.

"This *is* off the record," Stephen continued in a tone that left no doubt that it was. "But it looks like an inside job. The police know that it's a group of their own that's behind these heists."

Before I could ask any more questions, a trio of political types introduced themselves to my father and started talking about Social Security and some energy initiatives in public buildings. I wanted to continue the discussion with Stephen, but there wasn't a polite way to do that now that the conversation had shifted to weightier matters.

I used this interruption as an opportunity to slip away. In all the fund-raising events I'd attended at my dad's request—er, demand—I had developed a survival technique of finding moments where I could take a break in a different room of the hotel or home. Since this event was in a tent outdoors, there wasn't any place to escape to. So I stood near the corner of the bar and pretended to look at my phone as I thought about what Stephen had said. Was he right about this—police officers being responsible? Was that why Jake had said the police had put a cone of silence around the investigation and spoken cryptically about "someone spending a lot of time and money to orchestrate these burglaries and not for the reasons we all suspect"?

Or was Stephen just a disgruntled estate owner, blaming the police out of frustration that they had no suspects and no leads?

After the brief speeches made by a number of politicians, including my dad, and after the exclusive group had dug into the braised beef short rib with fingerling potato hash, I found my opportunity to leave.

"I'm taking off," I told my dad, who had been seated next to me at dinner but had spent most of the first and second courses engrossed in a conversation with a Nebraska senator to his right.

"You'll miss the dessert," he said, putting his arm around my shoulder.

"I'll be at the fund-raiser at Stephen Bening's on Sunday. I'll get dessert then."

"Please don't go after Stephen to talk about the heist at his estate. Promise me you'll respect his privacy."

"I will," I said, kissing him on the cheek.

As I left the tent, I scanned the room to see if Stephen was still at the event. He wasn't. But if he had been, I wouldn't have kept my promise.

Hurricane Juanita had expanded to become a superstorm with high winds covering about five hundred miles, cutting a swath from Charleston, South Carolina, to Virginia Beach. Drenching rains and high winds had traveled up the East Coast, causing massive flooding, toppling trees and power lines, and plunging cities and towns into darkness. Three days had passed, and I still had not heard from Eric. Now my worry was at its peak. Had he been injured—or worse—in the hurricane? Twenty-seven people had already died in the storm, and dozens more were reported missing. Had the storm wiped out cell communications? Or had he simply lost his phone?

I rose early the next morning, skipped my run, and jumped online from home to gain access to the station's news databases. I searched all of them, looking for information on the firefighters who were trapped in the collapsed school building, but according to the Associated Press, the names still had not been released.

I wondered what other girlfriends, partners, and spouses of firefighters did—those who didn't have access to Reuters, Associated Press, and every news database in the country. How did they manage their anxiety when they couldn't comb through reams of reports and information?

I called the Los Angeles County Fire Department Station 8, where Eric's team was based. The firefighter who answered the phone said he couldn't release any information about the Urban Search and Rescue team in South Carolina, but he could connect me with the public information officer.

In my experience it could take hours and maybe days to hear back from a busy PIO, especially in the midst of a superstorm on the other side of the continent. "Would you put me on with your captain?"

I waited on hold for a long time until a man's voice finally came on the phone. "Cap'n Smythe." He sounded irritated.

"Captain, this is Kate Bradley from Channel Eleven News. We have reports that some USAR team members are trapped underneath a school building in South Carolina in the midst of Hurricane Juanita. Can you tell me if any of them are from the LA-based task force?"

"It's fire department policy not to release that information. We don't make announcements until we know everything, until the family has been notified. We don't want to give out the wrong information. That's why Firefighter Heyman suggested you contact the PIO."

"Can *you* tell me anything?" I said, my voice wobbling. "This is not just a news story for me. It's . . . personal. I'm worried about Eric Hayes."

His voice softened. "Even our own families can't get information about us at an incident. All I can tell you is that some LA firefighters have sustained injuries in Hurricane Juanita. I can't tell you who or the extent of the injuries."

I kept it together after I hung up. My hand shook as I clicked on the website for the NBC affiliate in South Carolina, but otherwise, I was oddly calm as I watched a report on a small town that had been swamped by a huge morning tide, which raged over a concrete seawall.

I tried to grasp the allure of traveling three thousand miles to rescue strangers from rushing water, fires, and disaster. Eric's training had instilled in him a real understanding of the dangers involved, yet he still woke up every day ready to put himself in harm's way in order to help others.

On the surface, the lives of a fire captain and a TV news reporter might seem very different, yet in many ways we understood each other. After a particularly difficult rescue, I could look into his eyes and know exactly what he was feeling, even though I had never been in a burning building or pulled someone out of rushing water. And he was the only one who understood why I had curled up on the couch with exhaustion after a long day reporting about a young boy lost in the Angeles National Forest.

Now I wanted him home. Away from the excitement and action he loved. I wanted him here with me. I'd never been one to long for things or to pine for another person. So this feeling of needing him—the hollow place inside that yearned for him—was new territory for me.

"Overnight flooding led to a dramatic rescue this morning after a family of three was caught in rushing water on a road, overturning their car," the reporter was saying. "Large chunks of asphalt and boulders cascaded down the road as firefighters from the Urban Search and Rescue Task Force used ropes to stabilize the vehicle, then evacuated the family."

In the blinding rain, a team of rescuers was lowered into the churning waters. Then the tall rescuer wrenched open the car's door, and the others brought out a little girl, no more than four years old, and then her parents. I stopped the video and studied the profile of one of the rescuers.

I would recognize that face anywhere. Handsome, even wearing a yellow dry suit and bulky black flotation vest. Eric's gaze was locked on the little girl he was carrying, reassuring her as he waded through rushing waters in the powerful storm.

I peered again at the screen, making doubly sure that the blurry image was Eric.

"Come home," I whispered to his image on the screen.

The assignment meeting had already started by the time I arrived in the Fish Bowl that morning. David was in the midst of a mini-lecture and, thankfully, didn't seem to notice my late arrival.

"This is clearly a sophisticated operation," he was saying. "Folks, already ten million dollars in cash and high-priced items have been stolen in what are easily the largest hauls in LA history. The thieves are going for high-end, highly salable items that only the ultrarich can afford. Susan, tell us what was stolen from La Villa de la Paz."

My blood pressure rose as Susan opened her leather-bound notebook and flipped through the pages. From the satisfied expression on her face, I had no doubt she was gunning to make this her story.

"The owner of the estate refused an interview. But her assistant gave me a list of a few of the items reported stolen. I have a feeling he's going to get in trouble for that, but here it is: a Hublot watch worth thirty-nine thousand, a Lana Marks Cleopatra bag worth two hundred fifty thousand, a rare Cartier gold bracelet that sells for nineteen thousand dollars, a Patek Philippe Reference 1436 watch that goes for two hundred ten thousand, a Fendi dyed mink-and-fox bag that retails for seven thousand dollars. They also took a case of wine that she bought at auction for a hundred twenty-three thousand—"

"That's crazy," Russ interrupted. "What kind of wine costs a hundred and twenty-three thousand dollars a case?"

Susan shot him a withering look. "You're missing the point. The owner—a billionaire named Donna Chase—has a wine cellar with over two thousand rare bottles. The thieves knew exactly which case was the most valuable and didn't disturb any of the others."

Russ shrugged. "Clearly an inside job, then. Did they interrogate the sommelier?"

That got a few laughs from the group, even though I suspected some in the room thought a sommelier was someone from Somalia.

"Let's be vigilant on this story." David took a gulp of green juice from a sixteen-ounce jug. "It's got stickiness with our viewers, and sweeps start next week. We need a bump this month."

In the last ratings period, Channel Eleven had jumped from fourth to second place out of seven stations, but a lot of that gain had been attributed to my Good Sam reports. I knew our senior VP of news, Bonnie Ungar, and the executive team were worried we'd slip back to fourth place.

"Police aren't talking about the heists," David continued. "What we really need is to talk to the billionaires whose estates were robbed."

"Good luck with that," Russ said. "We'd be more likely to score an interview with the president than one of those highly guarded plutocrats."

"Actually, I am going to be meeting Stephen Bening, the owner of Château du Soleil, at a fund-raiser at his home on Sunday," I said.

Susan turned to look at me. When she realized I wasn't joking, her face turned pale with surprise.

David smiled. "Exactly what we need."

Apparently Andrew Wright, the executive vice president of news at ANC, had a short list of places where he'd meet for lunch in LA. All of them were on the Westside, which meant a thirty-minute commute for me; all of them had low noise levels so we could speak without shouting; and unfortunately, all of them were fairly high-traffic restaurants where I was likely to run into colleagues and news sources.

Which was why I argued with my dad's assistant, Lisa, about where I would meet Andrew for the lunch my dad had set up. Smart people didn't argue with Lisa. In the twelve years she'd been working with my dad, she had developed a way of making her intentions clear without ever raising her voice. And she almost always got her way.

But thankfully she was also practical. When I explained that I couldn't take off in the middle of a news day to meet Andrew across town, she tried to make it a dinner. And when I relayed that it wouldn't be smart for a reporter under contract with one station to be seen meeting with a highly placed news executive of a cable network, Andrew agreed to move the lunch to a small restaurant on Melrose Avenue, the kind where you sat at rough-hewn wooden tables and chose from a menu of organic items like couscous and quinoa salads. Because the restaurant was on the ultratrendy part of Melrose Avenue—between a vintage shop named Resurrection and another named the Way We Wore—I was pretty confident I wouldn't run into anyone I knew.

Andrew might have been dressed like a network executive in his gray suit and polished shoes, but he had reporter blood in his veins. Before he'd risen through the ranks to executive heights, he had been a field reporter for local news—first for an all-news radio station in Buffalo, New York, then as a reporter for the ABC affiliate in Washington, DC.

"I get it," he said as we lunched on winter quinoa tabbouleh and hummus. "My news director would have put me on the shit stories for weeks if he found out I was meeting with another network."

"I hope I'm not wasting your time. Because, as my father knows—and I hope he told you—I'm not interested in shifting focus into political reporting."

"I've known your dad a long time, and I know his agenda. But I'm not here to do his bidding. I've watched your reel, and your reports are excellent. I mean it when I say you're probably one of the top breaking-news reporters out there right now."

I felt warm at what he said. David and Bonnie weren't ones to dole out praise very often, and hearing it from someone with Andrew's experience felt good.

"I'm eager to hear what you want to do next," he continued.

Next. What did he mean by that? I had turned twenty-nine a few months before and hadn't given much thought to what came next.

He leaned forward. "Do you want to anchor? Report for a news magazine? Network news? Have your own news show?"

His words made me dizzy. "I actually like covering breaking news."

Andrew had seen a lot in his years as a reporter, and he had the wrinkles to prove it. In his early fifties, he still had a full head of curly brown hair. "I was like you, you know. I reported from Tiananmen Square the night of the government's crackdown, and it took me weeks to recover. But covering murders, disasters, tragedy . . . that can take a toll on a reporter. You can't do it forever." He rolled up his right sleeve. "You might find that reporting for ANC gives you a wider array of stories to cover."

I didn't know what to say. Where would a job in New York leave Eric and me? Our relationship was still so new that we hadn't talked about either of us leaving LA.

Andrew must have sensed my reluctance, because he took an unexpected approach. "I have an idea. Why don't you come on James Russell's show and talk about the heists?"

James Russell was a top political reporter on ANC who hosted a nightly hour-long talk show and was known for tackling big issues, but not without controversy.

"My news director—"

"They'll say yes. This'll be great promotion for you and Channel Eleven. If it's okay with you, I'll call this afternoon. It's Bonnie Ungar running that shop, isn't it?"

I nodded. He worked so fast he made my head spin. I'd come here expecting to declare all the reasons for my disinterest in political reporting, and within minutes, he had me coming aboard as a guest on a political talk show.

"I'm not a pundit—"

"I don't need another pundit," he said, waving his hand. "What I need is someone out there relentlessly investigating, reporting on the big stories firsthand." He smiled and leaned back in his chair. "I think you're going to like the experience more than you know."

CHAPTER FIVE

Stephen Bening's Château du Soleil was hardly a château. In fact, it probably dwarfed most French castles and manor houses. The mega-mansion, situated on ten acres of formal gardens, orchards, and ornate fountains, was located in what was called the Platinum Triangle—an exclusive area that included Bel Air, Holmby Hills, and Beverly Hills and was home to Hollywood celebrities, luxury shopping, and some of the most expensive estates in the world.

The fund-raising event, featuring a speech by the vice president, was held in a ballroom that rivaled those in most fine hotels. Priceless artworks lined walls graced by pilasters with gold crowns. A painted ceiling with majestic chandeliers soared twenty feet above our heads.

A symphony orchestra and a band entertained guests while they mingled with political stars. Unlike the other fund-raising event, however, there were no celebrities or famous athletes in attendance. I'd seen a few of the faces in the room in the pages of the *Wall Street Journal* and a few others from various lists in *Forbes* magazine.

While the house was completely ostentatious, the fund-raiser itself reeked of sophisticated wealth. This was not the kind of event where grand old ladies showed up dripping in diamonds and dragging fur coats. The men dressed in tailored suits, and except for the luxury watches on their wrists, they were mostly indistinguishable from each other. The women wore designer dresses with one or two pieces of classic, but never showy, jewelry.

My dad was standing with two couples in their late fifties, and even from a distance, I knew he had already launched into fund-raising mode. He was one of the best at raising money. So much so that NPR once dubbed him a "fund-raising rock star." He had the gift of small talk, a sincere laugh that put people at ease, and a chummy patter that sounded off the cuff and personal, even though he didn't often stray from the script. My dad and most senators spent shocking amounts of time raising money, thinking about money, and planning to raise money. In the House, the candidate with the most money won nine times out of ten. In the Senate, it was eight out of ten.

Most of that fund-raising didn't take place in high-end venues like this castle but in unglamorous settings that ringed the Capitol like the Capital Grille, Bullfeathers, and the Monocle. But it wasn't all drudgery. In the past year, my dad had attended four hundred fund-raising events, including golf tournaments, birthday celebrations, concerts, and even a pheasant-hunting trip.

All afternoon, I tried to get into a conversation with Stephen Bening, but he eluded me. He was clearly in his element here and flitted from one group to another, seemingly without a break. At one point I thought I'd caught his eye, but he looked past me as though he didn't recognize me.

All I needed was thirty seconds to make my case. I'd polished my pitch and even rehearsed it several times on the drive over. "This isn't about invading your privacy," I'd say. "This is about letting viewers understand what it feels like to be robbed. And it's an opportunity to help catch the thieves, because someone watching probably knows something about these heists."

It didn't look like I'd get thirty seconds with him, so I headed out of the ballroom and slipped into an open door across the hallway. When I saw what was inside the room, I exhaled sharply. This home library was a four-thousand-square-foot round rotunda with skylights at the top of its thirty-foot ceilings. Floor-to-ceiling bookcases that curved with the walls of the library housed thousands of books.

The room smelled of old books, a mustiness with a hint of vanilla that I had thought only existed in old dusty public libraries. Somehow Stephen had captured that scent in his home library. Maybe money could buy anything.

I walked the perimeter of the room, running my fingers along the spines of some of the books, soaking in the magnitude. It would take ten lifetimes to read all of them.

He had at least a dozen shelves of business and investing books and an impressive collection of children's classics—books about Robin Hood, Joan of Arc, King Arthur. And one entire shelf was devoted to identical copies of a book titled *Business Hacks: Secrets to Changing the World through Business*. The author was Stephen Bening.

I flipped past chapters titled "Disruption: Changing the Rules in the Marketplace" and "From Minnows to Sharks: The New Competitors" to the back cover, with a photo of a beardless Stephen Bening along with a brief biography.

"Stephen Bening, CEO of SalesInsight, was named Businessperson of the Year by *Fortune* magazine, Best CEO in the World by *Barron's*, and Best CEO in America by *Forbes*. He received the Innovation Award from the *Economist*."

I glanced at the trophy-stocked shelf above it. The centerpiece was a large, ornately filigreed silver cup trophy mounted on a wooden base. A plaque on the base read 1996 University of Southern California.

"Quite a behemoth, isn't it?" A man's voice startled me.

I whirled around and found myself face-to-face with Stephen Bening.

"National Debate Tournament." He nodded toward the trophy. "I was captain of the team the year we won it. It's the only time USC ever claimed that victory." He sat on the edge of the mahogany desk. "But you didn't come in here to look at an old trophy and stacks of books. Is the party that bad?"

"Your party is great," I said. "But as you can imagine, I've been to many of these events, and after a while they get—"

"Predictable. I agree, and I'm the host."

"Apologies for escaping in here."

"Not a problem." He gestured toward the book in my hand. "I see you've found my book."

With his book in my hands, I knew I looked like a busybody reporter snooping around his private library. "*Secrets to Changing the World through Business*," I said, trying to cover my embarrassment. "That's a tall order for a book."

"Read it and see for yourself. Everyone thinks the tech industry is about creating gadgets and apps, but if we do our jobs right, we can change the world." He glanced at his watch, a treasure I recognized now as a Hublot Big Bang: $110,000. "Maybe we should get back to the ballroom, or your father will be unhappy at both of us for deserting him."

I followed him toward the door and felt the blood pushing hard in my veins as I tried to figure out a way to get him to talk about the heist.

"Stephen," I said. "My father will give me a lecture for what I'm about to ask, so don't blame him. But I have to—"

"Ask about the burglary. It only took you two minutes. Not bad." He turned to face me. I couldn't tell if he was irritated or amused.

"Do you actually think some police officers are behind it?" I asked, setting aside my rehearsed pitch. "Or was that just cocktail chatter?"

"One hundred percent *not* cocktail chatter. They completed an entire investigation and yet never shared any information with me. Police claim they have no evidence, but that's impossible. How could there be absolutely no evidence, no clues of any kind?"

"They may have found some. A source of mine says they've found the Hidden Mickey."

He raised an eyebrow. "A Hidden Mickey?"

"Evidence powerful enough to potentially unlock the case. It's not usually shared with the media because it could compromise the investigation. I don't know what it is, but it may explain why they're not saying anything to you."

He thought about it for a moment. "I'm willing to bet the Hidden Mickey, as you call it, points to members of our illustrious police force. That's why I've hired a private investigator to look into police conspiracy."

"Police conspiracy. Would you be willing to talk with me on camera about that? It's an opportunity to—"

"The answer is no," he said swiftly. "And it's not because I have anything against you or reporters in general. I see how this story is developing in the media, and it's all about how the rich have *far* too much money. You can see why I don't want to be a part of it."

I couldn't let him get away with no. "Then let's change the story. What if we focused the interview on your investigation into police involvement in the heists?"

"Still a no." He reached inside his suit jacket and pulled out a business card. "Call me if you learn anything more from your police source."

"I never said my source was a police officer."

"It's obvious that he is, though."

"Stephen?" A thirtysomething blonde in a floor-length sapphire dress drifted into the library. Her hair was swept up in a jeweled comb, and her ruffled-hem dress was impeccable, as if she had just stepped off the runway during Fashion Week in Paris. "Everyone's wondering where you are."

"Margot, this is Kate Bradley, Senator Bradley's daughter." He turned to me. "Stay in touch. Keep me posted about what you learn from your source, and if you play your cards right, maybe I'll change my mind about an interview."

The party was in full swing when I returned to the ballroom. Dozens of people were dancing, swaying to a jazzy arrangement the orchestra and band were playing at full volume. The conversations had become louder, too, more boisterous and punctuated by peals of laughter. Now that the younger set of wealthy donors in their thirties and forties had arrived, the room was filled nearly to capacity. There seemed to be waiters everywhere. Dressed in black pants and crisp white shirts, some carried trays of appetizers and other delicacies, but most were offering an endless parade of signature mixed drinks, rare wines, champagnes, and even vodka and tequila shots.

Over the din, I heard my phone ping in my purse. I pulled it out, and a playful smile emoji flashed across the screen.

Who's this? I typed.

Eric.

I stepped into a corner of the ballroom to reply. *You okay?*

New phone. Old one lost in hurricane.

When will you be back?

You look beautiful tonight.

I smoothed my black dress and smiled, broader now, wishing he hadn't lost his cell phone for six days. I was enjoying flirting with him even from thousands of miles away.

Another text swooped across the screen. *Like your smile too.*

I looked up for a moment, confused by his texts.

That's when I saw him, standing near the orchestra, next to a group of older men who, despite the dance music, were engrossed in conversation. Our eyes met across the room. He was dressed in a jet-black suit, his wavy hair only slightly tamed. Most guys who looked like he did were keenly aware of their good looks and let you know it, but Eric seemed oblivious, unaware of the effect he had on me or anyone else in the room.

I could barely breathe from the thrill and surprise of seeing him. I wound my way through the crowded room, and when I reached him, he drew me into his arms.

"Do you know how much I've missed you?" he whispered.

"No," I said, meeting his gaze.

"You don't?" His smile reached his eyes. "Then let me remind you."

My pulse skipped a beat as he pulled me into a kiss that was as hot as it was brief. "Does that give you any hint?"

"Hmm, not enough." I leaned my head on his shoulder in a failed attempt to slow my breathing. "How did you find me here?"

"When you weren't home, I called the newsroom, and your producer, Hannah, told me where you were. I couldn't wait until you came home, so I came here myself."

I saw the extreme fatigue in his face and his red-rimmed eyes, but he was working hard not to show it.

"And they let you in? Everyone else here paid ten thousand dollars for the privilege."

"Your dad vouched for me."

"My dad? Was he in on this?"

He shook his head. "Not until I showed up a few minutes ago. I took a gamble and told security I was his guest, and he came to the door to let me in. He warned me, though, that you don't like surprises."

"Usually I don't. But this surprise is good. Very good."

"Dance?" he asked.

I'd never danced with Eric before—in fact, I hadn't danced with anyone since my cousin's wedding back when I was in college—so I wasn't exactly sure what to do at first. But then we eased into a rhythm together, a slow dance while everyone else, fueled by all the free-flowing liquor, was letting loose.

As we danced, I was both amazed and terrified by the strength of my feelings. I had never met anyone who made me feel the way he did. I needed him. It was a new feeling and not entirely a comfortable one. Desire I could handle. Well, maybe. But longing to be with him—being consumed with being with him—was shutting off the thinking parts of my brain.

The song ended, and a waiter came by, carrying a tray of sparkling champagne flutes. We both grabbed one; then Eric took my hand in his, and we snaked through the crowd, out of the ballroom, and past the library. "Where are we going?" I asked as we started down a winding staircase, away from the party.

He stopped on the stair below me and looked up at me, his face lit only by the fleur-de-lis wall sconces in the stairwell. "How often do we get to be in a place like this? Let's go explore."

I stopped. "What if we get caught?"

"Who's going to fault two lovers sneaking out under the moonlight?"

I liked the way he said *lovers*, but that wasn't enough to push away the gnawing feeling that we shouldn't go any farther. "My father will kill me for bailing on his party." Okay, not kill me. But I knew exactly what he would say: *A senator's daughter does not wander around a donor's estate.*

He smiled at me. "You'll cross police tape to cover a train derailment, but you won't sneak outside at a fund-raising event?"

He was right. How bad could it be to take a peek outside? We followed the staircase to the ground level, then walked down two long hallways until we found an arched wooden door that looked like it might lead outside.

Eric pushed the door open, and we found ourselves on a lush, expansive lawn in the back of the estate. The door closed behind us, and the laughter and music from the party fell away. The only sound was a lone cricket chirping slowly in the distance.

The scent of mint and night jasmine rode on a light breeze as we stood there for a long moment, letting our eyes adjust to the evening light. A second cricket joined to form a small chorus.

A full moon already hung high in the sky, casting its cool beams on a garden of white roses on the side of the house. Night fell slowly, and the sky behind the mountains in the distance was aglow with the last orange and pink hues of the day.

He took my hand, and we headed across a lawn that felt like a carpet beneath my feet. The night, the garden, and everything around us were transfigured by the luminous glow of moonlight. A quiet hush enveloped us as we slipped into a forest of mature fruit trees.

"Have you ever been anyplace like this before?" Eric whispered.

I shook my head. I had been in many paradises before on fund-raising jaunts with my father. I hadn't ever stolen away from a party, so I couldn't say exactly what the estates were like beyond the ballrooms and expansive lawns, but none had been quite as breathtaking as this one. But it wasn't the grandeur of the estate that was stealing my breath away. It was being with Eric again. I didn't believe in destiny, but I had the profound feeling that I was supposed to be here with him, that I was exactly where I belonged.

We stopped beneath an orange tree in full bloom. Around us a circuit of fireflies rose like sparks, lighting the trees with their glowing specks. Fireflies were rare in Los Angeles—but here they were, as though the orchard had become some kind of enchanted wonderland.

I reached out to catch one and missed, but Eric managed to corral a few in his cupped hands. I peeked through his fingers, mesmerized.

"It's like capturing a tiny star in your hands," I whispered.

He flung open his hands, setting them free into the swirling droves of twinkling fireflies. He leaned in to kiss me, and I tasted the champagne on his lips.

The squawk of a walkie-talkie interrupted our kiss. Peeking through the leaves of the tree, we spotted a security guard a few yards away, walking the perimeter of the orchard.

Eric took my hand again, and then we began running in the narrow grassy rows between the trees, deeper into the orchard and away from the guard. We started laughing, like silly kids who had just pulled an enormous prank. In the tender light he smiled at me, and then he was no longer the captain of a search and rescue team but a boy on a nighttime adventure. With me. We ducked beneath low branches heavy with fruit and skirted around small puddles in the dirt, giddy with excitement, our faces flushed.

We stopped when we came upon a small cabin surrounded by a thick grove of olive trees. Its gray clapboards were scraped and weathered, as though it had been around for a hundred years or more. It was clearly out of place on the immaculate estate. I cupped my hands and peered through the window to the right of the sagging front door, but a dark shade on the inside blocked my view.

"What're you doing?" Eric asked, catching his breath.

"Reporter's habit," I whispered and then peered into the other window. The shade on this one was lifted slightly, and I could see a sliver of the inside because a light had been left on in the corner of the small cabin. From my vantage point, I could see a long black table with tall banks of computer monitors. Considering Stephen was CEO of a software company, it wasn't surprising there'd be computer monitors everywhere. It was only odd to see them in a rundown old cabin.

"Come here, you," Eric whispered, drawing me away from the cabin. He pulled me close beneath the silvery leaves of a tall tree with a fat, gnarled trunk. "We didn't come all the way out here so you could play Nancy Drew."

I smiled and couldn't stop, even if I had wanted to. "What did we come out here for?"

He opened his hands and displayed a handful of green olives he had pulled from the tree above him. "To pick olives, of course."

My eyes met his, and then the night took on a magical quality. In the half light of that evening, the wind whispered through the trees, jostling their leaves, floating their fragrant blooms like fairy dust around us. I wanted the moment, the rush of it, to go on forever.

"How long has it been since you slept?" I whispered.

He brushed a lock of hair from my face. "Nineteen, maybe twenty hours."

But from the way he pressed his body against mine and planted a slow, deep kiss on my lips, I knew he wasn't going to catch up on any sleep that night.

CHAPTER SIX

I felt a glow of excitement as I headed into the newsroom the next morning. Eric was home. His dress shirt had hidden a deep gash he'd suffered when debris slashed at his neck during the high-winds rescue in the river. But otherwise he had returned unharmed. He was exhausted but safe, still asleep in my bed. Unless an emergency cropped up, he was going to spend the morning catching up on much-needed sleep.

I was hoping for a slow news day so I could slip out early, but that wasn't to be. When I arrived in the assignment meeting, Russ Hartman was pitching a story about an app that allowed users to take a photo of a key with a smartphone and get a duplicate of the key in the mail a week later.

David wasn't having any of it. "Let's see. We've got a gunman and another man dead in a veterans' clinic shooting this morning. There's a robber targeting elderly women in Koreatown elevators. A homeless man found a dead baby in a dumpster. And you want to do a story to promote some app that duplicates house keys?"

"We'd show viewers how vulnerable they are to having it happen to—"

"I've heard enough." David pointed at me. "Kate, tell me you have something to pitch on these heists."

"Actually, one of the billionaire homeowners has hired a private investigator to look into police conspiracy in the heists. He says police are withholding evidence they found at the scene. He's going to prove that it's a police cover-up."

His eyes lit up. "That's how you pitch a story, Russ. Police conspiracy. Cover-up. Missing evidence. *That's* a story. Kate, get on that angle right away."

The problem was Detective Jake Newton wasn't answering his texts or returning my calls. I'd even left a message on his home voice mail. When I called his office line without identifying myself, another detective told me he was "out." But despite peppering him with questions, he couldn't, or wouldn't, give any more information.

I tried sending an email to his LAPD address. When it bounced back as "mail undeliverable," my mind took a sharp detour. I wondered if Stephen Bening was right about police officer involvement in the heists and Jake was somehow caught up in that.

"Someone is spending a lot of time and money to orchestrate these burglaries, and it may not be for the reasons we all suspect," he had said. Could that mean police were behind the burglaries? They would certainly have the technology to bypass security systems and manage a sophisticated burglary operation. Was that why Jake had disappeared?

I bounced the theory off Hannah, who thought about it a moment as she sat in the chair next to mine in the reporters' bullpen. "If you look into past police officer corruption, it's always insidious, highly undetectable. It's never a string of high-profile megaburglaries that are being covered on nearly every news outlet around the country."

"That's because there never has been a string of megaburglaries like this before. The Château du Soleil owner is so certain police are behind it he's hired his own investigator."

She took a slug of coffee from a mug that read: HOME IS WHERE YOUR WI-FI CONNECTS AUTOMATICALLY. "Police aren't talking to the media and aren't sharing any information with the billionaire victims. Does that mean they're behind it? What does your source say?"

"My source has disappeared."

Hannah's eyes widened. "Disappeared as in 'on vacation'?"

I shook my head. "As in his personal cell phone is disconnected and his email bounces back as undeliverable. And when I call him at his office, they say he's out and don't give a reason or a return date."

Hannah cleared her throat. "I know you can't say who he is, but I might be able to use some tools on the deep web to figure out what happened to him. That is, if I happened to see his name written down somewhere."

I looked at her, trying to figure out if I could trust her.

"I wouldn't tell anyone," she said.

I wasn't good at trust. Trust the wrong person and you'd get your email hacked, your credit cards stolen, or worse. Lots of people trusted Bernie Madoff and lost millions in his Ponzi scheme. That was because most people suffered from unrealistic optimism, overestimating the likelihood that someone was trustworthy simply because they behaved a certain way. But almost every indicator of trustworthiness—making eye contact, feigning openness, smiling—could be manipulated or faked.

I'd only known Hannah for less than a year, and I wondered if she could really be trusted with the name of my source. My instincts were oddly saying yes. On every story we covered together, Hannah was not only resourceful but also loyal. There were plenty of story leads she could've given other reporters, but she nearly always came to me first. That counted for something in the trust department. Besides, I *needed* to trust her in order to find out what had happened to Jake.

I scribbled Jake's name on a slip of paper and pushed it across the desk. "I'm holding you to that promise."

"I'll see what I can do."

My cell phone buzzed on my desk, startling me. The call was from David Dyal.

"Hey," I answered.

"Come to my office, would you?"

"Sure." Before I could ask why, he'd hung up.

David was more of a "walk and talk" manager, so it was unusual to be summoned to his office by cell phone. Especially since I had seen him in the assignment meeting fifteen minutes earlier.

"Close the door," he said when I stepped inside his office. "Have a seat."

I dropped into a chair and glanced over the arrangement of framed photos behind his desk, waiting for him to speak. There were photos of David with his kids on a boat ride, David with a TV celebrity from the 1990s, David posing with the current governor of California, and another candid photo of him standing with a news photographer in front of a tank during what I was guessed was the Iraq War.

I braced myself to hear that he and Bonnie had decided to give Susan the heist story. It was sweeps week, after all.

"Something you want to tell me?" he said.

"About the heist story? I'm working—"

His tone was stiff. "About why you're meeting with Andrew Wright at ANC."

I hadn't expected that. "My father set it up. They're old friends."

He sat back in his chair and laced his hands behind his head. "Next time you meet with another network, you might want to choose a more private place. You probably didn't notice, but the station's general manager was having lunch in there."

"Lauren Hultmark eats lunch at a hole-in-the-wall on Melrose Avenue?"

He nodded. "Her favorite. Andrew knows it too."

I frowned. Had Andrew set me up?

"I don't like getting my ass chewed out by Lauren Hultmark—"

"The lunch was no big deal. He invited me to come on James Russell's show and talk about the estate burglaries. He told me he was going to call Bonnie to get her okay."

"Which he did. And Bonnie is livid."

"So she's not going to approve me going on the show?"

"No, she's going to let you do it. It'll be great promotion during sweeps."

I rubbed my eyes, trying to make sense of what he was saying. Few assignment editors got the position because they had great management skills. A lot of them got to be executives by being top reporters, a career path that wasn't always a great training ground for managing other reporters. David was that kind of executive. He had an almost superpower instinct for news, honed by years of reporting from the field, but he wasn't the best at the people part of the gig.

"I don't get it. What's this about?"

He took a sip of his green goo and grimaced. "We all know what Andrew is up to. He spots talent, talks to them about their aspirations and goals, then reels them in by bringing them on one of his shows. He knows you'll get a kick out of it and jump ship from wherever you are. He's a master at recruiting."

"He's not going to 'reel me in' by bringing me on one of his shows."

He laced his fingers behind his head and sat back in his chair. "You don't get it, do you? In Andrew's eyes, you are quintessential media royalty. Through your father, you have a recognizable name and connections to the most powerful people in the world. Recognizable names sell advertising, and Andrew knows it. Look at Chelsea Clinton or Jenna Bush Hager—"

"So this meeting is about you reminding me how valuable I am to Channel Eleven. So I don't even think about going to work for Andrew and ANC."

He shuffled some papers on his desk, then looked up at me. "No, it's about being smart, Kate. If you're going to meet with a poacher like Andrew, at least give me a heads-up. That way, I can act like I know what the hell is going on around here."

"Got it," I said, then stood, readying for my exit. His words stung, but I didn't want him to know he'd gotten to me.

He motioned for me to sit back down. "We're not done yet." He swiveled his laptop toward me. "Have you seen this?"

On his screen was a photo of me with Eric at last night's party at Château du Soleil. The photo had been snapped by the cabin in the olive orchard. In the silvery light, Eric had his arm wrapped around my shoulder, and we were beaming at each other, laughing at something, a fraction from a kiss.

"No doubt you two look good together," David said dryly. "Because of that, it will definitely get a lot of play in the media. Already is. My point here is that you are, again, not showing good judgment." He pointed toward the caption, which read:

"Senate majority leader Hale Bradley's daughter, Kate Bradley, sneaks away from a fund-raiser for Congressman Alan Blair with an unknown partygoer. The $10,000-per-person event at Stephen Bening's Château du Soleil featured a talk by the vice president. Bradley is a reporter for Los Angeles Channel Eleven."

"This is tabloid crap," I said, noting the *Globe* banner at the top.

But even as I tried to brush it off, it rattled me that Eric and I had been followed and photographed in the orchard last night. Worse, my dad was not going to be happy. This photo made it look like I was some privileged party girl.

"It's not what it looks like. It's not like I ran out of the party with some random guy."

He shrugged. "If you want to be taken seriously in this business, Kate, you're going to have to be more careful."

~

The rest of the morning became a huge time suck as several newsroom staff—and a few crew members—pointed out the post or asked me about it. What had been a beautiful and intimate moment between Eric and me had become the subject of light teasing, casual inquiries about the "unidentified partygoer" in the photo, and other prying questions that put me on edge. My private life had never been the subject of discussion or gossip before, and while I was proud of Eric, the whole situation had taken an uncomfortable turn.

My father's call came at noon. I grabbed my cell phone, slipped into the small conference room at the back of the newsroom, and closed the door.

"Dad," I said wearily, slumping in a chair.

"You already know what I'm going to say, so I'll make this quick. You know better. Someone else might be able to get away with wandering around Bening's estate, but as my daughter, you won't."

I sighed. "I know."

"I don't want to scare you, but I think this was a warning."

"A warning?"

"That photo was planted to send you—and me—a very loud message. I suspect the people who leaked it don't like how you're reporting on the heists."

"How *I'm* reporting on the heists? It's not much different from any other reporter's."

"You're a senator's daughter. Someone who's grown up with privilege. They expect you to speak out and condemn the criminals. But instead, your stories about the opulent wealth and extravagance are fanning the fires *against* the rich."

I felt a headache coming on. "Makes no sense. There are hundreds of reporters on this story, some of them with much bigger audiences than I have. Why target just me?"

"Because you're my daughter. As the chairman of the Senate Finance Committee, what is the biggest hot-button issue I'm wrestling with? Tax reform for the rich. Because of your reports, voters are demanding tax hikes on the wealthy. And the wealthy obviously don't want higher taxes and will do whatever it takes to make sure I know it. Think about that when you file your next report."

CHAPTER SEVEN

I wasn't an extension of my father. I made my own decisions, political and otherwise. And although I'd grown up in a household full of rules about what not to say to the media or how to behave so you didn't end up in the tabloids, my father had raised me to be an independent thinker.

Until now. I wasn't sure what to do about my father's request, but it weighed on my mind the rest of the afternoon as I filed updates on the heist story. I became suddenly self-conscious about what I wrote, thinking about how each choice of phrase would be perceived by the people who leaked the photo. All of it was giving me a bad case of writer's block.

And it was making me worried. My father and I had both experienced the dangers of his being a powerful name in public office. We rarely talked about it much anymore, but back when I was in elementary school, a militant group tried to set off a bomb outside my bedroom window. The bomb didn't explode because the city was experiencing rare below-freezing temperatures. After that, my father had a bodyguard trail me to and from third grade. I knew this event was on his mind, even if he didn't say it.

But there was no doubt he was right about the growing backlash against the wealthy. Later that afternoon, photos of the fireflies in Bening's orchard went viral on social media with this caption: "Billionaires spent over $150K to have thousands of lightning bugs flown in and released when the vice president arrived at $10,000-per-person fund-raiser for Congressman Alan Blair (Calif.) at Silicon Valley entrepreneur Stephen Bening's Bel Air estate. #TheTroubleWithBillionaires"

I tried to ignore all the social media posts and focus on writing a heist update for the station website, but that strategy wasn't working either. I was relieved, then, when Hannah waved at me from across the newsroom.

"You've got to see this." She pointed at her monitor.

I hurried over to her desk, grateful for the interruption. Her face was tense in the glow of the computer screen. On her monitor was a grainy video of a fire. "This is cell phone video of a house fire on Delfern Drive. I know we wouldn't normally cover a house fire, right? But what makes this one special is where it's located. Holmby Hills. This is an estate designed by Wallace Neff."

"Wallace Neff?"

"You need to bone up on your LA history." She ran her fingers through waves of thick brown hair. "Neff was old Hollywood royalty. The first 'starchitect,' famous for designing Pickfair, Mary Pickford and Douglas Fairbanks's estate. This one doesn't have an exotic name like the others, but it's one of the most expensive estates in LA. Eight acres of rolling lawns, tennis courts, and pools. A Wall Street broker named Thomas Speyer bought it for fifty-five million dollars."

"You think this is another heist?"

"All they're talking about is a fire on the scanner. But I'm willing to bet a month's salary there was a burglary too." She handed me a Post-it note. "Here's the address."

"I'll check it out."

I turned to leave. "Before you go," she said. "I did that deep-web search you asked me to. And your friend? Well, he's completely disappeared from all social media, when before he was pretty regularly on

Twitter. Looks like he had mostly tweeted about sports, particularly football, and now . . . it's like he's gone off the grid." Seeing my panicked expression, she added quickly, "But I'll keep digging."

I had no doubt her reporter's intuition was right about the Holmby Hills fire, so I convinced dispatch to assign Josh to work on the story with me. Minutes later, we jumped into the news van and raced to the address Hannah had given us.

Holmby Hills was a neighborhood west of Beverly Hills, with some of the largest properties in the city. We drove winding streets studded with English-style streetlights and named after places in Great Britain—Dalehurst, Strathmore, Westholme. But once we reached Holmby Park, ringed by a stand of mature sycamore trees, traffic came to a standstill. Up ahead we saw police cars, their lights flashing, blocking the street. I jumped out of the van and jogged past the line of cars to get a glimpse of what was happening. Farther ahead, police were instructing drivers to make U-turns.

"What's going on?" I asked a sandy-haired officer in a navy-blue Beverly Hills Police Department uniform. I had a theory they hired the Beverly Hills police officers as though they were casting a TV series, because all of them were as beautiful and handsome as the police heroes we saw on TV. Seriously, I had never met a Beverly Hills police officer who *wasn't* good looking. And this guy was no exception.

"Fire up in the hills," he said, laying a pair of piercing blue eyes on me.

"I'm with Channel Eleven. Any way you can let me through?"

His blue eyes were all business. "All access is closed. No one's allowed up there except fire and police."

I surveyed the scene. After my success sneaking past police lines on the Metrolink disaster, I was looking for a way to get past the blockade here too. But there were so many officers and squad cars in the immediate area that I couldn't see a way around them all.

"I hear there was a robbery as well," I said, stalling for time while I continued to scan for a way in.

"Don't know anything about that. But please get back in your car. It's not safe standing here in all this traffic."

Reluctantly, I headed back to the van and texted Jake. *Holmby Hills fire? Access?*

No response. Where was he?

A few minutes later, dispatch sent Chopper 11 to fly over the fire, and the news desk slotted our live report to open the four o'clock cast. Standing in front of a legion of police squad cars barricading the street, I delivered my report.

"As a fire rages in an estate in Holmby Hills, all lanes of traffic through this exclusive neighborhood are closed. Over one hundred firefighters are battling the blaze," I said. "Traffic is backed up throughout Westwood and Beverly Hills, creating a nightmare for commuters during the busy rush hour. At this time there are no confirmed reports that a high-stakes burglary has also taken place at the Holmby Hills estate, but we will continue to investigate further, given the recent series of multimillion-dollar heists in high-end properties."

Anchor Maria Vargas then cut to Stan McCort in Chopper 11, who was flying over the estate, giving viewers a bird's-eye view of the fire billowing out of the second-story windows of the massive colonial-style mansion.

"We're just getting word that the Los Angeles County Fire Department's Urban Search and Rescue team is working to rescue a man trapped in the fire. The man is believed to be a resident of the estate," Stan said.

I jolted to attention. If Urban Search and Rescue was on the scene, Eric was probably there too. No doubt his at-home recovery from Hurricane Juanita had been cut short, because I couldn't imagine he'd sit out a rescue like this.

Chopper 11's camera zoomed in as gray smoke billowed out of a second-story window and two rescuers scrambled up a ladder and into the mansion. Moments later, the smoke became thick and black, and there was no sign of the rescuers. My pulse shot up as I watched for any suggestion of movement at the window. Nothing. And as each second ticked by and the smoke became heavier, the rescuers' return seemed less and less likely. I sucked in a breath, unable to ward off the shaking fear that Eric was one of the rescuers in the fire. Then, out of a shroud of smoke, the rescuers appeared at the window and handed the victim to two firefighters on the ladder, who quickly carried him to a waiting ambulance.

"We've just heard that the victim is alive and being taken to UCLA Medical Center," Stan said.

Minutes later, Josh and I headed to UCLA. I texted Eric to let him know I was headed that way. Traffic was in a complete snarl, and even though Josh found a faster route that wound through a sleepy one-way street in Westwood, it still took over half an hour to travel three miles.

The six o'clock newscast was already underway by the time Eric and the Urban Search and Rescue Task Force stepped out of the travertine-marble-clad towers of the UCLA Medical Center. He looked surprisingly energized as he walked out of the building into the circular plaza, where a sea of reporters descended on him. I watched him scan the crowd—looking for me, I assumed—but it was already dark, and Josh and I were in the back of the reporter camp.

"The incident commander will be out here in about five minutes to give you all an update," a firefighter with thick blond hair announced. Then Eric and his team headed toward a fire department SUV parked on a side street.

Josh and I quietly slipped away from the pack and headed in the SUV's direction. Eric smiled when he saw me. "This is getting to be a habit, you stalking me for interviews."

"Actually, you haven't given me one single interview since the rescue of the boy in Malibu Canyon. Want to break your streak?"

He put his hand on the small of my back. "That could be a yes." He motioned to another firefighter getting into the SUV. "Give me a couple of minutes."

The firefighter turned to look at me. "Don't listen to the captain, because no matter what, he's going to give credit for the rescue to someone else on the crew. But *he's* the one that pulled that guy out."

Eric smiled. "Ignore him. This one's nuts."

The firefighter, bright-blue eyes on a face smudged with dirt and sweat, grinned. "Here's how it went down, 'cause I was there. There was a deadly river of flames rolling across that ceiling, and smoke on the floor. Can't see nothin' but black everywhere. But we can hear someone calling for help. And there the captain goes past me in the smoke—like he's got x-ray vision or something—and homes right in on the victim. Next thing I know—'cause I'm searching for the guy, too—here comes the captain dragging him past me. I hear him through his mask. 'Grab his legs.' We pulled that guy out just as the fire lit up."

"I think she's heard enough," Eric said with a laugh, clearly uncomfortable being the focus of the crew member's praise.

Josh called the news desk to ask them if they wanted a report from one of the rescuers and whether they had time in the already-jammed cast. He flashed me a thumbs-up.

"Two minutes," he said. "We're next after they come out of this piece about a multicar crash in the Crenshaw district." I put on the earpiece that connected me with the newsroom and quickly applied some lipstick as Josh set up the camera.

"Any idea how our photo made it into the tabloids?" Eric whispered.

"All my reports about the heists are putting the superwealthy in a bad light. Some well-connected individuals are trying to discredit me by making it appear that I'm some kind of party girl who runs off with unidentified men at expensive fund-raisers."

"Well, we know it's not *unidentified* men," he said with a smile. "But practically every reporter is covering that story. Why did they only target you?"

"My dad is chairman of the Senate Finance Committee. He thinks the people behind this photo leak want to make sure he knows what kind of damage they can inflict if he doesn't make the 'right' decisions about tax reform for the rich."

"So putting our photo in the trashy tabloids is about getting your dad's attention too," he said. "My crew has been giving me all kinds of heat about the photo. Getting in the tabloids isn't usually part of my job description."

My guilt skyrocketed. In the macho world of the fire department, I imagined that a captain making the tabloids for kissing someone at a political fund-raiser probably would be met with endless teasing. "Your life would be a lot less complicated if I weren't a senator's daughter *and* a reporter."

"My life is better with you in it." His eyes met mine. "Besides, I like the way you look in the photograph. I'm keeping that one."

"One minute," Josh interrupted, handing me a microphone.

"Ready?" I said to Eric.

He nodded, blinking in the glare of the camera lights. After years doing hundreds of live reports, I felt a quick kick of nervous energy as the clock ticked down. The report started out fine, but the way Eric was smiling at me was distracting.

"There's gratitude and a sense of relief among residents after a fire raged through an estate here in Holmby Hills," I started, but my voice wavered. I actually sounded . . . flustered. "With me is Eric Hayes, captain of the Los Angeles County Fire Department's Urban Search and Rescue team, who freed a man trapped in the estate. How did you rescue the man?"

"We used ladders to get to the second story of the home, and we located the victim in the north bedroom. Once inside, the room was black with smoke. We crawled on the floor, staying close to the wall, until we reached the victim. We had about two minutes to get him out before that part of the house was engulfed in flames."

I looked at him while he was speaking. Everything about him was throwing me off—from the warm, authoritative way he spoke to how he looked in his snug blue uniform to the bandage peeking out of his collar, proof of his past bravery. His story was riveting, but I was actually having a hard time focusing on what he was saying.

"So there was only one man inside the house?" I asked firmly, determined to get my mind back on track.

He shot me a sly smile. I could see he was enjoying the effect he was having on me. "One man. He was heavy, so once I found him, it took two of us to lift him. In order to get him down the ladder, we had to dump everything out of his pockets."

My focus sharpened. "What was in his pockets?"

"He had two specially made pockets that ran the length of his legs. They were loaded with watches and small jewelry."

CHAPTER EIGHT

Eric and the USAR team had rescued one of the thieves. They had gone in there thinking they were rescuing a resident trapped in the fire, but they had actually rescued a burglar.

"Once you realized he was one of the thieves, did that make you angry you'd risked your life to save him?" I asked when the interview was over.

He looked at me as though the concept was foreign to him. "We're saving lives. We don't make assessments about who's worthy or not."

I admired that about him. I often struggled with bias on the stories I covered. When a high-level member of the MS-13 gang was killed in a car accident in Echo Park over the Fourth of July weekend last year, I reported that story with less empathy than when a family of four was killed in a similar accident. And viewers were equally conflicted. When Channel Eleven aired a story about a prostitute who was beaten by a customer in Hollywood, many viewers wrote in questioning the newsworthiness of a story about someone injured while engaging in criminal activity.

"What makes you willing to risk your life to save someone who was in the midst of committing a crime?" I said. "You must have altruism DNA the rest of us are missing."

He broke into a smile. "There you go again. Seeing something more in me."

The final tally of the Holmby Hills haul was far greater than the jewelry and watches firefighters found in the victim's pants. Several small art pieces were stolen off the walls in the living room, along with numerous purses—a Hermès Scheherazade clutch worth $25,000, a Gucci crocodile shoulder bag, which once sold for $30,000, and an ostrich-leather tote by Prada worth $10,000. And in addition to the watches found in the victim's pants, several others were stolen, including a Cartier, a Patek Philippe, and a Jaeger-LeCoultre Tourbillon.

Early the next morning, police called a press conference downtown to issue a statement. As Josh and I raced to get there on time, I texted Jake once more: *Are you getting my texts?!*

Still no response.

About two dozen reporters gathered in front of police headquarters as the chief, Charlie Harris, spoke. Flanked by two uniformed officers and standing in front of a screen emblazoned with the LAPD logo, Harris delivered his statement dressed in a light-gray suit and striped red tie.

"At approximately eleven o'clock yesterday morning, thieves forced their way into a Holmby Hills estate, breaking and entering, stealing over five million dollars in valuables, and setting the estate on fire." He looked up from his notes and addressed the reporters directly. "UCLA Medical Center just informed us that the victim in yesterday's fire is in a medically induced coma as doctors work to treat him for head injuries sustained when he fell while trapped by the fire. The man has not yet been identified, but we have evidence to believe he was one of several individuals robbing the home. Investigators have determined that the fire was deliberately and maliciously started and caused over seven hundred and fifty thousand dollars in damage," Harris said firmly. But despite his efforts to only state the facts, his rising tone made it clear he was angry.

"We are offering a five-hundred-thousand-dollar reward for the capture of the key suspects involved in this escalating crime," he continued. "Funds are coming from various private and public donors, including the owners of the properties that have been robbed."

He paused for effect. The only sound in the room was the clicking of the digital cameras. Then he brought out the main attraction. On a screen to his right, he played a brief and pixelated video clip of a man walking past a security camera. For a moment, the man looked in the direction of the camera, and we got a glimpse of him: about thirty, with closely cropped blond hair and muscled shoulders. The image of his face was too blurry to get any sense of what he looked like otherwise. Then he quickly pulled down his ski mask and exited the room.

Police Chief Harris looked into the dozens of television cameras and issued a warning to the man on the screen. "This is one of the men involved in the Holmby Hills heist who is still at large. Let me be clear: we will not tolerate this reign of terror. It's not a matter of *if* we catch you, but *when*. We will be vigilant, and we will be steadfast. We will not allow you to remain at large and will expend all resources to capture you."

The crowd of reporters erupted with questions after that, but one thing was clear. The story that had started out as a string of multimillion-dollar heists had now taken a bitter turn as arson was added to the list.

It took me three attempts to be heard over other reporters' questions. "Some of the estate owners say police are withholding information, that they're not sharing key evidence found at the scene."

He shook his head. "Absolutely false. We share everything we can, as long as it doesn't jeopardize the investigation."

"You say the thieves 'forced their way' into the estate. What were the signs of forced entry?"

"It was a forced entry. That's all we can say at this time."

Harris tried to motion to another reporter, but I kept talking. "An estate owner claims that some police officers are actually responsible for the burglaries."

I saw a muscle twitch in his jaw. "I'm not even going to respond to such absurd speculation. Next."

I wondered what Stephen Bening would say. I dialed his number, but an efficient assistant on the other end of the line informed me he was in meetings and would have to return my call.

I flopped in a haze of exhaustion on Eric's leather couch later that evening. But my fatigue was nothing compared to what he'd gone through. After his six-day, round-the-clock stint battling Hurricane Juanita, he hadn't been back in LA for more than twelve hours before he and his crew had been called out to rescue the man at the Holmby Hills estate fire. Despite all that, he seemed completely relaxed on the couch, looking at some photos on his iPad, the bandage on his neck being the only visible sign of his hurricane ordeal.

I doubted I'd ever get used to coming home to a firefighter on the couch in shorts and a T-shirt. Ever. Damn, did he look good. He wasn't one of the overmuscled heroes the media thought we women admired—the ones with the giant pecs and the bulging veins in their necks, with thighs the size of tree trunks pumped up from endless hours spent in the gym. Eric looked like he earned his muscles doing real work. Authentic.

I kicked off my heels and snuggled next to him, luxuriating in the feeling of having his arm around me again. I'd missed him—missed this—more than I'd expected. I looked at him and suddenly felt hot.

What was wrong with me? Every time I was with him, I had the attention span of a kid in kindergarten. I was also pretty sure I had a perpetual dopey grin on my face. I felt a bit crazy, yet exhilarated, and wondered if he felt the same way.

Even Josh teased me about how flustered I'd been during my interview with Eric after the Holmby Hills fire. "You are rock solid out there when you interview the police chief or the mayor; then you're like a nervous cub reporter when you interview that fire-captain guy."

I hadn't told Josh about my relationship with Eric, but once he'd seen us together at the interview, he'd put two and two together and realized that the guy in the tabloid photo with me was Eric Hayes. I hadn't wanted him to know that when I was staring out the van window or seemed distracted, I might be thinking about Eric, not mulling over a story. Besides, I rarely shared private information with him or any of the cameramen. "In politics and in life, what matters is what *isn't* said," my dad had often reminded me.

After the Good Sam story, Eric had proposed to me on his sailboat, *Andromeda*. It was what we later called a "soft" proposal, not an official one, and we'd both decided that we weren't ready to rush into anything yet. In the months since then, I'd expected we'd settle into some kind of predictable routine—that the excitement might even wane a little—but our work schedules kept getting in the way, making our reunions more exciting, not less.

I glanced at his iPad and realized he was looking through photos of the devastation from Hurricane Juanita.

"Looks bad," I said as he flipped to a photo of a house that had been ripped from its foundation and dragged to the middle of the street.

"We were operating on three hours' sleep most of the time, rescuing people trapped in cars, trucks, attics. We could handle the water, but then we'd have five-foot-tall piles of debris or fallen trees blocking the roads. The stuff we saw . . . homes reduced to rubble, drowning victims. It still stays with me."

"Was yours the search and rescue team trapped in the collapsed school building?"

He nodded, his eyes darkening. "Ramirez broke his leg in three places when part of that building collapsed. We went in to get him. With the wind howling and the chaos of water and debris inside, there was a point there where I wondered if we'd all make it out alive. Once we got him, all I kept thinking was that I had to make it back home. To you."

My eyes met his, and I wanted to stay in the moment forever. Then my phone buzzed and dinged, alerting me to a text and breaking the spell. A text at ten o'clock at night probably meant I was going to be sent to cover some breaking-news event. Reluctantly, I pulled the phone out of my purse. The text was from Andrew Wright. *Cleared with Bonnie. Want you on James Russell's show tomorrow. Can you do it?*

I glanced out the window at the streetlights casting shadows through the trees on Eric's street.

This was really happening.

"Everything okay?" Eric asked.

"I'm going to be a guest reporter on James Russell's show on ANC tomorrow to talk about the heists." I sounded casual, like it was an everyday occurrence to be on a national news show, even though it wasn't.

"Wow, James Russell? A lot of people watch his show. That's big."

"Yeah."

"You don't sound excited."

I rubbed my shoulder. "The head news exec at ANC is recruiting me to come work for them. In New York."

"New York." His voice sounded hollow.

"He's talking about expanding the kinds of stories I get to work on beyond breaking news."

He looked away for a moment, and I wondered what he was thinking. "This is what you've always wanted. Bigger stories. A wider audience."

My voice came out like a whisper. "Yeah."

"I knew this moment would come eventually," he said, running his hands through his hair. "I just never thought it would be this soon."

"Me neither."

"You can't leave LA, Kate. It's in your blood. It's a part of who you are. Every time we go anywhere, you have a story about a report you filed from this street or from that neighborhood. You have an almost sixth sense of the stories this city has to tell and what LA viewers want to see."

I looked at him, speechless even though I made my living talking. My heart was pounding high in my throat, and blood rushed to my face. "Would you come to New York with me?" There, I said it.

His brown eyes met mine, and he was silent for a long time. "I don't know, Kate. I can't walk into the New York City Fire Department and get a job. It takes years to get certified by the department there, and then more years to wait around hoping a job like the one I have opens up."

The air came out of the room. "Years," I said quietly.

He nodded. "And after all that there's a good chance I wouldn't be doing anything close to what I'm doing here, captaining a search and rescue team."

"But if the same position was available in New York . . ."

"There aren't many search and rescue teams in the country like the one I lead." He swallowed. "I can't see how I would move to New York."

~

I had made a mistake agreeing to be on the ANC talk show. My pulse was doing a nervous jig as I sat in a chair with the Channel Eleven News set as a backdrop, waiting for the interview to begin. A camera was set up to beam my interview in real time via satellite to James Russell, and it would air live on ANC.

The makeup-and-hair stylist had done an outstanding job making me network ready, and I'd chosen a lavender silk blouse and black skirt, a blend of smart and feminine that looked good in the harsh glare of the lights. I'd done hundreds of reports from the field, but it was a lot more intimidating going on a live national news show where someone else was asking me questions, instead of the other way around. Worse, after my father's warning, I wasn't exactly sure what to say about the heists and the wealthy victims.

To calm my nerves, Hannah had done some research on James, showing me photos of him as a young Peace Corps volunteer and a father of two kids, as well as some vacation photos she'd found on the internet of his recent trip to Prince Edward Island. She had prepared the materials to make me more comfortable with being interviewed by the iconic journalist. But it wasn't stage fright that was making me jumpy. It was fear. What would the payback be if I spoke my mind about the heists in this interview? Would the people behind the tabloid photo escalate their attempts to rein me in and put even more pressure on my father?

A few minutes later, I saw the show opening and James on the monitor in front of me. Once James addressed me, my job was to talk directly to the camera like I always did. The producer had said my segment would be early in the show and advised me that James often veered away from the planned interview questions, so "be ready for anything."

James Russell had a haircut like a boy in high school, with long bangs swept to the side. They were blond with a warm russet tone, but since he was well into his sixties, that likely meant the beautiful color came from a bottle, not from nature. He sat in front of a wall of monitors, which projected a photograph of the White House at night. Soft, diffused lights below the news desk gave him the appearance of being much younger than he was. Until he started talking. Then he shouted at the camera in a stentorian tone, a rapid-fire delivery that was his trademark style but also seemed old fashioned.

Then a Billionaires Bilked graphic flashed on the screen, and James introduced the segment. "Millions of dollars stolen from billionaires in Southern California! Are we crying yet? Ha!"

He proceeded to show clips of the kinds of luxury goods that were stolen and some of the estates involved.

"Going now to Kate Bradley, a reporter who's been covering the story for Channel Eleven in Los Angeles. Kate, in less than a week, these thieves have hauled away over fifteen million in luxury goods and cash. Why can't police stop them?"

"This is a sophisticated, high-tech operation where the thieves leave behind no clues. They specifically target items that have high resale value and are easily carried out. Watches worth hundreds of thousands of dollars—each. Jewelry. Cash. Now they've graduated to exclusive cars that cost nearly a quarter of a million dollars each. But the people orchestrating these heists are careful, swift, and discerning. They get in, target the specific goods they want, and leave quickly, without a trace."

"Which seems to be delighting a lot of people," James said. "The amount of attention these heists are getting is insane. Everyone is talking about them. The barista at the coffee shop around the corner. Even Washington notables. Why should people care if a bunch of billionaires get bilked for millions?" Then he went on a tirade about the investment banker who earned $275 million a year before he was convicted of securities fraud. He finally came back to me a few minutes later. "Kate, it seems to me that there's a side effect to a story like this. People are now realizing how extravagantly some of the superrich live. Agree?"

I drew a deep breath. I knew my answer wasn't going to please my father or his wealthy donors. "It's very hard for viewers to imagine anyone owning, for example, dozens of watches that are worth twenty or thirty or one hundred thousand or more—each. And when they see the extravagance of these estates—indoor pools, ballrooms, tennis courts, spas that rival the world's finest—they can't help but be mesmerized. Especially here in Los Angeles, where less than twenty minutes from these estates, tens of thousands of families live below the poverty line."

"This is a war on the überwealthy, the one percent of the one percent," Russell said. "All of these estate owners are on the *Forbes* list of the top hundred richest Americans. Last year the *three hundred* wealthiest people in America were worth over three trillion—people, that's *trillion*—dollars. And America's megarich are getting megaricher at an unprecedented rate. That's why people are following this story so closely, right?"

"I think people are drawn in by all the extravagance and intrigued about how the thieves have pulled off these sophisticated heists. And yes, I think people are wondering how the estate owners have amassed such stratospheric wealth while millions are struggling."

"Now this story has taken an ugly turn. They've set fire to a Hollywood landmark, and one of their own is in critical condition. What kind of criminals are we dealing with here?"

I swallowed hard because now he was asking me to give an opinion about the thieves when nothing—absolutely nothing—was known about them. "I don't think we have all the facts about the heists yet, so it's hard to know what kind of people are behind them. I spend a great deal of time covering murders and assaults, and there it's easy to characterize the perpetrators as malevolent. But it's not yet clear here. After covering the Good Sam story a few months ago—the story about the anonymous Good Samaritan who left one hundred thousand dollars cash on doorsteps throughout LA—I've learned that things are often not what they seem."

James didn't seem to like that answer either. I suspected he'd hoped I'd paint a more threatening and sinister picture of the criminals.

The interview was over before I knew it. I assumed David and Bonnie would be satisfied because the Channel Eleven logo was in the shot during the entire segment. I suspected Andrew would call to recruit me. And I knew my father would let me know how disappointed he was with my comments about the wealthy victims.

But I never expected what happened next.

CHAPTER NINE

I struggled with my run around Lake Hollywood the next morning. By mile three, my calves were burning, and I was finding it hard to push through the strain. I hadn't run for nearly a week and was paying for it. That, and I was bone tired from the news events of the last two weeks, and even my morning run wasn't reviving my energy. I yawned, then switched my smartphone to an indie-rock song, one with a faster cadence, and tried to find my rhythm again.

I ticked off another mile of trail, and the calf pain was beginning to ease when my cell phone rang. I didn't recognize the number that flashed up and usually sent unidentified calls to voice mail, but I hoped the call might be from Jake, so I pressed accept.

"We didn't set the fire," the man said quickly. "It was an accident."

"Who is this?" I stopped in midstride.

"I'm the idiot they caught on camera."

A jolt of adrenaline shot through me as I realized who I might be speaking to. But years in the journalism business had taught me that often what seemed to be true wasn't.

"How did you get my number?"

"Found it online. Not easy. But I know how."

I tried to catch my breath, but my voice was squeezed in my throat. "How do I know you're the real deal?"

There was a long pause on the line, and I worried that he had hung up. "Because I'm going to tell you things no one else knows, not even police."

I moved to the side of the running path to avoid being trampled by a pack of runners. "Why are you telling *me*? You could tell your story to just about any reporter or network in the country."

His voice, thin and raspy, shook a little. "I saw your interview with James Russell. Online. You said something like, 'Things are not always what they seem.' Which is true, especially about this. You're the only reporter I've seen who hasn't rushed to judge us for what we're doing. So yeah, I thought you might give me a fair chance to tell my side of the story."

"What *is* your side of the story?"

"I'm not a bad person. I don't want police to continue to twist this and make it out like I am some kind of bad guy."

"You broke into an estate, stole five million dollars' worth of stuff, then set fire to the house, seriously injuring one of your comrades. That doesn't exactly make you a hero."

"I didn't break in. The door was already open for me. I was told to open the safe with an angle grinder. I didn't take anything. I had one job—open the safe and leave."

"After you set the house on fire."

"Like I said, it was an accident. The grinder threw off some sparks that hit the antique rug, and it caught fire. That's what I want people to know. Our instructions were to do the job and get out, without harming anything or anyone."

I wiped the sweat from my face. "Those were your *actual* instructions?"

"One hundred percent. What we were doing was important. He started every mission by saying he was 'summoning the champions' and telling us we were changing the world. And you can't change the world if you're destroying stuff."

"Who said that?"

"The leader guy."

"Who is the leader?"

"No idea. He spoke to us through an earpiece during the mission. We wore GoPro cameras so he could see where we were and tell us what to do. I only knew him by the name Locksley."

"How many of you were in on this?"

"Maybe five or six. I don't know exactly. None of us knew what anyone else was doing or anyone's names. We wore masks so we wouldn't see anyone's face."

"Still, you got caught. On camera."

"Yeah, about that. He had a way to disable the security system and cameras, but I guess there was a nanny cam or something that wasn't hooked into the system. I just happened to be the dumbass who walked by it without my ski mask on."

"So if you didn't know the leader, how did you get involved in these 'missions'?"

I heard him draw in a long breath. "We talked, you know, online in games and stuff. We knew we could change the world with what we were doing. And sometimes you have to break the rules to do that."

"How were you changing the world?"

I heard the sound of several male voices on his end of the line. "I gotta go," he said quickly. "Tell your viewers we aren't bad." He hung up.

I tried dialing his number back but got a recorded error message, making me realize he had disguised his caller ID. He was probably using the app that Jake had talked about that concealed your phone number.

I stood on the running trail for a long moment, staring at the Hollywood sign tucked in the hills in front of me and trying to make sense of what I'd heard. My gut was telling me this wasn't a fake confessor. This guy had facts that not even the police might know, and he had something else, a nervous quake in his voice that felt genuine.

But what struck me as odd was his agenda. He didn't want people to think he was a "bad guy." I didn't get to interview many criminals, because they were usually long gone or being taken away by the time I got to a crime scene, but the ones I had met never seemed all that worried about their reputation. Yet this guy believed he was changing the world and had asked me twice to tell viewers that he wasn't bad.

I met with David and Bonnie in the Fish Bowl to dissect the call. The last time I'd spoken to Bonnie, she'd been reprimanding me on the Good Sam story. She had been harsh with me then, speaking in clipped tones that made it clear she was in charge and my job was to follow her directives. But now as she sat in the brightly lit conference room, she was actually smiling at me. Okay, not smiling. Her lips were curved upward instead of pressed in a firm line like they usually were.

She was dressed as though she were about to be photographed for *Harper's Bazaar*—a tailored black suit-dress with a trendy upturned collar and five-inch Christian Louboutins.

"The attorneys have cleared your report for air," she said. Then she went on to explain that because we didn't have any identifying information about the caller—what he looked like, his name, his whereabouts—we weren't required to share what we knew with the police. She laid out a long explanation studded with legal terminology, then finished with "Don't be nervous, and if the police call you, direct them to me. I'll determine if or how we'll share information with them."

I swallowed hard. The story had taken on a gravity beyond anything I'd experienced before. I'd never had the police chase after me for information. I had always been the pursuer, often successful—but frequently not—at getting the information I needed from the police. But instead of being nervous, as Bonnie suggested, I saw a potential meeting with the police as an opportunity to delve into Stephen's theory about police officers' involvement in the heists.

David paced the floor, his hands shoved in his pockets. "Glad the attorneys are happy, but this makes for lousy TV. No visuals. There's no recording of the call. We don't even have the guy's name."

"True," I said. "But we know how many people are involved, how they opened the safe, how the fire got started. That's far more than the police know. And we know something about their tactics. By giving his team members the instruction not to do any harm or damage, the leader deludes them into thinking they're doing the *right* thing. The caller actually believes he didn't do anything wrong because he didn't break in or take anything."

Bonnie leaned back in her chair and stared at the ceiling. "If you spread out the parts of a crime over several people, no one feels like they're doing anything wrong. Clever."

Bonnie made sure my report opened every newscast for the rest of the day, with the anchors giving the story a powerful lead-in. "Channel Eleven has exclusive, new information about the recent burglaries that have hauled away over fifteen million dollars in stolen items from estates throughout Southern California. One of the burglary suspects spoke with Channel Eleven reporter Kate Bradley and gave her exclusive insight into the heists."

"According to an unnamed caller who claims he was the individual caught on camera at the Holmby Hills estate, a team of five or six is responsible for the high-stakes crimes," I said. "The caller wasn't able to identify other team members because they all wore masks and none of the team knew who the others were. He says the group was directed by a leader on a headset and given specific instructions not to damage anything or harm anyone. He claims the fire at the estate was an accident, caused by sparks falling on an antique rug. Meanwhile, motives behind the heists are unclear. Team members believe they are 'changing the world.' They are not, he says, 'bad guys.'"

After filing my last report, I headed to Eric's home, a sage-green California ranch house tucked deep in the shade of a rambling oak tree in the Hollywood Hills. I pulled in to his driveway and parked behind his midnight-blue pickup. You didn't see many pickups in car-congested LA, which defined itself by its Lexuses, BMWs, and Mercedeses. But there was something comforting about Eric's pickup—sturdy, reliable, and strong.

"I'm making naked stew," Eric called from the kitchen.

"Hmm, what are the ingredients?"

"What do you think they might be?"

I tossed my purse on the couch, curious to find out what he had in store. He stepped into the living room, wiping his hands on a towel. And fully clothed.

"Disappointed?" he said, with a twinkle in his eye. "What were you expecting?" He leaned in to kiss me. "It's called 'naked' because it's made with no spices. Makes up for it with two pints of Guinness."

I wrapped my arms around his waist. "Homemade stew and Guinness. Some might think you're trying to seduce me, Mr. Hayes."

"Is it that obvious?" he said with a sly smile, then slipped out of my arms and back into the kitchen. "Let me get you a real drink."

A large cardboard box was planted in front of the stone fireplace. Rising from a drift of Styrofoam chips scattered on the oak floor was a model sailboat with tall cloth sails and a wooden hull. I was no expert on model sailboats, but this one was clearly handmade and meticulously detailed, down to individual wood planks on the hull and deck.

"Brian's assistant sent it to me," Eric said, presenting me with a glass of wine. "He and I built it when I was ten or so. We couldn't sail for a month while our full-size sailboat was under repair, so Brian and I spent weeks working on this one."

Brian was Eric's only brother, who'd died a year earlier while sailing with Eric. Twenty-foot swells had pummeled their sailboat, and when it hit a reef, the boom swung loose, hitting Brian in the head and flinging both of them into the convulsing sea. In the midst of the howling wind and waves, Eric tried to rescue his brother, but Brian died of massive head injuries.

"I can't believe Brian kept it all these years. And not buried in his attic but on a shelf in his office."

"It must have been important to him."

"We would sneak out of bed late at night to work on it." He stepped over to the model and pointed to two tiny white lifeboats. "The kit didn't come with lifeboats." His voice shook a little. "But I complained so much about it—I had to have lifeboats—that Brian spent hours, weeks even, making them by hand. Carved them out of wood. Just for me."

"What a cool brother."

He brightened. "He probably did it to stop me from whining about it."

I took a sip of the wine. "I can't imagine you were much of a whiner."

"Actually, I was. And if Brian were still alive, he'd tell you that I was a big complainer. Especially on the boat. If a line wasn't pulled right, I'd be the first to point it out and complain about it."

"Those aren't bad skills to develop if you're going to be a fire captain someday."

"Maybe you're right." He squatted next to the sailboat and adjusted the masts. "I wish you could've met him. He was the keeper of my memories when we were kids. Like, he could remember what we ate for dinner on a sailing trip we took to Catalina when we were in high school. I don't have that kind of memory. Now that he's gone, I . . ."

His voice trailed off, and his eyes locked onto the sailboat as if he were lost in his memory of it.

"Sometimes it just hits me," he said quietly. "And knocks the breath out of me. Out of the blue, you know? I can be fine, and then . . . I get this sailboat, and I'm back where I was when he died."

I sat on the floor next to him, placing my hand in his. "He may not be here anymore, but he'll always be a part of you."

He adjusted the rigging on the sails. "I'd like to think that's true."

For months after Brian's death, Eric had grappled with crushing guilt for failing to save him. He'd trained his whole life to rescue strangers in swift water yet was unable to save his own brother. But as the months went by, he talked less and less about Brian. I often believed that his silence about it meant he was over it, that his grief had gone away. But now I wondered if I was wrong about that. Perhaps his grief had only changed shape.

My cell phone rang, ruining the moment. I ignored it, sending it to voice mail. But whoever was trying to reach me called back, and the ring seemed even more insistent this time.

"You should get that," Eric said.

I pulled the phone out of my purse. Andrew Wright.

"That was one heck of a report," he said excitedly. "You got the story every network—every reporter—wanted."

I glanced at Eric still sitting there, adjusting the sails. "Can I . . . call you back? I'm in the middle—"

"Let's talk seriously about you coming aboard ANC, where you'll have a bigger platform for your special brand of reporting."

I tried not to sound impatient. "I'll call you in the morning?"

"Actually, I'm still in LA. Let's meet for breakfast. Tomorrow. Seven thirty."

"Okay," I said quickly, trying to get him off the phone. "I'll text you where we can meet."

"Terrific. Congrats again."

When I hung up, Eric was back in the kitchen, chopping carrots.

"That was Andrew at ANC," I said, snapping up a carrot from the cutting board. "They want to talk specifics about me coming aboard."

"They're moving fast," he said with a catch in his voice. "Must really want you."

"It's a bit overwhelming. Especially after getting an exclusive interview with the thief who was caught on camera in one of the heists."

"The story was everywhere. How did you find that guy?"

"He found *me*. Said he chose me because he saw me being interviewed on ANC and thought I might give him a 'fair chance.'"

He was silent for a long moment, turning up the burners on the stove. "That's more proof that you belong at ANC, Kate. But what happens to *us* if you go to New York?"

When I was in college, my father had cautioned me about putting a relationship ahead of my career. On our Sunday-morning five-mile runs together, he'd tell me stories of women he knew who had left college to get married or quit promising jobs in order to follow their boyfriends to other parts of the country. The stories always ended up badly, with the woman dumped and left without a way to support herself or turning thirty-five and regretting the career or goals she'd never attempted. I had the feeling my dad took liberties with some parts of the stories in order to make his point. Still, the message had sunk in.

But as I drove to meet Andrew the next morning, I questioned whether that was good advice now that the relationship involved Eric instead of the boyish college guys I was dating back then. I couldn't imagine leaving behind everything I loved for any career opportunity.

I had asked Andrew to meet me at IHOP in a sketchy part of Koreatown. He hadn't balked, even though it wasn't on his list of preferred Westside restaurants. When I arrived, he was already waiting for me in a corner booth covered in faded red vinyl. With his sport coat and crisp white shirt, he looked out of place among the locals in their baggy shorts and flip-flops. He wasted no time getting down to business.

"Very impressive report yesterday. That guy could've told his story to any number of journalists, but he chose you. It's proof that viewers relate to you, Kate."

"Apparently criminals do too," I said, pouring a cup of coffee from the thermos on the table. "You know, he saw me on James Russell's show. He thought I came across as open minded and was likely to give him and his side of the story a fair shake."

Andrew grinned. "See what a platform like ANC can do for a reporter like you?" He removed his sport coat and laid it carefully on the bench next to him. "Look, I want you on the ANC news team. I'm not going to be subtle about it. I know you're under contract, and I'm willing to wait until it expires next month."

"You've got some pretty good intel."

"The way I see it, at ANC you could expand beyond these breaking-news reports into stories of nationwide significance. Politics, the economy, education, national security—"

The waitress, a middle-aged woman with smudged red lipstick and frizzy black hair in need of a hairdresser's attention, came by to take our order. I scanned the menu, avoiding the dozens of thousand-plus-calorie items, and settled on a vegetable omelet, easy on the cheese.

"I'm flattered," I said when she left. "But I'm not so sure those beats are for me. My real strength is covering breaking news."

"I understand why, Kate." He leaned forward and lowered his voice. "I know about your mother."

A nervous buzz coursed through my veins. I suddenly felt vulnerable and exposed and didn't understand where this conversation was heading. "My mother?"

"Reporter's habit, I guess. But I did my homework on you."

"What does my mother have to do with any of this?" I said, feeling my face flush.

"Look, I may be out of line here, but it seems to me that the way she died might be at the root of your interest—and perhaps even some of your ability—in breaking news. Not every reporter can handle the tragedy you witness every day. Unless they've been through what you have."

I felt my head go light. Before he'd become an executive, Andrew had been one of the best reporters in the business, so it made sense that he'd done some research on me. Then again, the story of my mother's death wasn't a secret; it had been widely reported in news media across the country.

My mother had died in a fiery car crash caused by a hit-and-run driver on a busy highway north of San Francisco. I had just turned five, too young to have formed many lasting memories of her or to fully understand what had happened.

Because my father was a US senator and my mother, Sarah Bradley, had been senior adviser on education and family to the mayor of San Francisco, the tragedy was covered in newspapers and magazines and on TV and radio around the country. For many years afterward, my father had shielded me from seeing any of the news reports. But in the summer before my junior year in high school, I'd interned in his Senate office, and I'd found a storage room stacked with notebooks my father's staff had assembled of every newspaper clipping and magazine article, along with carefully cataloged videotapes they had recorded of news reports about it. I'd snuck the materials out of the archives, rereading the laminated, yellowed clippings and replaying the grainy news tapes over and over in the VCR until I had memorized every word, hoping that watching the reports might reveal something about the mother I could not remember—the mother my father rarely spoke about.

In a strange way, most of what I knew about her came from those reports. There was videotape of her, wearing a red tweed coatdress and a chunky gold necklace, on the 1978 campaign trail with my father. Many reports showed a snapshot of her holding me days after my birth—a portrait I hadn't seen anywhere else, not even at home. There were photos of her busily at work with San Francisco's mayor during her years as senior adviser and a photo of her on her wedding day, wearing a white gown with filmy lace sleeves, all high cheekbones and raven hair, like a noblewoman in a European painting. And there were the inevitable photographs of the fire-scarred, mangled car—images that became indelibly carved in my memory.

The stories were covered by some of the most recognized reporters and anchors of the time: Dan Rather, Jane Pauley, and Tom Brokaw. For months, I'd watched the videotapes and searched through the notebooks in secret. Sometimes I would catch a glimpse of the way she held her mouth or the downward slope of her eyes, and it would be obvious that I resembled her. But most of the time, she appeared steeped in mystery, someone I only vaguely recalled in the corners of my memory.

I had never considered that watching those news tapes had inspired me to become a breaking-news reporter, yet now I understood in some unconscious way that they had. It baffled me that Andrew had made that connection. He had known my father for decades, so perhaps he knew more about my childhood—and me—than I realized.

"My father was a marine pilot killed in Vietnam when I was in my teens," he said quietly. "I have no doubt that's the reason I studied political science and journalism in college and then covered overseas wars for most of my twenties. For me it was a way of looking for my father. Of understanding him. We're alike that way." He took a long slug of his coffee. "What I'm saying—in my very clumsy way—is that maybe it's time for you to consider putting the breaking-news beat aside and try something new."

I wasn't sure what to say. I was irritated that he thought he had figured me out even though he didn't know me well at all. And if I denied it too vehemently, it would only prolong the discussion about my mother. A subject that was making me unsettled.

I managed a smile. "It's an interesting theory. But even if I wanted to change my reporting beat, I'm not all that excited about leaving LA."

"I can understand that too. Your father told me about the fire captain you met on the Good Sam story," he said, straightening the flatware by his plate. "You know, they have a damn prestigious fire department in New York City too. Second largest in the world, in case you're wondering."

I laughed. "With all the personal information you know about me, you're sounding a lot like a stalker."

"I don't mean to make you uncomfortable. I want to connect the dots and make a transition to ANC very appealing to you." He clasped his hands together. "Look, I want you on my team at ANC, Kate. What do you think? Can we do this?"

David had warned me that Andrew was in recruitment mode, but he was fast. And persistent. "What exactly would you see me doing?"

"At first, we'll have you cover a broad range of beats. You'll be a correspondent for crime and justice—where you already excel—*and* a part of the national news reporting team. And, if you're interested, you could take on the political beat. We'll give it time to see what's a good fit and then down the road think about developing your own show."

My own show. He said it casually, as if it were something I'd thought about before, but I hadn't. Unlike many reporters, I never imagined myself behind a desk or anchoring a newscast. I liked being in the field—digging up leads, interviewing subjects—and I lived off the adrenaline rush of the live news report.

I steadied my voice. "Can I think about it?"

"I probably don't have to tell you that there are dozens of top journalists who would jump at an opportunity like this. Take a few days to think about it. But I won't wait forever."

CHAPTER TEN

Breakfast with Andrew made me late to the assignment meeting. Again. The Fish Bowl was less crowded than usual, as several members of the news team, including Hannah, were absent—working on a breaking-news story in Venice, California, where lifeguards had rescued more than twenty-eight people caught in a single powerful riptide. The lower attendance made my ten-minutes-late-to-the-meeting hard to conceal.

Russ was rambling on about something as I slid into a chair. Whatever it was, it was irritating David, who stood in front of the whiteboard, frowning and rubbing his right ear.

"If the thieves keep this up, at some point they're going to make a mistake and get caught on camera again," Russ said. "These estates probably have cameras in places not even the smartest thief would expect. It's a matter of time before the leader gets caught in the lens too."

"I don't think he will be. Caught on camera, anyway," I said.

Russ turned to look at me. "Why do you say that?"

"Because he's not in the estate with his team. He's leading them from somewhere else."

He shrugged. "Not sure why you think that. None of the other networks have put that theory forward."

"Think about it. The masked operatives don't know each other. Or the leader. If one of them gets caught, the team stays intact. If you're that leader, you don't want to be calling the shots alongside your team. It would be too easy for them to identify you. The crew wore GoPro cameras so the leader could call the shots from somewhere else. Somewhere he can't possibly get caught."

David clapped his hands. "People, we're missing the point. It's all well and good to theorize *how* they're doing it but more important that we figure out *who's* behind it. Any leads on that?"

"The FBI is looking into a group from Oakland who has been on a bank-robbery spree. They've hit twenty-six banks in eight months," Russ said.

"Track that," David said, pointing at Russ.

"The burglar caught on camera told me he met the leader—who goes by the name of Locksley—through playing online games," I said. "I'm going to look for Locksley online."

Russ laughed. "Good luck with that. No offense, Kate, but I'm betting you don't know a thing about online games."

Could I find Locksley in the online-gaming world? Russ was right about it being a Herculean task and that I didn't play online games. But I knew someone who did: my cousin Max. His father was the mayor of Princeton, New Jersey, so Max was in college in Princeton. Not *at* Princeton but at Rider University, which was only eight miles from Princeton University yet far removed from the Ivy League education my uncle, his dad, had planned for him.

At six foot two, with curly blond hair and an athlete's physique, he didn't look like the nerdy stereotype of a gamer, but Max was the closest thing to a true internet native of anyone I knew. Within weeks of YouTube coming online, he had launched his own channel, and he had owned every game console ever made over the last decade, from Atari to Xbox to PlayStation. I didn't talk to him much, but in his texts or emails to me, he regularly used so many gaming acronyms that I had to look them up online to decode what he meant. I learned that *MOBA* meant "multiplayer online battle arena" and *WoW* was not an interjection with a typo but an abbreviation for *World of Warcraft*, an MMOG—a massively multiplayer online game—with over eighty million subscribers.

Max was in his fifth year of college, working on the six-year plan, after wasting nearly his entire sophomore year playing video games and "forgetting" to go to class. My uncle had made him get counseling for his gaming addiction, and while he was getting to class more often, he still spent forty-plus hours a week playing video games.

I called Max's cell. It was the middle of the day in his time zone, a time when he probably should have been in class, but I wasn't surprised when he picked up on the second ring.

"'Sup?" he answered. In the background, I heard a burst of gunfire, which, given the affluent area he lived in, was most likely coming from whatever game he was playing.

"Hey, Max, quick question. In what online games could you have a conversation with another player? With someone you don't know."

"All of them, pretty much. Why? You finally getting into gaming?"

"It's for a story I'm working. You know, the heists of the one hundred richest Americans' estates?"

He brightened. "Yeah, heard about that. Crazy how much money those dudes have."

"The guy I talked with said he met the leader of the group by 'playing games online.' I'm wondering if we could find the leader online and what games might allow him to talk to other people?"

He sounded distracted. "Like I said, most of them do. Too many to count."

"The leader goes by the name of Locksley. Could you find him by looking up that username on various games?"

"You got any idea how many games there are out there? Thousands."

The conversation was halting and awkward. He was clearly focused on the game he was playing, and I could tell he was annoyed with my questions. "So could you look for someone across the games you play if you knew his username?"

He hesitated. "No. He might call himself Locksley, but his username could be something else. So, yeah, sounds like a lost cause."

I could hear him feverishly clicking the controller. He sounded frustrated, which probably meant I was making him lose. "He starts every heist by saying he's summoning the champions and telling his team they're changing the world and—"

"He actually says 'summoning the champions'?"

"Yes."

"Like in *League of Legends*?"

"What's that?"

"How's it even possible that you haven't heard of it?" he said, without tempering his disdain. "It's a MOBA played by seventy million people. A player is called a 'summoner,' and they start the game by 'summoning a champion' into the Fields of Justice."

"What's a champion?"

He sighed as though I'd asked him to explain what a light bulb was. "A champion is a character. Each one has a special ability."

"What do you do with your champion?"

"You team up with other champions to try to destroy the other team's base."

"How do I find Locksley on *League of Legends*?"

I heard a couple of loud explosions on his end. "Lost cause. Gotta run, Kate. Catch you later?"

Hannah knew what *League of Legends* was. She was a rare girl who'd played it in college as a way to relax from the stresses of the journalism program at Columbia University. To the envy of her male classmates, she'd become good enough to earn a respectable platinum ranking.

"It's hard for outsiders to understand the allure," she said in the newsroom that afternoon. "Because it's a game that's very difficult to master and there's no easy way to learn it. So the people who achieve the highest rankings have a kind of cultlike following."

She opened the game on her laptop to see if she could find a summoner named Locksley.

Her face lit up. "Found one. He's got the highest ranking, what's called a Challenger. He's in the top one hundred."

"So someone with that ranking might be able to convince another player to help him rob an estate?"

She pressed two fingers to her lips. "Many players would be flattered if a Challenger reached out to them. Maybe he targets certain kinds of players—risk-takers, ones who chart their own paths in the game, or people he thinks would spark to his idea of a small group changing the world."

"How can I send Locksley a message?"

"We can send a request, but it's up to him if he wants to accept our invitation." She typed the name Locksley into the invitation box and pressed send. "A request has been sent to the user" flashed on the screen.

"What if he figures out you're a producer from Channel Eleven?"

Hannah shook her head. "He can't find out who I am from my summoner name. That's impossible."

I watched the cursor blink on the screen until my vision started to blur. All we could do was hope that Locksley would respond. I knew it was a long shot, and even if he did respond, there was no guarantee this was the Locksley we were looking for.

I turned to leave. "Let me know if he answers."

"There's something else." Hannah spoke in a low whisper.

I turned to look at her.

"I finally found something about your . . . source." She typed a few keystrokes on her keyboard and pulled up a newspaper article. "It took a lot of digging, but he's with his brother in eastern Kentucky. His brother heads up a group that calls itself the Kentucky Preppers."

"Why's he there?"

"No idea yet. He's still completely silent on all social media."

"So how *did* you find him, then?"

She smiled and pointed at the screen. "Don't laugh, okay? Where he's staying, Dawson Springs, Kentucky, is such a small town—less than three thousand people—that the local paper still publishes a column of local comings and goings."

I scanned the article, and right after an announcement about a visit from Connie Gaynor's four grandchildren, there it was: "Tom Newton and his brother, Jake, a detective with the Los Angeles Police Department, attended the opening of Lil' Cozy Kitchen, a new restaurant opened in Dawson Springs by owners Otto and Thelma."

I looked at her in amazement. "How *do* you find this stuff?"

She smiled. "Not saying. Job security."

"Any way to contact him?"

She shook her head. "His brother doesn't even have a phone."

"What do we know about his brother's group?"

"Many prepper groups share fairly normal self-reliance stuff like storing your own food and stocking up on water and medical supplies. But this one . . . well, take a look."

She pointed to their website. In bold letters it read: "**WE'RE PREPARING FOR THE BREAKDOWN OF SOCIAL ORDER CAUSED BY ECONOMIC COLLAPSE.**" Beneath the caption was a photo of a stockpile of guns, knives, axes, machetes, and ammunition. The photo was followed by a post showing how to make a device out of plastic piping and compressed air that shot out fishhooks to immobilize intruders.

The idea of Jake Newton joining some kind of survivalist group in Kentucky seemed impossible to me. He was ambitious, high minded at times, and never anything like the stereotypical police officer with a drug problem, an ex-wife, an estranged child, or a secret past. He had been raised in Portland by parents who were college professors. Sure, he liked to unwind with a drink and probably worked too many long hours, but I couldn't imagine him as someone who'd throw his promising career away and go off the grid.

"They're definitely on the fringe," Hannah said quietly.

~

My stories about the burglar caught on camera had rocketed Channel Eleven to number one for two days running, and to celebrate our new status, David and Bonnie had gathered all the reporters and anchors on the set to pose for a group photo. Some of the reporters grumbled about taking a photo so early in the morning. But in a market like Los Angeles, getting to number one was no easy feat, so everyone smiled long enough for one of the cameramen to snap a few photos.

I felt a pang of guilt as I stood shoulder to shoulder with the Channel Eleven News team while seriously considering leaving them for ANC. No doubt we were competitive, as each of us jockeyed for the best stories and airtime, but we were also like a family—celebrating milestones and playing petty pranks. I didn't have much time to dwell on my guilt, because David was obsessed with the heists story.

"There's one thing in this story that no one's been able to get," he said, pacing the Fish Bowl later that morning in the assignment meeting. "Not any of the networks, not CNN or ANC—not even Anderson Cooper or Diane Sawyer—have been able to get it." He took a slug of his green drink. "Anyone know what it is?"

He scanned the puzzled faces in the room, mine included.

"An interview with whoever is behind these heists?" Conan asked.

He shook his head. "If you had that, we wouldn't be sitting here." He slammed his hand on the table. "Come on, people. I'm talking about the kind of interview that catapults us straight to the top. National . . . worldwide attention." He threw up his hands. "We need to interview one of the *victims*. The billionaires who've been robbed."

"We've struck out with all the estate owners," Susan pointed out.

"That's exactly why we have to get an interview," David urged. "This is our moment, guys. We're crushing the competition. Even our movie-studio owners are paying attention to what we're doing. But if we want to capitalize on all the attention Channel Eleven is getting—if we want to stay on top and keep rising—we have to get on the inside and interview one of the billionaires." He pointed a finger at me. "Kate, you met one of them—Stephen Bening. Why can't you interview him?"

"It's not that easy—"

"I'm not looking for excuses. Find a way in," he said, waving a hand in the air. "Just bring back an interview."

I didn't have a "way in" to Stephen Bening. And given his relationship with my father, it wouldn't be smart to hound him like an ordinary interview subject. He'd already turned down two of my requests for an interview, so I needed a compelling reason to reach out to him again. A reason for him to say yes. I found the copy of his book, *Business Hacks*, and scanned through the biography:

"Bening, a twenty-five-year veteran of the software industry, began his career at the age of eighteen by founding an entertainment-software company, Liberty Software, to develop games for the Atari platform. From there he worked as an assembly language programmer at Apple, then at Oracle Corporation and Symantec. From a rented apartment in 2005, he launched SalesInsight.com, now a multibillion-dollar global organization. Bening is a graduate of the University of Southern California and has an MBA from Harvard."

The book was aimed at the captains of corporate empires. There was a chapter about the development of his Delfina software system, which revolutionized the way businesses tracked sales and serviced customers and became the leading customer-relationship software used by Fortune

500 companies and boutique businesses around the world. But nothing I read was a way into an interview, so I asked Hannah to do a deep-web search on Stephen. Fifteen minutes later, she handed me a white paper Bening wrote when he oversaw the Security Technology and Response division at Symantec, a computer-security-software developer.

She pulled up a chair next to mine. "Bening writes that cybercriminals use sophisticated techniques to leapfrog over company and private defenses. Maybe you can ask him if cyberattacks were made on his security system."

I shook my head. "Police say the security systems in the estates weren't breached. Even the security expert who designed the system at El Mirasol confirmed that the system wasn't compromised. There's no evidence of cyberattack."

"That's exactly Bening's point in this paper," she said, running her fingers through wavy hair that fell to her shoulders. "Hackers can hide their digital fingerprints with something called a rootkit. It's malicious software—malware—that *hides* the intrusion. Makes it appear that the systems were not compromised at all."

I straightened, then swung open my laptop and typed an email. *Stephen, were rootkit tactics used to evade the security systems in your home?*

~

It took Stephen Bening twenty minutes to call. That was breakneck speed in CEO time, because most executives responded in days, if they returned a reporter's call at all.

"It's a good theory," he said. "The problem is that we've run multiple scans and analyses and memory dumps and haven't found a shred of evidence of any malicious software or rootkit on my system or any of the others."

"Maybe their ability to hide is greater than your ability to find them," I said quietly.

"Without a doubt. That's why I've got some of the world's top cybersecurity experts working on it. But here's where you're missing the big story. For years, police have used high-end cyber tactics like installing undetectable rootkits and malware to spy on terrorists, drug dealers, and other criminals. *They* have the ability to pull this off."

"But why would they do it?"

"Isn't it obvious? They can steal millions of dollars in minutes and know they won't get caught. The police chief may be blustering on TV about how he's going to catch the criminals, but my investigator says the chief knows that it's actually some of his own officers who are behind it. That's why they're not sharing critical evidence with the owners or the media."

"Would you talk with me on camera about your findings?"

"No," he said firmly. "We're still gathering evidence."

My voice went up a notch. "You have evidence that police are using undetectable malware to hijack high-end security systems and rob estates of millions, yet you don't want to talk to the media about it?"

He exhaled sharply. "Look, let me help you another way. I'll set up an interview with the owner of the Holmby Hills estate."

Thomas Speyer, the owner of the Holmby Hills estate and CEO of a major Wall Street brokerage firm, was not the imposing figure I expected. He was only five foot seven and rail thin, but he had intense dark eyes and a deep, wide forehead that sloped sharply and gave him an almost hyena-like appearance. He looked like someone who, if provoked enough, might actually physically attack you, even if his size would put him on the losing end of that battle.

Stephen had done more than make an introduction. He'd also persuaded Speyer to meet with me Saturday morning in his home. I didn't often do interviews or file news reports on Saturday mornings—unless it was a breaking-news story—but if Speyer was willing to grant me an on-camera interview, I was willing to drag my sleep-deprived self out of bed to meet him.

Our cameraman, Christopher, waited in the news van—ready to bring in a camera on a moment's notice—while a uniformed butler ushered me inside Speyer's colonial mansion. He paused a moment to allow me to take in the grandeur of the foyer—the set of spiral staircases, soaring forty-foot ceilings, inlaid-marble floors, huge Palladian windows, and opulent gilded crown moldings.

Although a wing of the estate was badly burned, the home was so expansive that we were able to meet in a white oak-paneled dining room overlooking the tennis courts and not even be aware there had been a fire at all. When I arrived, Speyer was in the midst of devouring a plate of ribs. He offered some to me, but the sight of barbecued ribs at ten in the morning was turning my stomach.

"I tell you what, they stole from the wrong guy," he said. Dressed to perfection in a blue linen suit jacket and crisp white pants, he looked like a Ralph Lauren advertisement, albeit with a less attractive model. "I have one of the most high-tech security systems available. Yet they stole five million dollars in goods in under fifteen minutes. But do they have any idea who they're dealing with? No one gets away with stealing from Thomas Speyer."

I was always uncomfortable when people spoke of themselves in the third person. It usually came from interviewees who had inflated senses of self-worth, but it was also an indication that they were distancing themselves from me, which was something I had to change. I leaned forward and placed my palms down on the table, mirroring the placement of his hands. I shook my head in sympathy and tried hard to rally a similar expression. "What did they take?"

"What they stole from the others. Cash. Jewelry. But what makes my blood boil is that they stole my artwork. They left my Picasso and took my Mora. Go figure."

"Mora?"

He lifted his smartphone and pointed to his screen saver, which showed a painting of two impossibly stretched figures standing on a rocky precipice, trying to catch hold of the unattainable—the moon. One figure wore a bold red cape and yellow shoes, while the other was a somber black silhouette against a gray-blue sky.

"I fought for it at Christie's. *Man Reaching for the Moon* by Antonio Mora. Everyone assumed it would go for two million, but it ended up costing me two point four. You should have seen the looks on the faces of the other bidders when the auctioneer finally knocked his gavel against the lectern. They were kicking themselves—another fifty thousand, and they would've won it instead."

"Whoever stole it will have a hard time selling it on the black market."

He laughed, a throaty laugh that put me on edge. "That's not how it works. There are people around the world who would be ecstatic to get this piece, for the prestige of having something Christie's sold at auction for two point four million dollars."

"Stephen's investigator says that police officers are behind the heists. What do you think?"

He wiped his mouth with a wet napkin and laid it on the table. "I think he's right. They're hiding something. They won't share any evidence with me. And they took something from the crime scene and refused to show it to me."

"What was it?"

"Can't say for certain, but it looked like a silver coin. I saw a detective taking it away in one of those plastic evidence bags. I asked to see it, but he refused."

"Could I interview you on camera? I think viewers would like to understand what happened from your perspective—"

He stiffened. "Look, this robbery and this fire is a tragedy. But there's no way I'm going on camera talking about all the luxuries I've lost. People don't have sympathy for the other wealthy schmucks who had millions stolen, and they won't have any for me."

A young woman dressed in a black-and-tan sheath dress came into the room bearing a tray. "May I offer you some coffee?" she asked.

"No, thank you," I said.

"Mistake," Thomas said. "This is coffee grown on my private reserve in western Panama. The beans must be grown in a cold climate and carefully harvested, and my reserve is the only place on earth where they grow. This is our first harvest of the season, and the beans were flown in yesterday. Few people get to experience such a rarity."

His pretentious tone grated on me, but I hid my irritation. "I'll give it a try."

The woman poured the coffee into a porcelain mug decorated with a silver floral pattern, set it in front of me, then placed a silver-rimmed coffee mug in front of Thomas.

With bony hands, he picked up the mug and closed his eyes, savoring the coffee's taste. I took a sip and nodded my appreciation. It had a rich flavor, but if I hadn't known it was flown in from a reserve he owned in western Panama, I might have mistaken it for an ordinary coffee I could buy at Peet's.

"How can I help make the idea of a brief interview more comfortable for you?" I asked.

He set down his coffee mug and fixed an intense gaze on me. "You don't get it, do you? The way this is playing out in the media, the very wealthy are tasteless or crass for spending our wealth on beautiful and expensive things. People are enjoying the fact that we've lost so much. Many people even have sympathy for the burglars. People are rooting for the *burglars*, Ms. Bradley. But it's not a crime to be wealthy, so why are we being vilified for what we have?"

I thought about what I was going to say before replying. Really, I did. But clearly not enough. "It's hard for people to have sympathy for anyone who is buying western Panama farms that grow rare coffee beans or who owns paintings that cost more than most people will earn in a lifetime."

I saw a vein bulge in his forehead. He looked like he was going to jump out of his chair and hit me. Instead, his words sliced through me. "I agreed to meet with you because Stephen asked me to. I've done that. Now it's time for you to leave."

He stood and left the room.

CHAPTER ELEVEN

Losing the interview was my fault. I knew better than to say anything remotely controversial to an interview subject. Every beginning journalism student knew that. But somehow, I'd let my dislike for Thomas Speyer get in the way.

But what troubled me most was that while I prided myself on being objective—I had even chided Susan about treating this like any other heist or burglary—clearly I *was* biased. I *wasn't* objective.

I struggled with having sympathy for someone who lived as he did, a reported $15 million-a-year lifestyle that not only included the estate in Holmby Hills but also a Park Avenue apartment, a compound in Sun Valley, and a ranch in Connecticut. Worse, he was clearly out of touch, whining about his losses not because he would actually miss the stolen objects but because he was angry that someone had the audacity to steal them from him.

A crime had been committed, I reminded myself. No matter how many billions this man had or how pompous and self-absorbed he was, someone had committed grand larceny by stealing $5 million from him.

At least the meeting had not been a complete waste of time. Police were hiding evidence—a silver coin—found at the crime scene. Could this be the Hidden Mickey that Jake had alluded to? Were police holding back this key piece of evidence because they thought it would break the case wide open?

I was about to dial Hannah to talk through this development when Ben at the assignment desk called. "Kate, there's been a drive-by shooting at Washington and Fourth Avenue in Arlington Heights. David would like you to go there to cover it?" It was no mistake that he phrased his request as a question, because I was guessing even he didn't understand why David was assigning me to cover a drive-by shooting on Saturday morning at ten thirty. We didn't often report on drive-by shootings in the first place, unless the circumstances were unusual or the victim was very young.

"Dead teenager?"

"Sixteen years old. It happened this morning in broad daylight on a quiet residential street."

"I have my hands full with the heist story. Can't another reporter—"

"Conan and Russ are out sick. There's some kind of flu going around. You want me to tell David you can't do it?"

I thought about it for a second. It wasn't worth an argument with David. Not after his lecture about the meeting with ANC and the tabloid photo of Eric and me. I sighed. "No, I'll do it."

"Good. Josh is already on his way and will meet you there."

Less than eight miles separated the pricey estates of Holmby Hills and the densely populated Arlington Heights neighborhood just east of downtown LA, yet they were worlds apart. I left behind the exclusive enclave's lush landscapes, towering trees, and panoramic views and drove into streets scarred by graffiti and gum-splotched sidewalks littered with trash. On one street corner, a purple grocery cart lay on its side, a dozen broken compact discs scattered around it. The parkways were peppered with discarded couches and old-style tube TV sets.

Within minutes of each other, Josh and I reached the scene, a quiet street one block from busy Washington Boulevard. Police had cordoned off the crime scene, the victim had already been removed, and officers were busy interviewing family members and witnesses. The crumpled car that had slammed into a lamppost during the shooting was still on the scene. Yellow caution tape snapped and fluttered in the breeze.

I looked at the car, and then suddenly I was remembering the grainy photos and videotapes of my mother's crash. There had been so many, taken from every angle, that when I closed my eyes, it was as if I could walk through the scene.

I tried to remember something about her that I hadn't learned from the articles and news reports. Anything. The only memory I could conjure up was a brief glimpse of me sitting in a small kiddie pool in our backyard, my mother smiling as I held an inflatable beach ball. I couldn't make out her face, only the shape of her, but I could hear the buoyant ring of her laugh and its bright trill ending.

Yet the memories that came through the clearest were not of events I'd actually experienced with my mother but of the videotaped news reports from the scene of the accident and the disturbing photographs of the crumpled car and the grieving family members.

Was Andrew Wright right about me? Had my mother's tragic accident inspired my interest in breaking news? Was this why I had the "tragedy gene," as Josh had called it?

"Ready?" Josh asked, bringing me back to the moment.

I pulled my eyes away from the wreckage and nodded.

Tim Reynolds, a reporter from the *LA Times*, filled us in on the facts. The victim was Michael Gutierrez, a high school football star at nearby Los Angeles Senior High. In the off-season, he worked at a grocery store and had recently been accepted at a nearby college, where he had planned to study to be a paramedic. The son of Salvadoran immigrants, he had no known gang affiliations. He was on his way to football practice when he was shot six times from a gray sedan, which then fled the scene.

It's the kind of story where the newsroom expects you to interview the victim's family or get them to make a statement. But when I spotted a woman who I suspected was Michael's mother, her face ash white and stained with tears, I knew I couldn't do it. Standing on each side of her, gripping her arms and practically holding her up, were two other young women. Their shock was palpable as they spoke to two police officers. And the sound the mother was making was something I would never forget. It was a haunting sound on the far side of grief—a lament so boundless it canceled out every other sound around us.

I looked away. A couple of other news stations were already working the story, interviewing witnesses and people on the scene who had known Michael. Instead, Josh and I recorded a stand-up down the street from the shooting. I was usually one of the best reporters at covering tragedy, but today the right words totally escaped me, and I had to do four retakes before I stopped stumbling through the report. What could you say about such senseless violence and tragic loss?

~

I felt like the energy had been sucked out of me as I hurried back to my car after the report.

"You are with Channel Eleven?"

I turned to find a Latina woman with wavy black hair and big earrings running toward me. She wore slim-fitting jeans and a light-blue chambray shirt with ruffles.

I handed her my business card. "I'm Kate Bradley."

She smoothed her hair. "Blanca Rivera. I live near here."

I braced myself for her complaints. Many residents near a crime scene didn't like news reporters standing on their lawns, taking up parking spots, and blocking their streets and driveways. The list of grievances was often endless, and if it wasn't handled properly, it could verge on violence. Once, when I was filing a report about a murder on a quiet residential street in Culver City, an angry neighbor stormed out of his home and knocked the microphone out of my hand.

"Every time I watch the Channel Eleven News, all I see is this story about the robberies—how the rich live like kings and how much they have," she said softly. "But where is the story about the rest of us? The people who work two jobs but can barely feed our families? The people who struggle every day just to keep a roof over our heads?"

Was she right? Were we focusing too much attention on the superrich?

I was about to respond when my cell phone rang.

"Thank you for sharing that with me. Would you excuse me a moment?" I asked, then answered the call from Hannah.

"This is really strange," Hannah said, without even saying hello. "We just interviewed two top FBI officials investigating the heists who say they can't find *any* evidence of the millions of dollars in stolen luxury items. Not one item has shown up with any of the fencing rings or other networks that traffic in stolen goods. Nowhere."

"How can that be?" I asked. "With a haul this big, there'd have to be some trace of it."

"None. You should've seen the FBI guys, Kate. They both were . . . rattled. They say this is proof we're dealing with a well-financed group unlike anything they've seen before."

"Keep tracking that. Let me know if anything shows up."

I slid into the driver's seat and started my car, trying to come up with a solid theory for why the stolen goods hadn't surfaced. Was it simply because the thieves were highly sophisticated, as the FBI suspected? Or was it possible they had not yet sold the stolen goods—for reasons still unknown?

A mile later, traffic came to a standstill, and the streets were barricaded up ahead. My nerves tightened as I considered the possibility that there had been another shooting.

I called Ben at the news desk to see if he knew what was going on. He checked the scanners and online databases but couldn't find any mention of an accident, a crime incident, or any event in the area.

"It doesn't sound good," he said. "I don't think you should go in there alone."

He was right. This area of LA was gang territory—prime turf for one of the world's most brutal gangs, MS-13. The evidence of their dominance here could be seen in the large-scale graffiti scrawled in blue and black paint on the sidewalks and on retaining walls throughout the neighborhood.

I looked for a driveway to turn around, but then I felt foolish as I saw mothers pushing baby strollers and old men shuffling up the street. How dangerous could this be? I angled my car into a tight parking spot behind a rust-pocked pickup truck loaded with old TVs and scrap metal. I followed the people in the streets and on the sidewalks, all streaming in the direction of the barricaded street ahead. All around me, people spoke Spanish in a variety of accents. I heard words like *bueno*, meaning "good," and *comida*, meaning "food." Was it a street fair?

Thousands were lined up in about two dozen lines that led to a high school football field. A band played mariachi music on one side of the street while farther ahead another group played some music I recognized from Top 40 radio.

I headed slowly to the front of the crowd, hoping it didn't look like I was trying to cut in line. Dozens of tables had been set up, staffed by people wearing yellow T-shirts. Thousands of stacked cardboard boxes covered more than half the high school football field behind them.

I picked out a woman working behind the tables, her waist-length hair scraped back into a long ponytail. "I'm Kate Bradley from Channel Eleven. What's going on here?"

"We're handing out backpacks to ten thousand people today," she said with delight in her voice.

I looked across the vast football field. If all those boxes were filled with backpacks, her estimate of ten thousand wasn't far off.

"What for?"

She used both hands to wipe the sweat from her cheeks. "For the poor and the homeless. The people who don't have jobs. Most of us are volunteers, and when we heard what they were doing, we all wanted to be part of this day."

I scanned the crowd. One lady with wispy white hair held a backpack and dabbed tears from her eyes. A stooped man with a scruffy gray beard and a worn camouflage green cap patched with duct tape slung a backpack on his shoulder and grinned. A little boy in a striped red T-shirt, his two front teeth missing, did a kind of victory dance with his backpack, melting my heart with his over-the-top excitement. I was suddenly filled with awe, pure and unexpected. What I saw before me was an example of everything that was right and good in the world.

I felt like a desert flower in rain, soaking up the delight of the people around me. What was in these backpacks that was bringing such joy?

"Who's responsible for all this?" I asked.

"No one knows," the ponytail lady said. "We're told the donor wants to be anonymous."

I peered inside one of the backpacks. It was large—the kind a college student might carry. Inside there were about twenty-five food items: pasta, cans of soup, bottled water, cereal bars, granola bars, ready-made tuna salad, crackers, grape jelly, peanut butter, and small boxes of cereal.

I walked over to a woman who was looking through her backpack's contents. She was in her early seventies, with dark hair streaked with gray and skin freckled from a lifetime spent in the sun.

"How do you get a backpack?"

She looked at me as though I might take it from her. "Well, you sign up with the Food Bank."

"Anyone can do it?"

Her eyes fell on my designer jacket. "You won't qualify. You have to earn very little or be very sick or have a serious disability. It's very hard to get on the list."

I shook my head. "I'm not looking to get one. I'm a reporter with Channel Eleven. How did you hear about this event?"

"I received a letter from the Food Bank saying that I qualified. My husband passed away last year, and I have a heart condition. The medicine takes most of what I get from Social Security. For the next six months, I can come here every Saturday and refill this backpack. I can eat."

"This is a real lifeline for you, then."

She looked away. When she finally spoke, her voice shook. "It's everything."

This was exactly the kind of story I rarely got to cover. It was a story without victims, trauma, or disaster—ten *thousand* needy people receiving a free backpack of food from an anonymous donor. Every week.

I watched as a young boy wearing a Mickey Mouse T-shirt looked through the backpack, pulling some of the items out and showing them to his weary mother, who was struggling to strap another child into a stroller. Then he reached into the bottom of the backpack and brought out something shiny and small and showed it to her. I watched her inspect it for a moment, turning it over in her hand, clearly puzzled.

Curious as to what it was, I approached them.

"I'm Kate Bradley with Channel Eleven. May I talk to you about what you received in the backpack?"

She looked at me, a panicked expression on her face. "We would not like to be on the news."

"This won't be on the news," I said carefully. "I've noticed that in addition to food, your son pulled something . . . else from the backpack."

She started stuffing the items back in the backpack.

"May I see what it is?" I asked.

She looked at me for a moment as if deciding what to do. Then she opened her hand and showed me the shiny object her son had found.

It was a silver coin, triangular in shape and carrying the silhouette of a man standing in the fork of a tree, about to shoot a bow and arrow. The man looked like one of the Greek gods, Apollo or Orion, both of whom sported bows and arrows in many artworks. But the shape of the hat on his head made him look more like Robin Hood. Engraved on the other side was a phrase in another language. I recognized the Cyrillic alphabet from the reversed letter *R*. Russian, perhaps?

"May I offer you some money for it?" I asked, pulling a twenty from my purse.

The woman glanced at the twenty-dollar bill, then at me, as if I might have been trying to scam her.

"No, sorry." She took the coin from me, grabbed her son's hand, and hurried away.

It took me five attempts before I could get anyone to sell me one of the silver coins, but I finally got one from a woman with parchment-white skin who told me she needed cash for medicine more than she needed a "pretty coin."

I turned the coin over in my hand. There was no doubt that the image was of Robin Hood.

CHAPTER TWELVE

Everyone knows the story of Robin Hood. In one form or another—books, movies, cartoons—the story has been told for hundreds of years, maybe longer. But as the story has been transmitted and transformed, one aspect has remained constant: Robin Hood steals from the rich and gives to the poor.

My mind was whirring. Thomas Speyer said that police had found something at the crime scene that they had refused to show him. A silver coin. Could the people behind the heists be the same people behind this event that was bringing food to ten thousand people?

If a group calling itself Robin Hood was behind the heists, that would also explain why the leader of the group went by the name of Locksley, the village in Nottingham where Robin Hood was born.

But linking the heists to Robin Hood and this event was taking a giant leap of logic. At least David Dyal thought so.

"Yeah, I don't see it," he said after I called him on his cell and briefly took him away from his son's birthday party. "We don't know that the silver object police hid from Thomas Speyer was a Robin Hood coin. It could've been any number of metal objects. And the fact that the leader of the group is named Locksley is a coincidence. You're grasping at straws here."

"There's something to this theory. There are too many coincidences."

"The gut isn't infallible, Kate. Until you've got proof that the coin in the backpack is the same one found at the crime scenes, keep your hunch to yourself."

I frowned. I had the feeling he was too distracted by whatever was going on at his son's party to give any real thought to what I was saying.

"I'll find someone to translate the writing on the back of the coin and get back to you," I said with practiced calmness. "This isn't the last you've heard of the Robin Hood theory."

After I hung up with David, I flipped the coin and peered at the small lettering on the back. I tried calling the service Channel Eleven often used to translate documents from other languages, but it went to voice mail. But Google had a pretty spry and free translation service. Using its onscreen Russian keyboard, it took a whole three minutes to type in the letters from the coin. The translation came back:

"Take from the rich and give to the poor."

~

The last person I wanted to tell was my father. When my dad got angry, he glared, seethed, and scowled like many politicians. But strike at the core of something deeply important to him, and his white-hot anger often mutated into an edgy frostiness that could be devastating to be around.

My dad had planned to have dinner with a power couple who topped the list of the biggest political givers in California, donating over $1 million to an array of candidates. When their plane from New York was delayed because of another storm on the East Coast, my dad asked me to join him instead. I seriously considered not telling him about the Robin Hood coin, but I knew I couldn't keep quiet about it.

I met him at Cut, an upscale steak house in Beverly Hills where the waiters walked around with the raw cuts of meat and explained your choices before you ordered. Steak was not one of my favorite dinners, but it certainly was my dad's, and the restaurant had a legendary dark chocolate soufflé that even skinny Hollywood actresses who subscribed to the kale-and-celery diet couldn't resist. After seeing all the raw meat cradled like babies in the waitstaff's arms, I lost my appetite for it, so I skipped the steak and ordered the soufflé.

My stomach was a jittery mess as I weighed how to tell my dad about the coin.

"Headlines," my father said, a code word between us that stretched back to when I was seven and would scan the day's newspapers and give my father a two-minute summary of what I thought were the major stories of the day. Back then I was certain I was doing an important service for my busy father, who didn't have enough time to read every newspaper.

My idea of what was important news usually fell into two categories: politics, which I knew he always wanted to hear about, and the sensational, my favorite. When I led with a headline about the magnitude 7.8 earthquake that had launched a devastating tsunami on an island off Japan, my father gently sent me on a scavenger hunt to find stories "of substance," pointing out that the signing of the North American Free Trade Agreement would have a greater impact on the world than an earthquake on a sparsely populated island. Intentionally or not, he was honing my early news instincts, and over time I started developing broad knowledge of local and world events. When I was in fourth grade, the US attorney general resigned abruptly, and I told my dad my theory that she had quit because of her alleged involvement in a controversial wiretapping program. My dad was so proud that I had connected the dots that he let me eat ice cream for breakfast.

In the years since I became a reporter, *headlines* had grown to mean a list of the stories that were getting the most airtime in LA, even though they were often not "news of substance": A woman stabbed in a fight over a parking spot. Two bodies found on the exits of two different LA freeways. A violent encounter between three costumed superheroes who posed for photos with tourists on Hollywood Boulevard.

My father then ran down his headlines: Legislation aimed at increasing the federal minimum wage. The married congressman caught kissing one of his aides. Tax reform aimed at increasing the capital gains tax. The resignation of the president's national security adviser.

After my dad's steak arrived, I finally got the nerve to tell him about the Robin Hood coin. When I got to the part about the translation of the Russian words, he stopped chewing and, almost in slow motion, set down his fork and steak knife on the table.

"You're certain it's Russian lettering on the coin?"

"Positive."

The muscle in his jaw twitched. "What I'm about to tell you, I'm telling my *daughter*, not a reporter. That's a very important distinction. Do we have an understanding?"

"We do."

"Last month, Russian-speaking cybercriminals hacked into the biggest US bank and compromised information for more than eighty-five million households and businesses. They also infiltrated another seven financial institutions in the US. Kind of like a burglar casing a house before breaking in. A friend at Homeland Security says the hacks were meant to send a message that the Russians could cause financial chaos if they wanted to. They have evidence the hackers are connected to the Russian government, which is reeling from economic sanctions we put on them in response to their aggression in Ukraine. This Robin Hood stunt could be yet another way to point a gun at our head to ease the sanctions."

The waiter came to check on us, probably to see if we needed anything. But seeing the way my father was leaning over the table and the intense expression on his face, he kept moving.

"If this is true—that someone is targeting the superrich and giving to the poor—this is a powder keg ready to blow." In the restaurant's muted lighting, my dad's face took on a ghostly appearance. "There would be copycats and plenty of them. People who like this Robin Hood's idea and join his 'merry band.' No telling how out of control this could get."

"But if he's helping the poor—"

"You can't steal from the rich simply because the poor are suffering." He wiped his mouth with a napkin. "That's why we have government programs and charities."

We were silent for a long moment, both of us pretending to focus on our food.

"You need to get yourself off this story now," he said firmly. "If not, you're going to get caught in the cross fire, and it won't be pretty."

"I'm not going to take myself off one of the biggest stories of the year."

His response was strong, almost desperate. "Let me tell you why you will. Because no matter how you report this story, it's going to be positioned as though you're making a political statement. If you come out against Robin Hood, people will say that you're a privileged senator's daughter who's out of touch with how the rest of the country lives. And if you support Robin Hood, the wealthy will feel that you—and to some extent me—are attacking them. That you're advocating theft. And they've already fired a warning shot at you by putting your photo in the tabloids. What will they come up with next?"

The air in the restaurant suddenly felt stiff and unbearably hot.

"I don't have to take a position about Robin Hood."

"You already have on this story, Kate. You may not say it directly, but anyone watching your reports can see that you're pointing out the gap between the haves and the have-nots." He fidgeted in his chair as though he suddenly wanted to be somewhere else. Then he lowered his voice to a raspy whisper. "Have I ever told you not to cover a story before?"

"No," I said. Even when I covered the story of a young senator friend of my father's who had been killed in a small-plane crash with a woman who wasn't his wife, my dad never said a word about how or if I should report it.

This story was different.

The rush of blood in my ears made it hard to make out his words. "Trust me on this, Kate. If there is a connection between these heists and some kind of Robin Hood—Russian or otherwise—you've got to get yourself off this story and onto something else."

"Even if I dropped the story today, it wouldn't make the rest of the news media stop telling it."

"The rest of the media doesn't have Bradley for a last name."

Throughout the rest of the evening, my dad tried to lighten my mood by sharing some stories of crafty political maneuvering on a bill called the Reliable Home Heating Act. Usually those stories made me laugh, but I found myself distracted, forcing a laugh here and there when I thought my father was expecting one.

When I returned home, I couldn't sleep, so after tossing and turning for most of the night, I shuffled into the kitchen at 4:13 in the morning. I sat at my counter staring at the silver coin underneath the soft glow of the glass pendant lights. The Santa Ana winds had swept in from the mountains earlier in the night, bringing stifling hot, dry air into the LA Basin, but the temperature in my apartment was even hotter than it was outside. I opened the kitchen door for some relief. The only sounds were the whir of the neighbor's air-conditioning unit and the distant hum of the freeway as early risers began their morning commutes.

I rubbed the hollows beneath my eyes, willing away the pounding headache that was forming over my right eye.

I was steeped in the heists story. It didn't happen often, but there were some stories that became so embedded in my head and emotions that it felt like I was physically saturated with them, like a tea bag steeped in hot water. I felt the story in every cell of my body, and even though there was a physical world in front of me—a kitchen table cluttered with unopened mail, a stack of unread magazines, a sink full of dirty dishes—all I saw, all I felt, was the story.

The first time this feeling had come over me, I'd been afraid of it, certain it was evidence that I had become too obsessed with a story. Proof that my life was out of balance. I'd shared this experience with David and was surprised when he confessed he'd had similar experiences on certain stories. He called it "reporter's intuition" and urged me not to ignore it.

Eventually, I came to accept it as a gift. In these immersions, I often had my most useful flashes of insight on a story. But like the light from a firefly, they didn't last long.

As a gentle breeze swept through the room, I had no doubt that there was a connection between the heists and the generous act of giving away a backpack of food to ten thousand people every week. The Russian words on the coin were the beginnings of proof. What I needed was evidence that the same coin had been left at crime scenes.

And who was the Russian group who was stealing from the rich and giving to the poor? Were they a known crime ring? Part of the Russian government? Did they have other motives, as my father suggested? Was this why police had hidden the evidence from the estate owners and the media?

I resolved then that I wasn't going to drop this story simply because my father demanded it. I knew I was putting him at political risk and causing problems with his wealthy donors. But if there was an organization stealing millions from the rich and giving to the poor, I was going to be the reporter to figure out who it was.

CHAPTER THIRTEEN

On my way into the newsroom the next morning, my cell phone rang. The number flashed up as "Unknown." I hoped it was Jake finally surfacing, but instead it was Bonnie's shrill voice on the other end of the line.

"Kate, are you on your way?" she asked, not even bothering to say hello or identify herself.

I glanced at the clock in the car: 7:42 a.m. I wasn't late. Why was she checking on me?

"I'm about five minutes away."

"LAPD is here. As expected, they want to talk to you about the call you received from the burglar caught on camera."

"Am I required to talk with the police?"

"No, but from what you told me, I can't see any reason why you wouldn't. You've already shared with viewers everything the thief told you."

A sharp pain pierced my chest beneath my ribs. It physically hurt to think about being questioned by the police—not because I had anything to hide but because of what I was planning to ask.

I had expected a couple of police detectives to be waiting for me in the small conference room on the second floor, but instead there was only one. Detective Julie Haney stood looking out of the glass windows at the newsroom below, her hands tucked in the pockets of navy-blue slacks. Around her waist was a thin black belt with a handcuff holder, pepper spray, and, yes, a gun and ammunition clip. Her dark-brown hair was pulled back in a tight bun on the back of her head, and a sweep of bangs across her forehead made her appear younger than she probably was.

But any hope of getting an inexperienced officer faded when she opened her mouth. "I understand you've got a tight schedule, so let's make this quick. Have a seat."

I sat across from where she had neatly arranged a file folder and a police radio on the conference table. She didn't join me but instead kept looking out of the window, watching some action unfolding on the newsroom floor.

She spoke rapidly, with a husky tone. "Have you had any contact with the suspect since the call that's been detailed in your news reports?"

"No."

"Did the suspect give you any indication of his name or location?" She kept standing, watching the newsroom, which felt odd. If this was a tactic to make me nervous, it was working.

"No."

"Did he have an accent? Anything out of the ordinary about the way he spoke?"

I had a talent for detecting regional accents, but the voice I remembered didn't seem to be from anywhere specific. "No accent that I can recall."

"Think on it again. Did you hear anything that made you think he was from somewhere outside of the country?"

"You mean like Canada or Latin America . . . or Russia or something?" I said innocently. I knew what she was getting at even if she wasn't going to say it.

"Yes, anywhere. Perhaps eastern European . . ."

"He sounded like English was his first language. Like he was from here."

"What proof did he give you that he was one of the burglars?"

"None. As I said in the report, he's an *alleged* burglar."

She turned from the window and fixed a pair of gray eyes on me. "But you think he was one of the thieves."

I shrugged. "Does it matter what I think?"

She registered a half blink, then forced a tired smile. "Your news director, Bonnie Ungar, assured me that you would be helpful."

The door swung open then, and Channel Eleven's attorney, Ryan Nord, breezed in, dropping his leather briefcase on the table. "I hope you haven't started without me."

"No," I said. "Detective Haney was making small talk."

Her face was a stoic gray mask. If she was irritated, and I guessed she was, her expression didn't show it.

Ryan extended a hand to the detective. "Ryan Nord, Channel Eleven's general counsel."

She shook his hand briskly and then turned to me. "Had you met or talked with the suspect prior to his phone confession?"

I glanced at Ryan, who nodded his approval of the question. "No."

"Then why did he call *you* and confess?"

"He saw my interview on another network and thought that I'd be open minded about not labeling them as 'bad guys.'"

She shoved her hands in her pockets. "You don't think they're bad guys?"

"It's what *they* think that's important. And they believe they're doing this to change the world."

She looked skeptical. "You say you don't know him? Then how did he get your cell number?"

I shrugged. "He said he found it online. If these guys can bypass high-end security systems, finding my cell phone number wouldn't be hard."

"What is your relationship with Detective Newton?" She slipped the question in casually, as though it was routine.

Ryan straightened. "What does this have to do with the robbery suspect Kate interviewed? That's what we agreed to talk about today."

It was the first time I saw her blink. "Is there a problem if I ask Ms. Bradley questions of a general nature related to the heists case?"

"Please confine your questions to the matters at hand," he said firmly.

Detective Haney drew a deep breath and scanned through the documents in her folder.

"May I ask a question?" I asked quietly.

She hesitated for a moment. I could see she was figuring out how to appear cooperative without becoming a doormat. "Go ahead."

"Have you been at the heist crime scenes?"

She nodded. "All of them."

I reached into my purse and pulled out the silver coin. My hand trembled as I placed it on the table and slid it in her direction. "Was a coin like this one found at the crime scenes?"

She picked up the coin, examining it in her palm. "Where did you get this?"

"From a source on another story. Is it like the silver coins that were found at the crime scenes?"

She snapped a photo of the coin with her cell phone. "What makes you think there were silver coins left at the crime scenes?"

"One of the estate owners said there were. Coins just like this one."

"Which owner?" Her hand was firmly clasped around the coin now, and the volume of her voice rose a notch. "Where did you get this?"

Ryan cleared his throat. "Sorry, but I'm not following here. What's this coin have to do with the subject of today's questions?"

She flipped through the papers in her folder. "I'm asking your client how she received evidence from the crime scene."

"So it *is* evidence, then?" I said. "You're confirming that there were coins like this found at the crime scene?"

Her face flushed, and I could tell she was kicking herself for what little she had said. "I'm not saying that at all." Her voice held less conviction now. "You've misunderstood. In fact, this discussion is over."

She closed her folder and stood.

"What just happened here? Weren't we supposed to be talking about the phone call with the robbery suspect?" Ryan asked.

I rose. "You can't take my coin with you."

She opened her hand and made a show of placing the coin on the table. "Thank you both for your time."

~

Thirty minutes later I was live on Channel Eleven with my report linking the silver coins found at the estate crime scenes with the coins given out at the giveaway of ten thousand food backpacks to the poor. Within hours, the story went viral. The hashtag #RobinHood trended on Twitter and Facebook, and clips of my report started getting thousands, then hundreds of thousands, then millions of views online.

Many journalists seized on the Russian connection and delved into theories about the possible groups that were behind it. CNN did an entire segment with a Russian linguist who was decoding the Russian words to determine if there was any hidden meaning. Apparently there wasn't.

Hannah had jumped into finding the manufacturer of the silver coins, hoping that would lead us to uncovering Robin Hood's identity. But she reached a dead end when she found there were thousands of custom silver-coin mints across the globe and a local coin expert pointed out how easily and inexpensively someone could mint these coins at home.

Most news outlets focused on Robin Hood and ran clips from movies in their news stories. There was swashbuckling and debonair Robin Hood as played by Errol Flynn, complete with green shirt and brown hat. We also showed world-weary and mature Robin Hood played by Sean Connery, boy-next-door Robin Hood created by Kevin Costner, and gritty, armor-wearing Robin Hood portrayed by Russell Crowe. We even saw the swinging musical version of Robin Hood featuring Frank Sinatra and his "merry men," Sammy Davis Jr. and Dean Martin.

The images captured viewers' and reporters' imaginations. "Robin Hood's appeal comes from primal desires for justice and equality," one scholar said on our morning newscast. "And though medieval in origins, this is a fantasy broad and deep enough to possess the imaginations of people in almost all times and places, but especially in these disillusioned days of Wall Street robber barons and Bernie Madoffs."

"Whoever is behind these robberies couldn't have chosen more vibrant imagery," a pundit on our noon cast said. "Robin Hood is seen as someone who is bold and courageous and a beacon of hope to the poor. Somehow, breaking the law seems more forgivable if there is a noble and just cause behind it, carried out by someone with pure and honest intentions."

Meanwhile, I was interviewed for all the network's news shows, including the morning news magazine at a bleary-eyed three in the morning. My reports ended up on every national cast, a heady experience and a physically draining one.

My cell phone voice mail was full, and there wasn't even a free minute to listen to the messages or cull through the texts and emails viewers and friends were sending. As I watched the frenzy the story was creating, I knew my father would be angry with me for divulging something he'd told me off the record. But the first angry call I got wasn't from him. It was from Stephen Bening.

When he called the station, his tone was so urgent the station receptionist paged me several times rather than sending him to voice mail.

"Kate?" he said when I picked up the phone. "Do you know what's happening at my home? About a hundred people are protesting outside my gates."

"Protesting what?"

"Good question," he said loudly. "Apparently . . . my wealth."

I was silent for a long moment. "Maybe it's time we did an interview together?"

"You're right," he said finally. "It's time your viewers heard the other side of the story."

I was excited about nabbing the interview with Stephen—the first and only on-camera interview any reporter had scored with a superwealthy victim—but he couldn't schedule it until his return to LA a few days later. I offered to send a crew to record the interview wherever he was in San Francisco, but his schedule was too packed to fit it in. We settled on an interview in four days.

Hannah had pulled together information about some of the Russian groups the FBI suspected were behind the bank hacks, and I began to sift through them. But as I sat at my desk, I couldn't believe what I saw on the monitors around the newsroom. Protestors were assembling outside estates throughout the country, not just at Stephen Bening's. A hundred or so people stood outside Thomas Speyer's mansion in Bel Air hoisting signs that read TAKE FROM THE RICH, GIVE TO THE POOR and ROBIN HOOD IS RIGHT! Another group, mostly in their twenties and thirties, assembled outside a CEO's $55 million estate in San Francisco. By one count, as many as twelve protests were underway.

My cell phone buzzed in my purse, startling me. Andrew Wright's name flashed on the screen.

"Congrats on cracking the Robin Hood story wide open! This is exactly why we want you on our team."

"Thanks," I said, then ducked into the nearest edit bay to get some privacy.

"Look, we're getting on the phone with your agent to make an offer today. It's still Sharon McCarthy, right?"

He moved fast. "Yes, but—"

"I'm not going to talk numbers with you, but I promise you what we're offering is at least double what Channel Eleven's giving you. And with the exposure you're getting on this Robin Hood story, you're going to find ANC a great home to work on the kind of big stories where you excel."

He certainly was good at the flattery thing.

"We're all very excited. In a month, you'll be calling New York your home."

Most reporters would be overjoyed at this opportunity. In journalism school, many of us dreamed of working for an all-news channel someday, covering stories of national—even international—importance and working with some of the best in the business. But following that dream would mean leaving Eric behind, and that thought made my spirits sink.

I called his cell, but it went straight to voice mail. It was nearly impossible to get hold of him when he was on duty, but two days had passed, and we hadn't texted or talked to each other. Something felt off.

I texted: *Call me when you have a sec.*

When I returned to my desk, I found Marc Beck, the national sales executive, waiting for me. He was busy looking at his phone, so at least he wasn't rifling through the papers on my desk. While it was common practice for another reporter to sit in my chair, I was irritated that he had the audacity to do the same.

When he saw me coming toward him, he jumped up and shoved his phone into his tailored pants. "Marc Beck. We met before—"

"I remember."

"Hope it's okay that I . . . I want to tell you something. Off the record. You're going to hear about it anyway, but I figured you'd want to know before . . . well, before the top brass in the news department tell you."

"I'm listening."

He lowered his voice. "PowerTrade just pulled their advertising on the Channel Eleven News. Indefinitely. They are one of our biggest clients."

"And? I think we had this conversation before. I don't care if a brokerage firm advertises on Channel Eleven or not."

"But it's about *you* this time, Kate. They're pulling their ads because they don't like the way you're covering the Robin Hood story. They think it's wrong for a senator's daughter to be advocating for people to steal from the rich and give to the poor."

My mind reeled, trying to figure out what I'd done in the reports that appeared to be advocating. "They said that?"

"Word for word."

"I wasn't advocating anything."

"Hey, I'm just telling you what they said. In case, you know, you get pressure to stop doing this story or get assigned to something else. Well, you'll know why."

"I think you know there is a clear division between editorial content and advertising—"

"Absolutely," he said, his tone condescending. "But advertisers have a right to associate their brands with some messages. And not others."

"I'm sure my news bosses won't bow to pressure from some brokerage firm."

"They're not 'some' brokerage firm," he said with a dry chuckle. "They're what keeps the lights on here." He shoved his hands into his pockets. "Everyone around here says you're a really sharp reporter, but you don't get it, do you? That brokerage firm writes your paycheck. Mine too. You've angered someone with your Robin Hood reports, and they're going to take you down where it hurts most—the station's pocketbook."

CHAPTER FOURTEEN

I was only two minutes late, but the assignment meeting was already in full swing by the time I arrived the next morning. David was in rare form. Instead of sipping green juice, he was gulping from a cold can of Dr Pepper. The caffeine was clearly affecting him, because he was talking quickly and his cheeks were flushed.

"Nice of you to join us," he said as I slid into a chair.

I glanced at the whiteboard, where David had scribbled my name under "Breaking News" with the words "kidnapped woman in trunk." I frowned and scanned the board for the Robin Hood story but didn't find it anywhere.

"Kate, a Pomona woman made a 911 call from the trunk of an abandoned SUV off the 101 at Vineland. Says she's been kidnapped. You and Christopher should get on the road while police are still on the scene."

I considered protesting. But the last time I'd argued about an assignment, I ended up covering a story—for the station website—about some horses that got loose from the equestrian center in Burbank.

"Great," I said, as though I were eager to get started on the assignment. "I've got notes on the Robin Hood story. Who should I give them to?"

David paused. I knew he was irritated because he started rubbing his right ear, but his tone was unruffled. "I think we're going to give that story a rest. For the moment."

"Are we bowing to advertiser pressure?" I heard my words come out and then drop to the floor like lead balloons. Reporter Kevin Chen shot me a look that made it clear he thought I was an idiot for tackling that hot-button subject. I had the feeling he was right.

"We're focusing on more urgent stories," David said calmly. As though it were true.

I nodded, pretending I believed him. "Glad to hear that some big advertiser can't influence our agenda on a story of nationwide importance."

He faked a smile and raised his Dr Pepper as if in a toast. "You're right about that."

I knew he was giving out the party line while the executives at the top scrambled to figure out how to deal with the loss of a major advertiser. But I'd wanted to be in the news business not because I expected to change the world with every story but because I hoped it was a place where the truth could be told. In journalism school, my professor often talked about Stanley Walker, a *New York Herald Tribune* editor from the first half of the twentieth century who said that a good journalist resents lies and anyone who attempts to corrupt his profession.

Back when Stanley Walker was working, few women were journalists, and the preferred mode of journalism was still the ink-stained newspaper. But antiquated words and genders aside, the truth of what he said still lived on. For reporters like me, anyway. In a time when the mighty dollar ruled over all enterprise, were we becoming dinosaurs?

"Why are we dropping the Robin Hood story?" I asked.

"Folks, what Kate is referring to is that PowerTrade has pulled all of its advertising from Channel Eleven. These are their words, not mine—they are 'offended that a senator's daughter is advocating for the thieves by trumpeting what they're doing with the stolen funds, igniting anger and protests against the wealthy, and using her platform as a senator's daughter to campaign for tax reforms against our economy's job creators.'"

The sting of his words left me breathless. "I haven't done any of those things."

He took a slug of his Dr Pepper and pointed at me. "We'll talk about this later."

I straightened. "There are hundreds of other reporters on the Robin Hood story, but PowerTrade is only offended by what *I've* reported. Why?" The room went silent. I looked down at my hands and realized they were clenched in tight fists. "Last year PowerTrade spent a hundred forty *million* dollars lobbying the government, primarily over issues of taxation of the wealthy. Removing their advertising from Channel Eleven has *nothing* to do with me or this news department and *everything* to do with my father, who's head of the Senate Finance Committee—which is working on tax reform proposals for the wealthy. If you take me off this story, you're letting PowerTrade use Channel Eleven to lobby my father, to lobby the government."

He crushed his Dr Pepper can and tossed it into the trash bin. "That's not what we're doing. When we take you off this story, we're telling our shareholders that if a particular reporter is causing us to lose millions in advertiser dollars, we'll make the right business decision."

What kind of editor took a reporter off the very story that was driving ratings through the roof? How could he possibly call himself a journalist when he buckled at the first hint of pressure from an advertiser? Was this a sign it was time to leave Channel Eleven?

White-hot anger burst through me. I wasn't one to rage or throw a tantrum, but I could feel a raw and volatile energy brewing. The intensity of it frightened me for a moment, but then I felt the power of it coursing through my veins. I knew the next words to leave my mouth would be brutal but precise.

"David—"

"Don't," he said. "I know exactly what you're going to say. And you'll regret it if you say it out loud in here."

~

My stomach was still shaking when I returned to my desk, where I found a folded note on my keyboard. "Find me ASAP," it read. "But act like nothing's happening. Hannah."

I looked over the reporters' bullpen and saw Hannah hunched over her computer, a set of headphones over her ears. I reread the note. Hannah wasn't one to send handwritten notes—texts or emails were the norm—so I wasn't sure what to make of the old-fashioned communication. I also didn't know how to act like "nothing's happening," since a lot *was* happening, so I strode to her desk like I always did.

"What's this about? Have we heard from Locksley?" I asked.

She shook her head. "I'm listening to the police scanner, and there's a huge gathering at the site where that boy was killed in the drive-by shooting. The one you covered. I know you're on the kidnapping story, but I wanted you to hear about it first."

As I said, Hannah was loyal. "Is it peaceful? How many people?"

She scanned her notes. "At last count police were saying over a thousand. Peaceful so far. There's some people playing music, handing out candles. Looks like they're holding a vigil."

I shook my head. "Sorry, Hannah, but a vigil for a drive-by in Arlington Heights will never get any airtime."

"But—"

"This is the news *business*. Sometimes doing the right thing isn't the *best* thing for getting an audience," I said, then cringed because I hated when David said those words to me. I knew she didn't like my answer—neither did I—but as I raced to the parking lot to find the news van and get on the road for the kidnapping story, I had the sudden feeling that I was making a big mistake. It started as a pang in my gut and then spread up my arms, an ache that felt like I'd overdone it lifting weights, even though I hadn't been anywhere near a gym.

I found my cameraman, Christopher, sitting in the news van, engine running, and finishing a cinnamon bear claw. "Ready?" he asked.

I didn't answer. With one foot on the curb and the other in the van, I tried to think this through. The last time a large group assembled in Arlington Heights, ten thousand backpacks of food were given out. Was that a onetime event, or could Robin Hood have more things planned?

"Give me a sec," I said to Christopher and then called Hannah on my cell. "I think that gathering in Arlington Heights has something to do with Robin Hood."

Hannah's voice was soft but insistent. "You should go. I'll cover the kidnapping for you."

"I've been taken off the Robin Hood story. David will probably—"

"Not if your story turns out to be what we both think it is."

There was a good chance she was right. But that didn't stop me from focusing on the consequences if we were both wrong. I was not only putting my job on the line but hers too.

"I'm okay to take the risk," she said, as though reading my mind.

"Change of plans," I said to Christopher. "Hannah is going with you in my place."

He shrugged. Christopher was a go-with-the-flow photojournalist, not easily ruffled. He never got caught up in newsroom politics, and as long as he got to cover something visually interesting, he didn't complain.

I ran back into the building to find Josh—the one cameraman who knew the Arlington Heights area as well as I did—and spotted him in the lunchroom. His face was red and smudged with dirt.

"Would you come with me to cover a story in Arlington Heights?" I asked.

He slumped in the chair and rubbed his face. "I'm beat. We just got back from covering a fire at the Port of Los Angeles, and Conan had me running everywhere on the story. We got some awesome shots, but I can hardly move."

There was a sound of admiration in his voice that I didn't like. "You were on a story with Conan?"

He nodded. "He's really good at the breaking-news stuff. He got us an exclusive interview with the captain of the Long Beach fireboat *and* one of the fire department's scuba divers."

I was usually the breaking-news reporter Josh raved about, so I felt a sting of jealousy. "I think this gathering in Arlington Heights has something to do with Robin Hood. No evidence of it, but if I'm right, I'm betting we'll get an exclusive."

I could tell he wanted to say no. And from the exhausted expression on his face, he should've.

"If you think this is another Robin Hood story, I'm in," he said finally.

A few minutes later, we barreled down Olympic Boulevard in a news van loaded with remote broadcast equipment, hoping I wasn't making the stupidest move of my career.

CHAPTER FIFTEEN

By the time we got to Washington and Fourth Avenue in Arlington Heights, the crowd had grown to what looked like two thousand people. Josh dropped me off at the corner and set out to find a place to park the van on the packed side streets.

A few minutes later, a yellow school bus lumbered down the street and stopped in front of the crowd. The front door squealed open, and about two dozen teenagers, mostly African American and Latino, slowly filed out of the bus. They were dressed formally in brand-new suits and ties for the boys and cocktail dresses for the girls. Their clothing was so finely coordinated that they almost looked like an ad from a magazine, or at least like a stylist had been involved.

"What's going on here?" Josh said, rushing up beside me, his camera already hoisted on this shoulder.

"I have no idea," I whispered, and as I gazed around I could see everyone near me was similarly puzzled. A sense of anticipation hung in the air, as though we all knew we were about to witness something special unfold.

As several elegantly dressed women led the teens into the middle of the street, the teens looked both bewildered and a bit nervous. Then two men wearing headsets began jumping up and down and shouting, encouraging the crowd to form a ring around the teens.

What happened next I wouldn't have believed if we hadn't captured it on camera. A few people in the crowd started singing, and then others joined in, and then more, until the sound became so clear and powerful it was obvious this was not impromptu singing but a planned production.

The song was surprisingly upbeat, not mournful or soulful, like one would expect at a vigil. The teens seemed totally surprised. I had the feeling that they hadn't been told anything about whatever was happening in front of them.

Josh moved to get a closer shot. Who were these kids? Were they somehow connected to the boy who had been killed in the drive-by shooting?

Then, as the singing reached a crescendo, a dozen dancers dressed in black leggings and colorful T-shirts seemed to come out of nowhere, adding a dance sequence to the song and handing each of the teens a big blue envelope.

When the song ended, the crowd erupted in loud applause, cheers, and whistles. Then a tiny woman, as fragile as crystal, slipped through the throng and stepped up to the mystified teens with a microphone in one hand and a sheet of paper in another.

She stood there for a long moment, her eyes trained on the teens, her hands trembling slightly. I recognized her then as the mother of the boy who had been killed in the drive-by. When she finally spoke, her words reverberated on speakers that had been set up along the parkway.

"My name is Evelin Gutierrez. Michael Gutierrez is my son. Today, out of despair and tragedy comes hope," she said, reading from the paper. "Each of these twenty-five students here—they are the best and brightest from our neighborhood schools, top in their class, seniors with dreams and extraordinary talents and hopes of a better life. Each of them has received a four-year scholarship to the college of their choice. Whether they choose the most expensive school or a community college, their tuition, room and board, and living expenses are completely covered for the next four years. The blue envelope in your hands is a ticket to a future filled with excellence and prosperity, a lighted path to safety and security. *You* are our hope."

The crowd erupted in cheers and whistles again. The look on each of the teens' faces was of such profound surprise and awe that a lump formed in my throat as I watched them react to the news. Three of the girls hugged, their arms linked around each other's shoulders. A few of the students stood alone, staring at their envelopes with tears in their eyes as they realized the magnitude of what they'd received.

The woman tried to speak again, but the applause and cheers grew so loud that even her amplified voice was drowned out.

Three long minutes later, the noise died down enough for her to speak. "This ticket to your future comes from someone we all know as Robin Hood—but it comes with strings. You must finish in four years, and when each of you is a success someday—and notice I said *when*—you must find some teen with great potential and little opportunity and help them achieve their dreams."

She turned and faced the crowd. "And this is only the beginning. We're told that another five hundred students from our community will be selected to receive full scholarships to the colleges of their choice. Five hundred more of us." She wiped tears from her eyes, and her shoulders began to shake. "This is proof that you matter. *We* matter. Light has entered our world."

She lifted her hands toward the sky and started crying then, and many of the crowd did the same. I couldn't fathom the despair and tragedy of her loss, but somehow, through this transformative moment, she was given comfort and healing.

The singers began again—what sounded like Beethoven's *Ode to Joy* in an arrangement so upbeat and full of hope that people in the crowd couldn't help but smile through their tears. Strangers linked arms with strangers and swayed to the music. Others came up and embraced the startled teens. Many held up their smartphones and snapped pictures or shot video of the event.

Evelin slipped back to the sidelines, where she was greeted by hugs from people in the crowd. Josh and I inched our way through the crush, grabbing sound bites.

"It restores your faith in humanity," a man named Eliecer Amezcua said, carrying his four-year-old son on his shoulders so the boy could see over the crowd.

"It's melting my heart," his wife said, dabbing the corners of her eyes with a tissue.

I approached one of the teens, a young Latina with a luminous smile. "My dad is a carpenter. My mom works in a *panadería*," she said, clutching her blue envelope. "I will be the first in my family to go to college. And to Berkeley, where I've been accepted but could not afford."

"Did you have any idea this was what today was about?"

Her voice broke. "It's a complete surprise for all of us. I didn't think anyone was paying attention to people like me. Good students without money. But to think that they'd do this for me . . ."

Her voice trailed off, and she started to cry again. Another teen with tear-stained eyes and long brown hair that drifted to her waist came up and gave her a hug. Then she was enveloped in hugs from other people, and I lost sight of her.

I pressed my way through the crowd toward Evelin, the mother of the slain boy. I found her surrounded by a dozen other people waiting to talk to her.

"I'm Kate Bradley from Channel Eleven," I said.

Her eyes were flint gray, steely in their determination, but no amount of makeup could conceal the puffiness around them. She smiled brightly, but I could see it was forced, her last threads of energy.

"How do you know the scholarships are real?"

Another woman with a short bob replied for her. "The money's in a bank account at City National, and the bank has been appointed as the trustee. It's been verified."

"And you're certain it's from Robin Hood?" I asked.

Evelin nodded. "Yes. A Robin Hood coin came in all of the envelopes."

I called the newsroom, and despite PowerTrade's boycott, a few minutes later I was reporting live from the scene in a breaking-news report that interrupted the morning's highest-rated talk show. I was bursting with excitement when David told me the story would open the next newscast as well. Not the fire at the LA port. Or the kidnapped woman. Even the stolen-car chase down the 405 wouldn't open the cast.

Hope would.

"The hope for a savior to restore the balance of power is enduring," the pastor of a church in South Central intoned to anchor Kelly Adams on our evening newscast. "Robin Hood is a powerful symbol against inequality and injustice. In troubling times like these, he has come to the aid of the common man and woman. As it says in Isaiah, 'Share your food with the hungry and give shelter to the homeless.' Robin Hood knows that if you want to be perfect in the eyes of God, give to the poor."

The *Huffington Post* asked whether the kids would be allowed to keep the scholarships when they might have been funded by proceeds from stolen goods. But that sentiment was drowned out as news stations, including Channel Eleven, ran profiles of the kids who received the scholarships. All of the students came from staggering poverty or families broken by drugs or gang violence. All of them were achieving stellar grades in college-level courses, many winning awards in debate team or mathlete competitions—one had even won a national competition in robotics—against impossible odds. Some of them had already been awarded scholarships to attend the top schools in the country, but none of them had amassed enough funding to attend.

Two of the stories grabbed the most attention. Mario Hernandez had just returned from a funeral for his two uncles, who had been killed in a gang shooting, when he found out he had won a scholarship. And seventeen-year-old Shannon Johnson, a talented African American ballerina whose family of eight was living in a two-bedroom apartment just east of crime-riddled Watts, was enrolling in the dance program at Juilliard.

The story had taken on such enormous importance that the people at PowerTrade had no choice but to retract their position, saying their "thinking" had "evolved."

Even the pope seemed to be weighing in, although he was sidestepping the stealing element of Robin Hood's work. "The worship of the ancient golden calf has returned in a new and ruthless guise through the idolatry of money," he said to reporters aboard his plane back to Rome. "But we are all awakened when we see that money can have a truly human purpose."

Eric was waiting for me when I came home that night. He was sprawled on my living room couch, watching a football game on TV. Built in 1929, my apartment building in the hillside neighborhood of Los Feliz was considered historic by LA standards. It had the high ceilings, original tile, and vintage appliances that appealed to the LA history purists, but luckily it also had all the modern conveniences—high-speed internet and air-conditioning, which was on full blast to offset the unrelenting Santa Ana winds.

I dropped my purse on the floor, kicked off the pumps that had been digging into my toes all evening, and curled up next to him.

He paused the football game. "I'm surprised they're not interrupting the game for updates on Robin Hood," he said, pressing a kiss to my lips. "It's all anyone's talking about. Looks like you're becoming a fixture on ANC too."

"About ANC . . ." I dragged in a deep breath. "They've made an offer. They want me in New York next month."

"Next month?" His face turned pale.

I looked down at my hands. "I don't know what to do."

His jaw tightened. "This is serious, then?"

"They're saying I'll get to cover more important stories. And it is a worldwide network."

He sat up. "This is a huge opportunity for you," he said in a faraway voice.

"What if a position were available in the FDNY—"

"I looked into it, and there isn't. I talked with a friend of mine who's a captain there—and there are no openings for what I do. And I was right about the certification. Even on the fast track, it will take years."

I rubbed my forehead, trying to stall the headache that was forming. "What are we going to do?"

"I don't know," he said in hushed tones. "You also have to remember that Brian's family is here in LA too. I can't just leave them. They're all I've got."

Heat rushed to my cheeks. "All you've got?"

"I didn't mean—I meant that they're the only family I've got left. I'm still in the middle of helping settle his estate . . ."

I felt a rush of warmth as I looked at him. In the few short months we'd been together, he had become my best friend. He understood me in a way no one ever had. Why was I letting something as mundane as a *job* tear us apart? "This is happening so fast, so maybe I shouldn't . . ."

"No. You *should* do this. But I also want us to be together. I just can't see how we can have both at the same time."

"Maybe we can make this work long distance. What if we flew back and forth every other weekend?"

He placed his hand on mine. "I don't know if I could live like that. Apart from you for most of the time. Is that what *you* want?"

"No." I heard the certainty in my tone, but inside I was wavering. "What if we try it out for six months? See if I even like New York. I can always come back."

"If you go, we both know what will happen. At first, we'll see each other every few weeks. Then we'll get busy, and it'll become every few months until . . . we just drift apart."

"It doesn't have to be that way."

His voice became a raspy whisper. "I've been in love with you almost since I first laid eyes on you, Kate. I won't make you stay here—and I can't stand by while you build a whole new life in New York without me. That would kill me. I don't see how we can make this work."

As I headed into work the next morning, the decision that lay ahead weighed on me. I fumbled through the call from my agent, Sharon, as she rattled off the details of the ANC offer. Double your salary. Wardrobe allowance. Multiyear contract. Two free months in a furnished apartment overlooking Central Park. The perks blurred together into meaningless words. I couldn't even muster an excited tone, even as my usually laid-back agent gushed about the offer being "a career opportunity of a lifetime." I promised to get back to her with an answer.

A few minutes later, a text came from a number I didn't recognize.

$6M heist at Palazzo de Bella Vista. You on it?

I typed back: *Who is this?*

Jake. Back in town. Meet me later tonight?

I paused a moment before I typed back. What if this wasn't Jake? What if it was someone pretending to be him?

What was the name of the severed-head victim? If he was Jake, he'd know, as that was the first story we'd worked on together.

Bizarre question. Jaclyn Conway. Why?

Making sure it's you.

There was a long delay before his reply: *8 tonight. Howling Wolf Den. Silver Lake.*

??? I typed back. Since when did Jake hang out at a place called the Howling Wolf Den?

No one will be looking for either of us there.

He was right. Silver Lake, a small neighborhood just east of Hollywood, had been the hipster haven of LA for years. It was a place where you could pick up a cup of single-origin organic coffee. Or you could forage through organic vegetables at the farmers' market, then watch an indie band play on a small stage in a Moroccan café specializing in fresh mint teas. It wasn't somewhere I'd ever expected to meet Jake, which was exactly why he was right about no one ever discovering us there.

Will you be at Palazzo de Bella Vista? I texted.

Can't. But you should be. Big surprise coming.

CHAPTER SIXTEEN

The sixty-thousand-square-foot Palazzo de Bella Vista, owned by real estate magnate Elliot Wagner, held an IMAX movie theater, a thirteen-hundred-gallon aquarium, eleven master suites, and an underground garage with parking for thirty vehicles. The estate had so many Jacuzzis, waterfalls, fountains, and waterslides that the owners engaged a full-time "pool technician."

No reporters were allowed on the grounds, but Josh and I didn't need to go inside to see the over-the-top extravagance. The estate had recently been on the market for $135 million, and realtors had a website with over two dozen photos of the property taken by one of the top photographers from *Architectural Digest*.

So many reporters were swarming the streets outside the estate that we were forced to set up fifty yards from the front gates. Within minutes, the police chief, flanked by two police officers, strode through the tall iron gates. I hadn't seen the chief at a crime scene very often—most of his announcements were done from downtown headquarters—but the sheer magnitude of this story must have changed his approach to talking with reporters.

In a flash, all of the reporters were jockeying for premium space in front of him, and our cameramen edged to the back and sides to get unobstructed views. One reporter from Channel Four smacked me in the ribs with her clipboard, and another scraped my arm with his microphone. It was like the early-morning hours at a Walmart Black Friday sale—with the shoppers all dressed in suits and heels.

Without fanfare or introduction, Police Chief Charlie Harris—dressed in a dark-navy uniform punctuated only by four silver stars on each collar and the LAPD badge—started speaking.

"Palazzo de Bella Vista was the site of yet another robbery by the criminal known as Robin Hood. Early this morning the thieves forced their way into the estate and stole over six million dollars in valuables. In the course of the heist, a forty-year-old housekeeper was injured and was taken to the hospital. The woman came upon the thieves while they were making their escape, and it appears one of them pushed her aside and she tumbled down a stone staircase."

"Can you release the identity of the victim?" a reporter from the *LA Times* shouted.

"Not at this time."

"Any update on the condition of the alleged criminal caught in the Holmby Hills fire? The one previously in a medically induced coma?" I called out.

"He is improving, but his medical condition still prevents us from questioning him." He shifted his weight to another foot. "Folks, this story is getting a lot of traction because people seem to be enjoying the fact that these wealthy estates are being robbed for the benefit of the poor. But these *criminals* are committing grand larceny. Let's not forget another person has been injured in the commission of this crime spree. I urge you—let us not encourage these criminals."

Now that an innocent woman was injured, the sentiment about Robin Hood wavered a little. "Robin Hood's Merry Men Assault Housekeeper" read the headline in the *LA Times*. Viewers loved Robin Hood as long as he didn't hurt anyone, but this event had put even the most zealous fans on edge. One blogger with over a million followers wrote, "Now that people are getting injured, let's rethink whether Robin Hood is doing this for good."

One lobbying group seized this opportunity to fault Robin Hood's gifts to the poor. "No society ever thrived because it had a large and growing class of parasites living off those who produce." That set off a firestorm in social media as people debated whether Robin Hood was doing a good thing or simply enabling the poor to stay that way. This was the all-out powder keg my dad had predicted, and the story was quickly spinning out of control.

The twenty-five microbrews on tap at Howling Wolf Den attracted a crowd of hipsters I didn't see much in my line of work. As I waited for Jake near the outdoor bar, I overheard a group of young men and women in oversize glasses and thrift-store skinny jeans discussing the merits of the grilled gruyère cheese from the food truck they had just tried and whether an indie-rock band named Reel Big Fish was imitating or influenced by ska, which a slim, bearded guy described as the "primitive, raw, syncopated precursor to reggae." Their faces lit by the cool glow of their smartphones, they tapped on their screens, talked about ska, and sipped their craft beer from what looked like oddly shaped wineglasses. From the sounds of it, the Robin Hood controversy wasn't even on their radar.

"Want to take a walk?" I heard someone say, and I turned around to see Jake standing behind me. His normally clean-shaven face had the beginnings of a beard, and his once carefully clipped hair was now a bit tousled. It was the first time I'd seen him dressed casually; usually he wore a suit and a badge, so it took me a moment to adjust to seeing him in dark jeans and an untucked blue shirt.

We started walking under the warm glow of the café lights from the restaurants along the street until we found a park bench. Across the street, a crowd had gathered in front of a food truck, which sold gluten-free burritos—apparently the new trend in Silver Lake. Fortunately, we were nearly invisible in the shadows of a stand of dense California oak trees.

I was asking questions before Jake could sit down. "What happened to you? Why were you in Dawson Springs, Kentucky?"

His eyes widened. "How did you know?"

"What were you doing with the Kentucky Preppers?"

"Damn. You found out about that too? Like I've said, you'd make a great detective. That raised a lot of eyebrows at the department. I had no idea how deep my brother was into the stuff until I got there."

"But why were you there? What happened to you?"

He looked down at his hands. "Look, I'm embarrassed to say this. I was suspended."

"Suspended. What for?"

He drew a deep breath. "They caught me on camera showing you around El Mirasol. Remember I said those cameras were off-line? Well, they weren't."

"Are you kidding me?"

"It was a really dumb move on my part because my bosses made it clear they didn't want anyone at the crime scenes. Even the estate owners. Certainly not reporters. Things got worse when you met with Detective Haney and showed her the Robin Hood coin. They assumed that I had given you evidence from the crime scene and extended my suspension so they could investigate further."

"But you didn't give it to me. I got it from—"

"I know, Kate. And now that there are silver coins everywhere, they're starting to come around to that. But they still took my badge away for showing you around."

"Why was it so important for the police to keep the Robin Hood coins a secret?"

"The chief thought that if people knew that there was some kind of Robin Hood out there stealing from the rich and giving to the poor, it would ignite a media firestorm that would make it even harder to stop these heists."

I nodded. "He was right about that."

"That's why we withheld information about everything we found at the crime scene, not only from the media but from the estate owners too."

"*Everything* you found at the crime scene?" I asked. "Was there other evidence besides the silver coin?"

He looked away. "I've said too much already."

"There is, isn't there? Is it the Hidden Mickey you talked about?"

He rubbed the back of his neck. "Maybe."

As much as I wanted to know what it was, I didn't want Jake to get into more trouble. "Look, I'm going to stop asking questions. You've already done enough for me. And I feel terrible that you were suspended for helping me."

His eyes met mine. "I had my own reasons for doing that."

There was an awkward silence then, as neither of us knew what to say.

"I'm going to tell you what else they found at the crime scene because I think it'll help your investigation. I can't do anything more on the case. But you can."

"Are you sure you—"

"The thieves also left a green felt hat, complete with a red feather." He showed me a photo on his iPhone. "Do you get *why* the coin and the hat are the Hidden Mickeys that could crack the case?"

"Because they eliminate a lot of suspects? Most of them don't steal in order to help others."

He shook his head. "In real life, thieves don't leave calling cards—evidence deliberately left at the scene as a kind of signature. That's the stuff of TV crime dramas. Yet these sophisticated thieves left not one but two calling cards behind. Why?"

"To lead you to them?"

"Nope. Think harder. Why would the thieves want to send a message to the owners? I mean, why would they take the extra measure—and time in a limited fifteen-minute window—to leave behind two calling cards to owners they don't know?"

I thought about it for a long moment. "Because they *do* know the owners."

He beamed his approval. "Exactly. It's not random. They're sending *these* estate owners a message. If I could ever get myself back on the case, the first thing I'd do is look into everyone these estate owners know. They've angered someone. And I think this is payback."

"I'd like to follow up on that."

He flashed me a wide grin. "Wish we could work on this one together."

"How soon until you can come back?"

He shrugged. "Hard to say. Looks like it's going to be a long process. Months maybe."

"I'm so sorry, Jake. I feel bad about my part in this."

He placed a hand on my arm. "You didn't pressure me to do anything I didn't want to do. Really. After they suspended me, I was crazy with anger and went off the grid—canceled my cell phone, stayed off social media—and tried to escape from the hell of it all by hanging with my brother in Kentucky. But after being there awhile, I realized that I didn't have anyone to blame but myself. Wasn't my smartest career move, but it's no secret that I had other motivations for helping you, Kate."

I let that statement hang for a moment, watching the shifting shadows on the sidewalk as a light wind blew through the trees. I didn't know what to say. I knew I hadn't misled him about my feelings, but now I felt bad for not reciprocating them. Even if he did get his job back, there'd be a blot on his record for what he'd done to help me.

"Would it help any if I wrote a statement saying I didn't get the silver coin from you?"

He ran his fingers through his hair. "I think they're past that now that thousands of people have these silver coins. At this point, they think that if they lift my suspension, I'll compromise some other crime scene for you."

"But you wouldn't."

His eyes met mine. "I don't know, Kate. Even after my suspension, I'd still do just about anything for you."

My thoughts were spinning. In the shadows, he appeared especially attractive, and for a moment I felt a tug of affection for him. Something beyond friendship.

I knew he was expecting a response, but any truth I might say would only disappoint him. "I'm leaving LA at the end of the month," I said finally. "I'm moving to Manhattan."

"Manhattan?"

"ANC made an offer this morning."

"That's awesome." He leaned forward. "But you can't go without me."

"Without you?"

"New York? Heck, I'm packing my bags tonight."

"Jake, I—"

He touched his hand to my knee, and the tension rose between us. "I'm just playing around," he said lightly, but I didn't believe him. "Remind me to show you how to find a secret running trail in Central Park. Makes your run around Lake Hollywood look like child's play."

There was a long moment of silence between us, and I felt his feelings for me in the dark. They were palpable and real—exciting and overwhelming at the same time.

His voice was soft and low. "I know there's someone else. But until there's a ring on your finger, I'm gonna keep hoping."

As I left the Howling Wolf Den, my phone lit up with a text from Sharon, my agent. *ANC agreed to the big stuff we asked for. Want to close this up?*

ANC moved fast. Hadn't I just spoken to Sharon this morning? She had never been a high-pressure agent before, so this could only mean that ANC was pressing her to get this done. But I didn't have an answer. I needed to talk with Eric again. To figure this out.

I texted him. *You home?*

Yep.

Coming over.

It was nearly eleven by the time I reached his house. The streetlights were on, casting leafy shadows through the wide-canopied jacaranda trees that lined his quiet residential street. I found him in his driveway, unloading boxes from his pickup.

"What's all this?" I asked.

"Almost finished," he said, hoisting a box from the back and setting it on the ground. He was breathing rapidly even though the box didn't appear that heavy. "This is the last of it."

From the open box, I lifted a red waterproof jacket, the kind you saw on the guys who sailed in the America's Cup, and a pair of graphite waterproof boots. They looked to be for a man smaller and shorter than Eric.

"It's Brian's sailing stuff," he said quietly. "His wife is closing out the storage locker at the marina and told me to take whatever I wanted. Guess I took most of it."

"What do you plan to do with all this?"

He lifted another box from the van, dropped it on the sidewalk, and opened it. "Not sure yet. My second bedroom is already stacked to the ceiling with his stuff, so the bigger question is *where* am I going to put it?"

I lifted a red helmet out of the box. "Seems like a lot of gear for sailing."

"Brian always dreamed of racing sailboats one day." He picked up a pair of Puma high-tops. "He often practiced with the most expensive gear." He dumped the high-tops back in the box, took out a black flotation vest, and brought it up to his chest. On the front, in white letters, it read: HAYES. "He had a friend who was in charge of designing the technical clothing for a well-known America's Cup team, so he got a lot of free advice about what to buy . . ." His words trailed off.

I studied a pair of black Lycra pants. "Are you going to take up sailboat racing?"

His eyes softened. "Maybe I should, you know, to keep his dream alive," he said just above the threshold of my hearing. "But I don't . . ."

I waited for him to finish speaking, but he stood there, looking at the things in the box as though the rest of his sentence might be in there. "This is all I have left of him."

His eye fell on something in the box. "Here they are," he said, pulling out a pair of black TAG Heuer sunglasses. "These were Brian's lucky sunglasses. If he wore them in the morning when the skies were gray, we were guaranteed to get sunny bluebird weather. At least that's what he thought. One time he accidentally dropped them in the water while we were still anchored in the harbor. He had four of us in the water searching for them for nearly an hour. We couldn't leave the harbor until we found them."

He turned the sunglasses over in his hands, his mind miles away, remembering. The beginnings of a smile crept across his face, but in the shadowy light, I saw the weariness in the hollows of his eyes and in his slackened jaw, his shoulders hunched by the memory.

I reached out and pulled him close, hugging him tight until I felt him hug back. My questions would have to wait.

~

My cell phone was ringing.

What time was it? My heart raced as I tried to lift myself from a deep sleep.

My eyes snapped open. Five rings. Pause. Five more rings.

I sat up, realizing I had fallen asleep on the couch in my living room.

Where had I left the phone?

I stumbled in the dark, listening for the chime again and shuffling in that direction.

Bleary eyed, I found the phone on the kitchen counter and squinted at the bright screen.

Hannah.

"Did I wake you?" she said before I could say hello.

"What time is it?"

"We've heard from Locksley."

It took seconds for her words to sequence in my brain. "He answered on *League of Legends*?"

"He claims he's the leader behind the heists. I asked him if he was Robin Hood, and he said yes."

"Of course he did," I said, rubbing the sleep from my eyes. "Soon enough everyone's going to be claiming to be Robin Hood."

"Thought about that. So I asked for proof. He posted a twenty-second clip showing one of the robberies in progress. Looks like it was shot at La Villa de la Paz—that's the one with a safe in the sauna."

I shuffled back to the couch and sat down. "Still, the video could be a fake."

"I asked if he'd let you interview him. He said yes."

"He knows you're from Channel Eleven?"

"He knew before he even replied."

"I thought you said there was no way he could figure out who you were?"

"I was wrong. If he has the ability to rob these high-tech estates, he's probably got tech to do just about anything. He says he's responding to us because he wants to set the record straight about what happened with the housekeeper."

I swallowed hard. Part of me was damn certain this was a fake, but another part was hoping it wasn't. "I don't think Robin Hood will ever reveal himself. He'd go straight to jail."

"It's an interview by Skype. He has some kind of voice equalizer on his end."

"What does he look like?"

"Don't know. His profile is a painting of Robin Hood."

CHAPTER SEVENTEEN

I had a hard time convincing David to attend the Skype interview with the alleged Robin Hood. Not just because it would mean he would have to reschedule the assignment meeting, but because he was 100 percent certain this Robin Hood was fake. We'd both had our share of false confessors on big stories before, and given the number of fakes versus the real deals over the years, the odds were stacked against this guy being the real Robin Hood.

"If there's an organized group—Russian or otherwise—behind these robberies, I doubt they'd come forward on Skype to announce themselves," he said, pacing the floor of the Fish Bowl. "And if they're going the confession route, why reach out to *you* instead of the usual mea culpa icons like Diane Sawyer or Anderson Cooper?"

"Actually, Skype could be the best way," I said. "For him, anyway. He can keep his identity a secret and control exactly what we see and hear."

Hannah, who had been quietly looking at something on her laptop, piped up. "Diane Sawyer and Anderson Cooper have big followings, but if a story like this goes viral, Robin Hood doesn't need those brand names to get heard around the globe."

"Look, I'm as curious as you two are about whether this guy is Robin Hood," David said. "I think he's a fake, but I'll listen."

We set up the interview in one of the smaller recording bays, a room specially lit for Skype interviews. My hands were twisted in a tight knot as we waited for Locksley to log in to Skype. I stared at the blank screen, the blinking cursor ticking off the passing seconds, trying to wrap my head around the questions I wanted to ask. My radar for hoaxes and scams was on full alert, and I tried to imagine what he could say that would convince me that he was Robin Hood.

Our recording technician, Dan, sat across from me, clearly bored. He was a big guy, and the rising temperature in the bay was bringing out beads of sweat on his forehead. He kept rubbing his eyes and yawning to make it obvious he wasn't expecting anything of importance. I began to have the feeling he was right.

I was also worried. If this turned out to be Robin Hood, how would I explain to my father why I hadn't taken myself off the story, why I hadn't handed the story off to Conan or any other reporter who wasn't Hale Bradley's offspring? The answer was obvious to me, but it wouldn't be to him. Scoring an interview with Robin Hood would be one of the biggest coups of the year. What career was I forging if every story I covered had to be measured against the impact it might have on my father's political career?

Suddenly the image of Robin Hood flashed up on the screen. But not the icon Errol Flynn, Russell Crowe, or Kevin Costner made famous. This one was an older painting, one where an intense-looking Robin Hood wore a red hat and hawk feather and was poised to shoot an arrow as his merry men looked on.

David took a seat next to me, a few feet out of range of the camera but close enough that he could see exactly what was going on. He took a long sip of his green juice and put his feet, clad in his signature black loafers, on the table.

"No more Dr Pepper?" I asked.

He nodded. "Fell off the wagon for a day. But I'm good now," he said as though trying to assure himself it was true. He cracked his knuckles.

Seconds later, a blurry image replaced the Robin Hood painting, followed by a few other images. At first none of us could figure out what they were; then we realized they were photos taken at the heists. One photo showed two masked men using some kind of power tool to break into a safe. Another was of three men, their faces partially cropped, choosing items from a drawer filled with expensive jewelry and watches. In the final photo a person wearing a black ski mask held a painting I recognized.

It was *Man Reaching for the Moon* by Antonio Mora. The same painting Thomas Speyer had shown me that had been stolen from his estate.

I whispered to David, "This is one of the paintings stolen from the Holmby Hills estate. The owner, Thomas Speyer, showed me a photo of it."

David pulled his feet off the table and sat up.

"This is Kate Bradley," I said to the screen. "Who is this?"

"This is Locksley. I believe you and the news media are calling me and my team Robin Hood." The voice was clearly processed, like Hannah had said. Still, even through the processing, I heard the hints of an eastern-European accent.

"Where are you located?" I asked.

"Did I provide sufficient proof of my identity? Or would you like more photographs?"

David nodded.

"Please keep sending photos. But for now, assuming you are—"

"Let me tell you why I've agreed to speak to you today," he interrupted. "First, we want to apologize for the injury to the housekeeper in Palazzo de Bella Vista. That was an unintended consequence of our mission, and we apologize. We have made a hundred-thousand-dollar deposit into her bank account to compensate her for our mistake. Second, we want to talk about those from whom we stole. My organization took millions from a handful of the hundred wealthiest people in the United States. The combined worth of the wealthiest one hundred is over two *trillion* dollars."

"We've established that the victims are extremely wealthy, but—"

"Let's be clear that none of the people we took from will have lost anything. Zero. Their insurance companies will be reimbursing them for their losses. We took nothing of sentimental value and nothing that couldn't be easily replaced. *It is a victimless crime.*"

I tried to get control of the interview, but whoever Robin Hood was, he was a formidable interview subject. "But you can't argue that stealing is good—"

He was also intent on ignoring me. "Meanwhile, a few miles away from some of the greatest concentrations of vast wealth this country has seen since the Industrial Age, forty percent of people are living below the poverty line. I'm not only talking about the homeless but also the working poor, some of them working two or more jobs to survive, and nearly half of them—forty two percent of them—will *never* get out of poverty."

"But why help the working poor this way? Why not go through legal channels—get the government involved or work through a charity?"

"Government and charities can't solve this problem fast enough. But that's not why we are taking from the rich to give to the poor."

David leaned forward, clearly engrossed. He seemed to be changing his mind about this being a fake confessor.

"Why, then?" I asked.

There was a long pause, and I worried that Robin Hood had hung up or we had lost the connection. The silence in the room suddenly became deafening. David drew a giant question mark on his yellow pad and pointed at it.

Long seconds later, Robin Hood returned. "No one would pay attention to the problems of the poor if we quietly helped others and gave away scholarships and food to the needy. Charities and individuals are doing that kind of work every day throughout this country. Yet the news media rarely cover those stories. But we knew that if we created a sensation—crimes of unimagined proportions—the global media would be riveted. Suddenly they are bringing attention to the crisis of the poor. Now very few people on the planet can say that they aren't aware of the problem."

"But aren't you advocating that others steal from the rich and give to the poor? Aren't you encouraging others to commit crimes?"

"We are strategic and specific. We target those with the greatest wealth—none of the top one hundred has a net worth of less than five billion dollars—and we take what we know is valuable yet easily replaced. We do no harm to the property or to any individuals. No one should follow in our footsteps." What sounded like a laugh, or a cough, escaped his throat. "Do not try this at home."

"What is your connection to Russia?"

"This is our origin."

"Russian government?"

"No."

"Where are you?"

His voice rose. "In the United States. Like Robin Hood, we live in the slums."

My cheeks grew red hot. "Why me? Why are you telling your story to me?"

"You made the connection between user Locksley on *League of Legends* and Robin Hood. We're impressed. And curious how you did it."

I looked at David, who was apparently wondering the same thing. "You started each mission by telling your team that you were 'summoning the champions.' That's how you begin a mission in *League of Legends*."

"That kind of research is exactly why I am talking to you, not someone else."

I smiled a moment, happy that I'd scored kudos from Robin Hood even as David was still scowling next to me.

"I also understand that you start each mission by telling your team you are 'changing the world.' Do you really believe that?"

"This is a movement for shared prosperity. We know with one hundred percent certainty that we are changing the world."

I heard my father's words ringing in my ears and felt the pressure to say them. "Some would say you and your merry men are robbing the superrich because you're jealous of what they have."

His tone became brittle. Even through the voice processing, I could tell I had made him angry. "They would be wrong. We do not envy the rich. We see unused utility in what they have. They have money and resources even they cannot use or enjoy. And their unused wealth does not help the economy." He cleared his throat. "We are simply helping the ultrawealthy to bring light and hope into our troubled world."

The screen went black. Dan tried to get the connection back, but Robin Hood didn't answer.

We put a digital-forensics expert to work reviewing all twelve of the photos that Robin Hood sent over, verifying that they hadn't been doctored and that they were actually taken from the crime scenes. Then my report aired every hour on Channel Eleven and was picked up by the network and shown around the country in newscasts and breaking-news reports throughout the day. Viewers by the hundreds of thousands flocked to the station's website to download the Robin Hood interview, overloading the system and taking the site down for ten minutes—an eternity in the news business. It was a heady feeling watching the story gain momentum on air and go viral online.

I admired what Robin Hood was doing, but I wrestled with whether this was the right way to go about it. I couldn't argue with one fact, though: his heists had brought worldwide attention to the poor. If he hadn't been robbing all these high-end estates, no one would have paid attention to what he did helping others. And now that he had the nation's attention, people were listening.

In place of reports about the latest celebrity arrest, stories cropped up about how one in every five children in the US lived in a household without adequate food. Instead of updates on the latest sports cheating scandal, the media rolled out reports about the growing number of Americans who were homeless each night. Stories of people helping others even disrupted the hallowed litany of crime stories that usually dominated our newscasts. It was no exaggeration to say that Robin Hood was changing the world.

My dad didn't think so. He called on my cell phone and wasted no time expressing his frustration. "You're ruining my chances for reelection."

I was silent a moment, processing what he was saying. "How?"

"Because *your* Robin Hood reports are getting some of the most play across the country, my donors feel they are under attack by *me*. Some are saying they won't back my campaign for reelection."

"You'll find other campaign donors. You always do. You're one of the best at fund-raising."

He raised his voice a notch. "That's not how it works. There's an organization planning to spend nine hundred million dollars on the next election. If I'm not part of that campaign spend, I don't have a chance in hell of being reelected. And the men who run those funds have made it crystal clear that if I don't rein in this story—if I don't rein in *my daughter*—they won't spend a penny on my reelection."

"Your donors want to control the media and the world we live in. That's why they contribute millions to political campaigns each year. But I don't play requests on the news. It's time they found out that some things can't be bought."

"I admire your idealism," he said. In my line of work, idealists didn't last more than six months. But I was beginning to wonder if I was turning into one. Was the Robin Hood story changing *me*? "But you've crossed the line. When big donors become unhappy with politicians like me, they can carpet-bomb my campaign. My political career will be over. Finished."

My throat constricted. After thirty years in public service, my dad was doing his best, most important work as Senate majority leader. The thought that I might somehow be responsible for him losing the next election made me feel sudden, sinking dread.

~

By nine o'clock that night, I was exhausted and wondered why I hadn't heard from Eric. If he'd turned on the TV or even looked at social media, he was sure to have seen the story. It was odd that he hadn't texted me with his usual *Wow* or *Good stuff* when he watched a story I'd done.

I pulled up in front of Eric's house and was surprised to see that nearly every light in the house was lit. As I walked up the concrete path to his front door, I was also surprised to hear laughter and music coming from inside the house. As many times as I'd been here, he'd mostly been alone. Sometimes he'd have a few of his friends over to watch the game or hang out over a barbecue. But given the demands of his job, he wasn't home often, and when he was, his house was a place to rest and recharge.

The front door was unlocked, so I opened it without knocking. A woman was sitting next to Eric on the leather couch in the living room.

Her back was to me, and all I could see was that she was holding some kind of pink drink in her hand. Their heads were close together as they looked through a book. The music was loud, and they didn't hear me come in. I recognized the song as one by Maroon 5, not one of Eric's favorite groups by any stretch. Eric's face was flushed—probably from the red wine he was drinking—and when he looked up and saw me, an expression I hadn't seen on him before flashed across his face. Guilt.

"Kate," he said, standing. "I didn't—"

The woman turned to look at me. She had the face of a model, with high cheekbones and thick sable-brown hair that rested in waves on her shoulders.

"Hi, I'm Carrie Gilbert," she said, standing. She was petite, about five foot four, the kind of woman who had to have her size zeros taken in to fit properly.

I crossed the room. "Kate." I shook her hand and shot an expectant look at Eric.

"Carrie and I go way back," he said. He seemed uncomfortable, unsteady in his words. "We used to—"

"I went to school with his brother, Brian, and then met this goofball on one of many sailing trips."

Goofball. If there was any word I *wouldn't* use to describe Eric, it was *goofball.*

She swatted his arm with the back of her hand. "Remember all those pranks you and I used to play on Brian? We drove him crazy."

They both laughed, and an uncomfortable feeling crept into my veins. I could feel the intimacy between them, and even if it was a remnant from the past, I didn't like it.

Eric stopped laughing. "We used to move stuff around the boat, and Brian, who always liked having a solid sailing routine—"

"And knowing where everything was—" Carrie said.

"He didn't like it."

Carrie covered her mouth. "Remember that time he thought there was some kind of ghost on the boat?"

Eric nodded. It was one of the rare times I'd seen him smile at a memory of his brother. His eyes met mine. "Carrie lives in San Francisco. She's in LA visiting her dad."

Carrie put her drink on the table. "My dad, who turned seventy-two last month, broke his leg while skiing at Mammoth. At seventy-two! And this one," she said, pointing to Eric. "This one has been helping me out. I still can't believe how you were able to make that ramp for him so he could get down his front steps."

Eric shook his head, clearly embarrassed. "Just a sheet of plywood and some bolts."

Carrie touched a hand to his forearm. "All those years, I never realized you were so good with a saw."

I felt a flicker of nausea. How many times had they seen each other since Carrie had been in LA? And why hadn't Eric told me about her? Or that he was helping her father?

From the way she looked at him, all flirty smiles and misty eyed, I had no doubt she was attracted to him. Then again, who wouldn't be? At the same time, I couldn't imagine her ever being Eric's girlfriend. No doubt she was beautiful in a way that made most men pay attention. But she seemed somewhat vapid—or was that simply the alcohol?—and, from the rapid way she talked, a bit on the insecure side. But she kept touching his arm, and he wasn't stopping her.

"And then he goes and repairs my dad's screen doors too. While he's at it, he says. My dad thinks you're Superman."

I wasn't afraid to ask questions. Ever. But in that moment, the questions I wanted to ask were locked in my throat. I didn't even try to speak, because I knew my words would sound weak and thin. Or possibly like the demon's voice that came from Linda Blair's throat in *The Exorcist*.

Then Carrie fixed her light-blue eyes on me, and the smile left her face. I could tell she was trying to figure out who I was and how I fit in—or how I was going to disrupt this cozy picture. Was I a neighbor? A friend? Surely not a coworker at this time of night.

My cell phone rang then, annoying me. David Dyal's name flashed on the screen. David rarely called me on my cell. My stomach lurched at the thought that he'd found out about the ANC offer. Why else would he be calling me at eight thirty at night?

Carrie lifted the photo book from the coffee table. "Mind if I borrow this? My dad will get a kick out of it. I'll give it back when I see you tomorrow."

I looked at Eric, and then at Carrie, trying to decide whether to answer the insistent ring.

"Everything okay?" Eric asked, nodding toward my purse.

The phone rang again.

"I'll take this outside," I said finally.

I felt Eric's eyes upon me, imploring me to understand, as I stepped outside and closed the door behind me. "David?" I said, answering the phone.

"Kate," he said, with a surprisingly buoyant tone in his voice. "*The Morning Show* wants you on the show tomorrow. Just got off the phone with the executive producer, who's an old buddy of mine from way back when we worked the news desk in Dayton."

It was the longest, chattiest sentence I'd ever heard David say. "Doesn't Teresa usually coordinate—"

"Yeah, I'll put her on in a sec, but I wanted to call you first myself. To say that was one hell of an interview with Robin Hood today."

Was he sick? Dying? Quitting? David never gave out compliments. The closest I'd seen him come to it was when Chuck Raines, one of our anchors, received a Peabody Award for an investigative report he'd done on migrant workers in Southern California. Even then David only managed a brusque "Good work, Chuck," then changed the subject to talk about the Senate debate on immigration.

I wondered if David knew about ANC's offer and was hoping to guilt me into turning it down by being nice. If that was his plan, it was working.

"Chris Gallagher himself is doing it," he said. Chris Gallagher was the popular anchor of *The Morning Show*, a fixture for so many years that viewers had watched him age from a cute guy in his twenties with a full head of curly hair to a handsome middle-ager with a graying buzz cut. "Hang on and I'll put Teresa on."

I knew Teresa would do a quick rundown of the interview sequence. The timing was still likely to change, but we would go through the questions they were preparing and work out what time I needed to be in Channel Eleven's studios for the live shot by satellite.

But instead of doing the call in Eric's front yard, I started walking back to my car. As Teresa detailed the questions, I got in the car and sank on wobbly legs into the driver's seat. And as we sorted out the sequence, I started the car. The next thing I knew, I was pulling away and heading down the street. I glanced at Eric's house reflected in my rearview mirror, wondering where I was headed and where I belonged.

CHAPTER EIGHTEEN

Could we ever know where we belonged? As I sat under the hot TV lights at three o'clock that morning, waiting to begin my interview with Chris Gallagher by satellite, I wasn't sure. Did I belong here at Channel Eleven or at ANC in New York? Did I belong with Eric, or was that over? With Jake? With anyone?

Eric had texted me multiple times:

Call me back?

We need to talk.

On duty for the next 24. But I really want to talk with you. Call me?

I took a full thirty minutes to text back: *Interview on ANC. Call you tomorrow.*

I was still smarting about Carrie, baffled why he hadn't told me about her—or apparently told her about me. My head spun at how quickly he'd moved on to someone else once I had a serious offer to move to New York.

One thing I knew. There had been a relationship between them at some point. Past or present, I couldn't be sure. But it didn't take much to see that their shared history, especially her connection with Brian and sailing, was a powerful draw. And admittedly she seemed far less complicated than I was, what with all my baggage—reporter, senator's daughter, possibly moving to New York. Maybe uncomplicated was what Eric wanted.

Where did I belong? Whatever the answer was, trying to find it was distracting me from the biggest story of my career. While I was worrying about moving to New York and what would happen with Eric, our Channel Two competitors had homed in on a sophisticated group of hackers in Russia who had ties to Southern California. Their theories about the group's connections to the heists were strong enough to get police and FBI attention. What leads did Channel Eleven have? None.

We had scored the exclusive interview with Robin Hood, so all expectations were on us—and on me—to figure out who he was. But despite repeated attempts at contacting Locksley through *League of Legends*, he had gone silent.

The floor director gave me the signal that the interview was getting ready to start, so I sat up in my chair and tried to focus my attention on what Chris was saying as he introduced me. It was already into the breakfast hour on the East Coast, so the entire morning team there looked fresh and awake on their cheery set decked out with purple peonies for some reason they must have explained earlier in the show. It would take some work to match that tone from a mostly empty newsroom in the middle of the night in Los Angeles.

"Kate, there are lots of theories about who Robin Hood is, but you're the only one who's actually talked with him. Any thoughts on who he is?" Chris asked.

He had veered completely from the list of questions Teresa had given me. I hid my surprise. "He's someone with great technical ability. I suspect he has considerable charisma, enough to convince others to follow him in his mission to change the world. And I think he's someone who's guided by strong values."

Chris laughed, the staged kind of laugh that morning-show anchors perfected. "He's stealing. That's not exactly value-driven behavior."

"He makes a point of apologizing for the injury to the housekeeper at Palazzo de Bella Vista. And not only apologizing but depositing a hundred thousand dollars in her bank account. He marshals his team by telling them they are 'changing the world.' He orchestrates events of giving to the poor in staggering proportions. Ten thousand food baskets to the poor every week. Over five hundred scholarships. And I'm sure there's more to come."

"You sound as though you admire him."

I chose my words carefully. "I admire how he's bringing attention and help to the working poor in America."

"But is stealing the right way to go about it?"

I shook my head. "Whether he is good or bad, it doesn't change the fundamental nature of what he has helped us see. Two-thirds of Americans are living paycheck to paycheck, while a single year of income from just one of the top hundred wealthiest Americans could buy housing for every homeless person in the country."

"So are you saying he's a hero?"

"Here's what we know. The majority of Americans have stagnant or worsening living standards, while those at the very top have seen the most significant gains. I think what Robin Hood is asking us to consider is whether this is compatible with values rooted in our nation's history and the high value Americans have placed on equality of opportunity."

"If you keep making statements like that, you might find yourself running for office. And you'll have many people agreeing with you as we see minimum wage and tax reform bills going through Congress."

I shifted in my seat, uncomfortable with where this conversation was headed. Why did journalists always assume that the sons and daughters of politicians wanted to launch political careers?

He must have sensed my uneasiness, because he changed the subject. "Do you think we'll figure out who Robin Hood is? We know he's got ties to Russia, which makes the likelihood of tracking him down that much more complicated. What do you think?"

"There are a lot of people who want to find out who Robin Hood is. And we're going to drive ourselves crazy trying to pin him down. He's got enough technical sophistication to outsmart us all. But we're going to keep trying."

He flashed the trademark smile that had made him an American favorite for decades. "Well, if anyone does find him, I hope it's either you or me who gets the interview." He leaned forward and set his index cards on the coffee table in front of him. "All right, thank you. Kate Bradley from Channel Eleven in Los Angeles, the station that scored the exclusive interview with the man we're all calling Robin Hood. Next up, Gretchen takes a look at the record-breaking rain headed to the Midwest."

~

"Guided by strong values?" There was no mistaking the anger in my father's voice. "A hero? What has come over you?"

Sweat broke out on my upper lip. I couldn't remember the last time I'd been fearful of my father's voice. I gripped my cell phone tightly. "First, I never called him a hero—"

"You said you admired him. Wait until *that* appears in the headlines. 'Senator's Daughter Admires Robin Hood.'"

"It's about helping the poor, the disabled, the homeless."

"It doesn't look good. A senator's daughter admiring someone who is stealing—"

"Stealing from your would-be campaign donors. Your donor base. That's what's really causing the problem, right? If your donors weren't upset, this wouldn't even be an issue. You didn't raise me to agree with you on everything. You always wanted me to be an 'objective thinker.' Why has that suddenly changed?"

There was a long silence on the phone. My dad had hung up.

~

Who was Carrie Gilbert? While every reporter I knew was scrambling to figure out who Robin Hood was, I was wondering about the woman who'd been with Eric the night before. I didn't think of myself as someone who was overly insecure in relationships, but that certainly wasn't holding true here.

I googled her first. Carrie Gilbert wasn't an uncommon name, but I found her on LinkedIn. The profile was pretty meager—a listing of her current position as a wedding photographer in Pacific Heights, a neighborhood in San Francisco.

I clicked on her Facebook page. Apparently she hadn't made her page private, because I could see her entire timeline. She didn't post often, but there was a post of a poem about how she missed her mother. A few other posts were shares of funny videos or photo memes. Then I scrolled down to a photo of her with Eric in front of his fireplace. He was dressed in uniform, and one of her tanned arms was around him as they beamed straight at the camera. The caption read: "Love the Hayes family."

I stared at the post in disbelief. Anger and disappointment lit my nerves. She hadn't tagged Eric, probably because he wasn't on Facebook much, but the post had already generated thirty-eight likes and seven comments, including "Who's that hottie with you?" from someone named Tamara and "You two look great together" from a woman who looked like Carrie's sister. A few were more somber reminders of Brian's passing. "Miss Brian too. Love to the whole Hayes family."

But the shot to my heart was Carrie's comment. "You can't see it, but he's got a superhero cape under that uniform."

My call to Eric went straight to voice mail.

~

Rain was coming. We didn't get much of it in LA, so few Angelenos had developed a sense of when it was on its way. But I'd grown up in San

Francisco, where everyone seemed to be clairvoyant about impending rain. You could read it in the light shift of the wind, the earthy scent in the air. In Los Angeles, there was a peculiar quality to the light before it rained, a yellow-blue tint that scattered the sunshine.

The sky hung close as I drove to Bel Air that morning for the interview with Stephen Bening. Even after a full night of sleep, I was still dog tired, and the shadowy skies reflected my mood. Worse, I hadn't prepared for the interview. After hounding Stephen for it, I hadn't even found time to write questions.

The timing of his interview couldn't have been worse for him and the other wealthy heist victims. Robin Hood's interview was all anyone was talking about, and even if Stephen was engaging on camera, few people would see him as a victim.

I reached his Bel Air estate a few minutes past ten o'clock, just as the rain began to fall in big fat drops. I handed my keys to the valet and walked past a multicolored stone gatehouse capped by giant eagles, then along a stone pathway that meandered past a koi pond. As I reached the estate's covered front porch, the sun peeked out from the clouds, and the rain transformed into an almost invisible mist, giving the estate a timeless, otherworldly feeling.

A man dressed in a tailored black suit ushered me inside. "Mr. Bening will meet you in the study." Our footsteps echoed as we crossed the grand foyer decorated with oak paneling and gilded balustrades, past a staircase with intricate wrought iron railings, and into yet another foyer covered with an expansive yet faded Persian rug. Then, in a move he had clearly mastered from doing it many times before, the man flung open two enormous wooden doors into the study.

The room looked more like a cathedral than a study. It was easily three thousand square feet, with soaring thirty-foot-high ceilings that were adorned by carved wooden beams. On one end of the room was a vaultlike recess with floor-to-ceiling windows and a hand-carved wooden chandelier. Rays of watery sunshine slanted through the windows, bathing the alcove in the kind of golden light you'd see in a Botticelli painting. I was caught in a dream. Surely such a place was of the imagination, not reality.

Josh had already set up a camera and some lighting by two antique chairs in the middle of the room. The look on his face was of utter disbelief. "I shot a ton of B-roll because no one . . . no one's ever going to believe this room."

There was so much to see and absorb that my eyes wouldn't settle on anything for long. The hand-painted harpsichord, the antique fireplaces, the oil paintings in carved frames—even if I'd had stratospheric wealth, I could not have imagined the splendor of this room.

"Thank you for coming out." Stephen's voice brought me back to the moment.

He was dressed informally in a pair of blue jeans, a white shirt open at the collar, and a tailored navy sport coat. The beginnings of a wispy beard were creeping along his jawline, a look that was less billionaire and more tech guru. But it was his shoes that quietly professed his wealth—a $1,500 pair of Ferragamo semigloss leather sneakers in black with distressed off-white piping.

"I hope this room works for the interview."

Did he have any idea what level of wealth this house was trumpeting? No one was going to feel sorry for Stephen—no matter how much Robin Hood had stolen from him—with this room as a backdrop.

"We could set up somewhere else less . . . grand, if you like."

Josh shot me a panicked look. I knew he didn't want to leave this setting, not only because he'd worked hard to set up the lighting but because neither of us ever got to do interviews in a place like this.

Stephen glanced at his watch. "I'm tight on time, so if this works, let's go with it."

I settled carefully in a hand-painted antique chair, realizing it probably cost more than my yearly salary. Stephen sat next to me and laid a laser-focused gaze on me.

"A few ground rules," he said. "You may not refer to me as a billionaire. Or one of America's wealthiest one hundred. Understood?"

I nodded. We didn't allow interview subjects to give ultimatums, but they were hard to argue seconds before I started recording the interview and even harder to argue in an awe-inspiring setting like this.

"The estates of some of the wealthiest people in America have been targeted in a series of sophisticated, high-tech heists. The thieves—known as Robin Hood—have hauled away over twenty-one million dollars in cash, cars, and other high-end goods and have used the proceeds to fund several high-profile events giving away scholarships, food, and housing to the poor," I said, opening the interview. "Stephen Bening, owner of Château du Soleil in Bel Air, is the first and only estate owner to talk with the media. Thank you for talking with me today, Stephen."

He nodded, lifting the corners of his mouth in a slight smile.

"Stephen, why are you talking with us now?"

"A lot has been said in the media about the wealth of the people targeted by the band of criminals known as Robin Hood. We didn't steal to earn our wealth. We worked for it. We are tenacious problem solvers. We set goals, and none of them have been easy to achieve. But no matter how much someone has, stealing is wrong."

"Robin Hood says this is a victimless crime."

"How is this victimless? First off, our privacy was violated, and the thieves could've accessed sensitive information. It appears that they didn't make off with any data, but we are still confirming that. Second, my property was stolen. Yes, I can replace it with funds from insurance—although I haven't—but the insurance companies are taking significant losses that will eventually be passed on to other clients in the form of higher rates. And let's not forget the cost to taxpayers for all the police and FBI agents who are investigating the crimes. This is *not* a victimless crime."

"Does it make a difference that Robin Hood is doing good with what he stole from you and others?"

His neck flushed red. "Look, I give to charity. Most of us do. I don't go around talking about it, but I recently gave ten million dollars to diabetes research at UCLA. How I choose to give money is *my* choice. I don't need someone who calls himself Robin Hood to decide for me."

A blonde woman wearing a tan blazer and black pants strode into the room. She held a cell phone and nodded anxiously at Stephen.

"Beth has a very important call waiting for me, so let's end the interview here." Stephen rose and extended his hand. "Thanks, Kate. Be sure to say hello to your father for me."

~

Russ Hartman didn't like how much airtime my brief but exclusive interview with Stephen Bening was getting. Because of it, his story about the brush fire that had already burned seventeen hundred acres in Angeles National Forest was getting buried in our newscasts.

Russ was making a mistake venting his discontent. David ran the assignment meeting like the captain of a battleship and didn't tolerate disruptions, punishing outbursts with crummy assignments or withering lectures. But David was surprisingly silent as Russ railed about an interview with a billionaire beating out his exclusive footage of the out-of-control wildfire.

I tried to defend the station's decision. "This is the first time any of the billionaire victims has spoken to the media. We got the interview David asked us to get and one that every news outlet in the country has been vying to get for weeks."

"No offense, Kate, but the only reason you scored that interview is because your name is Kate *Bradley*."

That stung. Yes, I knew my father's name opened doors for me. I should've been used to people being insensitive about it, but it still managed to surprise me. "My father didn't arrange the interview. I did."

He nodded. "And the fact that Stephen Bening has contributed tens of thousands to your father's campaigns over the years, or that you attended a fund-raiser at his estate, has nothing to do with you getting that interview."

"None of that makes the interview any less newsworthy."

He lobbed an arrow at me. "Unless you consider that it makes you look like a mouthpiece for your father's rich friends."

I stared at him in disbelief. My father had begged me not to cover the story. How could Russ accuse me of doing my father's bidding?

My cheeks grew hot, but where it hit me—where it really hurt—was in the gut.

"Enough," David said. "We're losing sight of what's important here. And that is: Who is Robin Hood? Channel Four has an entire series of segments airing with theories about possible suspects. CNN has a similar series. What have we got, Kate? Anything?"

I fumed. We might have nothing on who Robin Hood was, but everyone seemed to have forgotten that I had broken the story with the only exclusive interview with Robin Hood. And I'd brought in the only interview with a billionaire whose estate had been robbed. That was the problem with the hungry beast called television news. No matter what success you had today, tomorrow the beast would be asking, *What have you done for me lately?*

CHAPTER NINETEEN

My pulse was hammering so hard I could hear it in my ears as I watched a fast-moving brush fire consume a stand of massive California oaks and dry vegetation, turning the skies orange and gray. Josh and I had set up across the eight-lane freeway from the firestorm that had already burned two thousand acres on the mountain pass that cut through the San Bernardino and San Gabriel mountains—what was called the Cajon Pass. We had a clear shot of the firefighters battling the blaze, upwind from the smoke that was quickly blackening the skies. When the flames rose up the hillside, they sounded like thunder, drowning out the rescue helicopter buzzing overhead and the whine of cars hurtling by on the freeway.

My cell phone vibrated in my back pocket. I pulled out the phone, and Eric's photo flashed up on the screen. I slipped inside the news van and pulled the door shut.

"Hey, sorry I missed your call yesterday." His voice sounded tired and hoarse. "We were on back-to-backs all day."

"I'm at the Cajon Pass fire. You here?"

"No. Just got back from an apartment-complex blaze in Covina. Our crew pulled out a family of five. Haven't been called to the Cajon Pass fire yet." Like me, he was trying too hard to sound casual.

"Why didn't you tell me about Carrie?" There, I said it.

There was a long pause on the line. "Maybe we should talk about this when you're not in the middle of covering a wildfire?"

Through the window, I watched a six-winged rescue tanker plane roar overhead, dumping bright-red slurry, a mixture of water and fertilizer, on the flaming ridge.

"It's a simple question," I said. "Maybe there's a simple answer?"

"You and I are trying to figure out some pretty big stuff, Kate. I mean, you're leaving for New York, and I can't go with you. The last thing you needed to hear was that an old girlfriend was in town."

"She was your girlfriend . . . ," I said, feeling my stomach knot up.

"A long time ago."

"If it was a long time ago, why didn't you just tell me?"

"It's not what it looked like."

Josh waved his arms, trying to get my attention. "The fire has jumped the southbound lanes," he shouted, then started running to capture the shot.

I glanced at the monitor showing Chopper 11's view of the scene and was stunned to see two semis and several cars engulfed in flames on the freeway. "This fire is out of control. I've got to run."

He sounded worried. "Be careful out there—"

"Can we get together when I'm done here?"

"We're all about to head north to help with the fires in Ventura. I'll call you when I get there."

"We're live in one minute!" Josh shouted, pointing at the fiery scene.

Eric's voice softened. "I miss you, Kate."

~

The phone on my desk was ringing when I headed into the newsroom late that afternoon after five hours covering the Cajon Pass fire. The station receptionist didn't put many calls through, because otherwise,

I'd spend my day talking to viewers with axes to grind and every LA resident with an event or product to promote.

The hot desert winds and thick smoke had left my skin and lungs parched, and even a bottle of water couldn't quench my thirst. I took another gulp before answering the phone.

"Kate Bradley." I sounded exhausted, because that was exactly how I felt.

There was a lot of street noise, and then a woman's voice came on the line. "Kate?"

"Yes," I said wearily.

"This is Blanca Rivera. You gave me your card when I met you after the drive-by shooting of Michael Gutierrez. Do you remember me?"

"Yes, of course." She was the woman who had said we were focusing too much attention on stories about the wealthy.

"There is something here you must see," she said. "You won't believe it unless you see it with your own eyes."

I didn't hide my cynicism. "What might that be?"

She paused. "Perhaps you could just come?"

"Can you give me an idea of what I'd be seeing . . . if I came?"

"The Star Apartments has been planning to build fifty new apartments for homeless families with young children. And for families whose homes are *embargada* . . . foreclosed. They've been trying to raise money for many years, but the project could never get off the ground. Today there's a line of cars at the construction site. People are driving in and giving money."

"What people?"

"I don't know exactly. But hundreds of them."

"When you say they're giving money, how much money?"

"I talked to the lady who's in charge, and she said they'd already raised a quarter-million dollars. In one day. From people dropping by and giving them checks and cash. Now there's a man here bringing a truckload of . . . how do you say it . . . drywall."

"Can you put the man on the phone?"

"I don't know. He might not want me to bother him."

I smiled. "Interview subjects never do. But let's give it a try."

There was a lot of street and crowd noise on her end, and for the next minute, I heard her walking, then her muffled voice telling the man that a "reporter from Channel Eleven is on the phone." It was so loud on their end that he asked her to repeat herself twice. The next thing I knew, a full, round voice came on the phone. "Hello, this is Ron."

"Ron, Kate Bradley from Channel Eleven," I said. "Forgive the unusual way we're speaking today. I understand you're donating a truck-load of drywall. Why?"

He cleared his throat. "It seemed like the right thing to do. Seeing as I work in construction and all."

"But why today? Why are there so many of you giving today?"

"My wife got a text telling us about this project for homeless families. From Robin Hood."

"A text from Robin Hood?"

"He said a lot of Americans are working full time but are still in poverty and can't afford a home. He said he'd give five dollars for every dollar others gave to the project."

"Have you done this before?"

"No. We kind of figured that, you know, the government or people with more money than we had were taking care of things. But Robin Hood, well, he got us to realizing how we had to do something. We thought we'd join him. Not in robbing people or anything. In helping out."

I was scribbling notes as fast as I could. "So Robin Hood inspired you to contribute today?"

"It's not only us. There are a whole lot of people here today. We all can have a hand in changing the world."

The Channel Eleven pundits estimated that millions of people had received a text from Robin Hood. We sent a cameraman to shoot a report about the thousands who'd responded to that text and donated to the housing project. The story had legs, as Channel Eleven and other stations started airing reports about the growing groups of people donating groceries to food banks, donating cash to emergency shelters, and bringing meals to homebound seniors and people living with disabilities—all sparked by the texts from Robin Hood.

Despite the story being played late in the newscast—as the feel-good story before sports—the report drew a huge viewer response. The number of comments on the station's website post was rising by over a thousand an hour. The report had gone viral, and the number of hits online quickly climbed from a few hundred to nearly 750,000 in a few hours. Our social media producer, Amy, was so happy with the response that she left a box of chocolate-covered strawberries on my desk.

In the next morning's assignment meeting, Hannah rattled off the growing list of Robin Hood's giving. "He's given five hundred thousand each to a cluster of schools in Inglewood to complete repairs and upgrades. He's donated ten thousand backpacks full of school supplies to the areas of the city with the highest concentration of children in poverty—Bell Gardens, Huntington Park, and South El Monte. He's given four million dollars to begin construction of a hundred apartments on Skid Row. And Associated Press reports that Robin Hood recently purchased a hundred and forty thousand acres of land in the Sierra Nevada area from a logging company for the sole purpose of its preservation."

"Starting Sherwood Forest, perhaps?" Conan said, evoking a few laughs.

"Can we trace his identity through the real estate transaction?" I asked.

Hannah shook her head. "We're trying that. But it looks like a dead end. He purchased it through a land trust that shields his identity behind multiple complicated layers." She glanced at her computer. "And there's more. A viewer called in this morning to say that at the bus stop at Crescent and Santa Monica Boulevard in Beverly Hills, a man dressed in a tuxedo asks every woman getting off the bus at six in the morning if she's a cleaning woman. If they say yes, he hands them an envelope from Robin Hood. With twenty-five hundred dollars cash."

"A rich Beverly Hills socialite could claim to be a cleaning woman and get twenty-five hundred dollars cash for a shopping spree at Barneys," Conan suggested.

"A Beverly Hills socialite isn't getting off a bus at six in the morning," I said wryly. "And she certainly isn't going to pretend to be a cleaning woman."

"Could the guy who's handing out the dough be Robin Hood?" Conan asked.

Hannah shook her head. "He's an out-of-work actor hired to do this gig."

"All this is great," David interrupted. "But let's not lose sight of what's important. True, our viewers want to hear these stories about Robin Hood's escapades. But if we want to score the story of the year, we've got to find out *who is Robin Hood.* Channel Eleven has got to break that story."

After that he launched into a pep talk about how he was adding two associate producers to the Robin Hood team. One was going to chase down theories that had been floated by other news organizations, scouring the flotsam for anything that might be a meaningful lead. The other producer was working FBI and police sources for information on suspects they were investigating. Even Bonnie had jumped into the fray, working with the FBI to try to force *League of Legends* to give us information on Locksley's account.

Later in the morning, Hannah and I sat across from each other in the bullpen, trying to write a story that would pull all the theories together. It was making my head hurt. And even after two cups of coffee, Hannah looked pale and tired. Troubled.

She threw her pen on her desk. "The FBI is investigating. LAPD. The State Department is involved because of the possible ties to the Russian government. This Russian group has such sophisticated tech that they can bypass security systems in billionaires' homes and send out anonymous texts to millions of people. What makes us think we even have a remote shot at figuring out who Robin Hood is?"

I took a swig of my now-cold coffee and grimaced. "You've got a point. No way someone with Robin Hood's level of tech smarts is going to be easy to find." I leaned back in my chair. "Don't you ever wonder why he agreed to talk with us in the first place?"

Hannah considered that for a moment. "I guess because he wanted to set the record straight about why he was doing it. To do damage control after injuring the housekeeper."

"Sure. And to make his case that this was a victimless crime and to raise awareness for the plight of the poor. Got all that. But was that why?" I wondered aloud. "Or did he see an opportunity to throw all of us off track? To mislead us."

Hannah pushed the hair from her face and held it there for a long moment. "I'm . . . not following, Kate. What are you getting at?"

I didn't know. But something about that interview still nagged at me. It was too easy. Planned. Safe. I stared off into the newsroom, letting my eyes settle briefly on the newscast that was currently underway. "What if we're looking in the wrong places?"

"Meaning?"

"What if the answer isn't in what organization is capable of such sophisticated heists but why these specific people were targeted?"

"Robin Hood said he was targeting the hundred richest Americans. These guys are all on the Forbes one hundred list. The poorest of them is worth over five *billion*."

"So we know they're all überrich. But what else do we know about them? The first house robbed was Stephen Bening's Château du Soleil. He's the CEO of SalesInsight, but what else do we know about him?"

Hannah typed on her computer. "Thirty-two million in compensation and bonuses last year."

I was dizzy at the number. *Thirty-two million.* "And El Mirasol in Malibu? Who owns that?"

"Richard Ingram. Owner of Enterprise Products, an oil-pipeline company. Earned sixteen point seven million plus a bonus of six million last year."

"Didn't their stock tank last year?"

She nodded. "Yep, it fell forty-four percent."

"We're in the wrong business," I said. "If our ratings dropped by forty-four percent, you can bet we wouldn't be bringing home twenty-two million dollars a year. We'd be looking for jobs in Nebraska. Who owns La Villa de la Paz?"

"Donna Chase. CEO of McMillan Pharmaceutical. Last year she earned seventeen point nine million. Laid off sixteen thousand staffers this year and just announced another twenty-eight thousand. Stock fell twenty-two percent."

"I don't get how someone earns that kind of money while their stock tanks. Guess I should've gone to business school. Okay, next. The Holmby Hills estate is owned by Wall Street CEO Thomas Speyer. Which firm?"

Hannah took a moment to reply. "Sterling Blair Investments. Speyer earned twenty-two point nine million dollars last year while the stock fell twenty percent and thirty thousand employees were laid off." She took a slug of coffee. "It looks to me like Robin Hood's targeting the one hundred wealthiest Americans who have stratospheric compensation even if their companies performed poorly."

"It's a good theory but, again, too easy. Let's do a deep dive on the owners of the estates. See what you can dig up and why someone would target *them*."

She stood. "I get where you might be going with this, Kate. Russians are heavily invested in our stock market. Maybe Robin Hood and his group lost money when these companies' stock prices fell."

I had a hard time imagining Robin Hood as a stock baron out for revenge because of poor price-earnings performance. But that wasn't what was bothering me most. "What if Robin Hood isn't Russian?"

I found Curtis Seifrid, an expert in Russian linguistics, at USC's Department of Slavic Languages and Literatures. Seifrid taught a class on the structure of modern Russian and was a native speaker of Russian along with four other languages. His research involved something called "formal modeling and cross-linguistic comparison from a synchronic and diachronic perspective." I had no idea what that meant, but a journalist friend of mine at the *New York Times* said Seifrid had been a lifesaver on a story she had written about the crisis in Ukraine.

I interviewed Seifrid by Skype from his office on the USC campus near downtown LA. He was dressed in an off-white tweed sport coat and a black T-shirt—a look that only a college professor could pull off without looking like a throwback to 1990. I played the recording of the interview with Robin Hood for him three times and asked him to identify clues to his Russian identity.

"Well, it is difficult," he said, his own accent readily identifiable as Russian. "In part because of processing. His accent, even through processing, is very convincing. But if he is from Russia, no doubt he was raised in an English-speaking household."

"How can you tell?" I asked.

"He pronounces the *ng* sound as in *nothing* and *talking* perfectly. That can be difficult for Russians to say correctly because we don't have that sound in our language. He also uses articles like *a* and *the*, which we don't have. And his grammar is good. Someone who learned English as a second or third language might say, 'He is good man,' but this speaker has none of that syntax."

"So it's possible he learned Russian and English at the same time? That's why he speaks English so well?"

"I don't hear any proof he speaks Russian. He even pronounces *Robin Hood* like an English speaker. Most Russians have trouble making a good, clear *h* sound, but this guy articulates it perfectly."

"You don't think he's Russian, then?"

He shrugged. "I think he has mastered a Russian 'accent,' but he has not studied or spoken the Russian language. I do not hear anything that points to him being a native Russian speaker, no."

I frowned. "Which leads to the question of why he would put Russian words on the Robin Hood coin if Russian isn't his first language."

Curtis looked baffled by my nonquestion. That kind of question was the staple of cable television news, because most pundits would rush to speculate even when they had little real information to go on.

Curtis wasn't a pundit. "I cannot say."

Was Robin Hood Russian? Or was the Russian phrase on the coin meant to disguise Robin Hood's real origin?

I watched the monitor in the newsroom as my interview with Curtis Seifrid aired on the newscast that evening. If Robin Hood was not Russian, that exploded the possibilities of who he could be. Without that as an identifier, where would we even start?

And did I want to find him? The station that uncovered his identity would surely win massive ratings and awards. But if he were caught, all this would end. The food banks, the scholarships, the gifts to build housing for the homeless and working poor. The story.

Yet what Robin Hood was doing was wrong. At least the *LA Times* thought so. They posted an editorial from ethicist Randall Wallace that read: "Robin Hood is not the only way to help the poor—political action might work better. Large-scale robbery produces pain for the wealthy, sets a bad example, and may inspire copycats."

As proof of their point, the *LA Times* reported that earlier in the day, a woman was robbed of her Rolex watch and gold bracelet as she left her car and entered a furniture store in Beverly Hills. In a brazen afternoon attack, three men in hoodies jumped out of a BMW, held the woman down, and cut the jewelry off her wrist. The *Times* trumpeted this as proof that Robin Hood was inspiring violence against the wealthy.

Yet viewers liked what Robin Hood was doing. The station had launched a poll with the question "Do you admire Robin Hood or think that what he's doing is wrong?" Already 71 percent said they admired Robin Hood. A Channel Eleven News poll wasn't empirical evidence of anything, but it was, at minimum, a gauge of viewer sentiment.

"You're not going to believe this." A voice startled me from behind.

I whirled around to see Hannah. Her hand trembled as she handed an iPad to me.

I stared at the numbers on the screen. "What's this?"

She shook her head. "The interns called the food banks, the places that are giving out scholarships, homeless shelters—every organization who received money from Robin Hood."

"And? Don't bury your lead, Hannah. Tell me, what am I looking at here?"

Her voice shook. "The amount of money Robin Hood has given away is far greater than the amount stolen."

"By how much?"

She pointed to the screen. "Fifteen *million* dollars."

CHAPTER TWENTY

It had to be a mistake. If Robin Hood had given away $15 million more than he had stolen, someone must have calculated wrong. Or Robin Hood had robbed twice as many estates as we knew about. Had police underreported how much was stolen at each estate?

I swung by David's office and shared the $15 million discrepancy with him, and by the time I finished, he was smiling. At first I thought it was a "You don't understand" smile that would precede a lecture about how I had gone down the rabbit hole. But there was no lecture.

"Ratings winner," he said, rubbing his hands together. "Now use your advantages to find out if Robin Hood has robbed more estates than police are reporting."

"Advantages? My inside source can't help me, my father hung up on me after demanding that I stop covering the Robin Hood story, and a few days ago PowerTrade dropped their commercials on Channel Eleven because they didn't like how a senator's daughter was covering the story."

He took off his reading glasses and laid them on his desk. "Most reporters don't get to rub elbows with America's wealthiest one hundred at political fund-raisers. Or get invited to their homes because some other wealthy guy sets up a meeting. They have no way into that exclusive world."

I hadn't looked at it that way before. I'd taken for granted the privileges I enjoyed being Hale Bradley's daughter and had focused primarily on the negatives.

"Susan says you're attending a fund-raising lunch with an appearance by the First Lady tomorrow afternoon. Go there and find out what the wealthy know about any unreported heists. That's one thing you can do that no other reporter can." He slung his messenger bag on his shoulder. "Now, when are you going to tell me your news?"

Did he know about ANC? I scanned his face for anger or frustration but didn't see any sign of it.

"Tell you what?" I knew it was a chicken move to feign ignorance in times like this, but I wanted to make sure we were both talking about the same thing.

"About ANC. I heard about it from an editor friend of mine there. You know I hate secrets. Why didn't you tell me they made you an offer?"

A pang of guilt shot through me. "I'm . . . not sure I'm going to take it."

He looked at me in disbelief. "Why the hell not?"

"It's . . . complicated."

"How many more train wrecks or mudslides do you need to report on before you decide you can do something else?"

"Wait. You're *okay* with me leaving at the end of my contract?"

His face reddened. "No, I'm *not* okay with you leaving at the end of your contract. We've built our reputation around your reports, and I'll be damned if I let Andrew Wright and ANC ride our coattails on this one." He picked up a can of Dr Pepper from his desk and popped it open. "Honestly? I think they're going to eat you alive at ANC. You're fearless, but you're not ready for the kind of politics and competition a place like that serves up every day."

I frowned. "Thanks for the vote of confidence."

"Bonnie's going to fume, of course," he continued, unfazed. "And she'll put up a big fight and make you some insane offer to stay here. But you shouldn't take a deal from Channel Eleven, no matter how good it is. And you know why?" He took a few gulps of soda. "With your last name, you can bet you'll be on every high-profile political story out there. From there, you could end up as a White House correspondent or a political commentator for any one of the broadcast networks."

I looked down at my hands. It was the first time I realized that it wasn't only Eric who was keeping me from going to New York. I was frightened, afraid of taking a big leap and failing. And equally afraid of staying exactly where I was.

A luncheon with the First Lady had specific fashion requirements. There wasn't a written dress code, but the unspoken rules were clear: Wear a dress or smart suit in conservative colors like black and darker shades of blue, gray, or neutrals. Jewelry should be minimal, hair down, and closed-toed footwear was best. Since this was a luncheon outdoors, I'd opted for a slightly chunkier heel, to avoid the novice move of getting stilettos stuck in the grass. I was digging in the back of my closet to find the right pair when my phone dinged, alerting me to a text. My dad.

Please don't attend fund-raising lunch today.

I felt a pang of guilt. My father had never disinvited me to anything before.

Why? I typed back.

Three blue dots danced on the screen, indicating he, or more likely his assistant, was typing an answer.

Need to distance myself from you and this Robin Hood story.

My father had never spanked me as a child. I'd never even had a time-out or been ordered to my room like most of my friends. My father had been around so little that he had rarely even raised his voice at me. Seeing the text felt like I'd been punched in the chest. Hard.

I stared at the perky green bubble on the screen, wondering for a moment if perhaps it had been mistyped or autocorrect had taken over.

I knew better.

Tears stung the corners of my eyes, and I willed them back. I wasn't going to let my father order me around like I was one of his aides or staff members. I was entitled to my opinions about Robin Hood, and I knew he wasn't thinking clearly about the positive impact Robin Hood was making.

I needed to talk with him face-to-face. Not through a text his assistant sent or a phone call. In person.

I dressed quickly and headed to the luncheon, determined to work this out with him. The event was held at the home of the chairman of Universal Studios, and his $13 million estate was small in comparison to the homes I'd been reporting from recently. Still, the ten-bedroom mansion sat on 1.2 developed acres of prime real estate in the tony La Mesa section of Santa Monica. Its fourteen thousand square feet nestled against the ultraexclusive Riviera Country Club, home of a legendary golf course and breathtaking ocean views—along with a whopping $250,000 initiation fee and one of the highest membership-rejection rates in the country.

The event was billed as a "closed-door roundtable," which meant that media were not allowed until the First Lady made her speech. Then reporters were ushered out again when the questions-and-answers session began.

The biggest hurdle was the check-in table, staffed by five well-dressed political aides and flanked by two security guards wearing highly visible earpieces and walkie-talkies. When I stepped up to the table, a woman in a dotted sheath dress searched through the invitation list for my name. My fingertips tingled with anxiety as she looked through a list in another binder, her mouth twisted in a confused frown.

"Here it is, Ms. Bradley," she said, brightening. "On the original invitation list. There's a notation, however, that says you are unable to attend."

I feigned the most sincere smile I could muster. "Oh, I thought I was going to be out of town, but my travel plans changed at the last minute."

"It's not like your father to have forgotten to notify us," she said with uncertainty. She turned to ask what to do from a harried-looking man working alongside her. They both glanced at the long line behind me.

"I've seen you at these events with your father before," she said quietly. "So . . . enjoy the afternoon." She handed me a yellow ticket and motioned toward the entrance.

Getting through a security screening for an event with the First Lady added another five minutes to the check-in, as all guests went through metal detectors. Lunch was held outdoors in a grassy backyard the size of a football field. A formal black curtain sectioned off half of the yard, where ten tables were set up in the grass with cheery yellow roses and bowls of lemons at each table.

I recognized several political figures, including the current and former mayors of Los Angeles, a congresswoman from the Thirty-Second District, and a few people I suspected were high-ranking entertainment executives—recognizable by their more casual attire and the cell phones seemingly glued to their ears.

This fund-raiser wasn't for a particular candidate but rather an event to raise money for the political party my father belonged to. The more you paid, the more you got. One hundred fifty people paid $10,000 each to attend. A smaller group paid $15,000 to stick around for a private chat and photo with the First Lady.

I spotted my dad engrossed in a conversation with the head of Christie's Auction House. I strode toward him as though things were as they'd always been.

"Dad." My voice was tentative and small.

He turned to me, and his face crumpled. "Kate."

"I know you said I—"

"Would you excuse me, Sonya," he said to the head of Christie's. "I haven't seen my daughter in ages and would like to have a few moments with her."

"Of course," she said and stepped away.

"We need to talk," I breathed.

"Let's not create a scene," he said firmly.

I inhaled sharply. "I want you to know that I'm not trying to ruin your chances for reelection."

He dropped his hands to his sides. "Your association with the Robin Hood story is already doing that. And your presence is going to distress a lot of people here. You need to leave. But don't call attention to yourself by making a swift exit. Drop in on a quick conversation, stay a few more minutes, and then politely excuse yourself."

I touched the sleeve of his suit, wanting to find some way to connect with him. "This Robin Hood story is changing the way people think about the poor. It *is* a movement for shared prosperity. That's *important*."

For a moment he seemed lost in thought. "You know, for a moment there you reminded me of your mother."

Before he could say anything more, a congressman with large eyeglasses and a receding hairline whisked him away to meet a group of donors from the health industry. I watched him walk away, wondering what my mother had to do with any of this.

I stood there for a long moment, unsure of what to do. Should I leave, as he'd demanded? Or could I, as David had suggested, use this opportunity to look into the discrepancy between what Robin Hood stole and what he gave away—to find out if Robin Hood had robbed more estates than the police were reporting? I'd been at enough fundraisers to know that the superwealthy weren't that different from the rest of us. They gossiped and told stories, and although it wasn't true that all wealthy people knew each other, they often knew a lot about what other wealthy people were doing.

I scanned the crowd. There were so many "brand names"—famous people—that I couldn't approach any of them without appearing to be fawning or stalking. Celebrities had a kind of radar for reporters, so even the friendlier ones would find convenient excuses to avoid conversation with me.

Then I spotted them. Two executive types gathered near the bar. I ordered a drink and briefly eavesdropped on their conversation. The tall bookish man with the tortoiseshell glasses was talking about the private airplane that had crashed in the Mojave Desert earlier in the day. He seemed to know the owner of the plane, who was fortunately not the one flying it at the time. The woman he was talking to, a brunette wearing a black tweed dress and Chanel sunglasses, hung on his every word.

I stood next to them while the man finished his story. At least he was talking about something I knew about instead of something like derivatives or bond prices, which were often the topic of conversation at fund-raisers. "I heard that right before the crash, the pilot had accidentally caused the tail to rise and create drag—a process known as feathering," I added.

The woman smiled at me and then launched into a brief story about how she had recently been in a private jet that ran into trouble. I was in.

As soon as she finished her story, she turned to me and said, "You're Hale Bradley's daughter, aren't you?"

"Yes, I'm Kate."

"Linda Paulson," the woman said. She had an easy grace about her, and I suspected she worked in fashion or art—but I knew better than to ask. The man followed with a first name–only introduction—James.

"There she is," I heard a voice behind me say.

I turned around to see Thomas Speyer, the owner of the Holmby Hills estate. He was smiling, friendlier than I remembered, so I returned the greeting. "Hello."

Only he wasn't talking to me. Instead, he hugged Linda. "We should grab lunch soon." He turned to me. "How is the news business these days, Kate?"

I knew he did it deliberately to alert his friends that a journalist was in the house. It worked. They both turned to look at me.

Thomas didn't keep them guessing. "Kate is a reporter at Channel Eleven. I thought they weren't letting the media in until later."

The two exchanged nervous glances. James started to say something—I think to excuse himself—but Thomas kept going. "Haven't viewers tired of your Robin Hood story yet?"

I felt an immediate shift in the mood from the other two. James's eyes darted around the yard, clearly looking for a reason to leave this conversation.

"Well, we've uncovered something unusual. Robin Hood has only robbed five estates for twenty-one million dollars total, but he's given away thirty-six million dollars."

"Sounds to me like Robin Hood has revenue coming in from other criminal activities," Thomas said. "We all know that organized crime is rampant in Russia."

"He's not Russian," I said firmly. "I interviewed a Russian linguistic expert who says Robin Hood has mastered a Russian accent but Russian is not his native language."

Thomas waved me off as though I were a child with a foolish idea. "Anyone can claim to be an expert these days. The simple answer is that there are many more estates being robbed than the media know about."

"It is possible, Thomas, but I seriously doubt it," Linda said in clipped tones. She had a graceful way of speaking with her hands that took some of the sting out of her words. "You and I—all of us—would've certainly heard rumblings if there were."

"I agree, Linda," James added. "I've heard a lot about the five estates that have been robbed. Even know one of the robbery victims. So how *would* this Robin Hood get hold of fifteen million more than he's stolen?"

CHAPTER TWENTY-ONE

"All of the billionaire victims have secrets," Hannah was saying later that afternoon in the Fish Bowl. The large monitor displayed a photo of each estate owner. "We looked for shared histories, shared connections—a single person who appeared in all their lives. Many of them are connected to each other in some way or another—maybe they're part of the same club or attended the same university. But we've found one unifying connection. They all have scandals in their past."

She handed me a treasure trove of information: a racially charged college essay written by Elliot Wagner, the owner of Palazzo de Bella Vista; a copy of a settlement agreement between Thomas Speyer and a bank accusing him of misappropriation of funds; and police records showing that Donna Chase, the owner of La Villa de la Paz, had been convicted of two counts of DUI a few years back.

She pointed to the photo of Stephen Bening. "Stephen's bio says he graduated from USC, and the media has widely reported that as well. But a search of the deep web shows no record that he either attended or graduated from USC."

I shook my head. "He told me that he was captain of the debate squad and they took first place in the National Debate Tournament. The trophy is on display in his library."

Hannah typed on her laptop, then swiveled it toward me. "This is the USC Trojan Debate Squad website. USC only took first place once. In 1996. And the captain of the debate team was named Esteban Diaz."

I scanned the photograph of the four members of the debate team and the faculty coach. The young man identified as the captain had a thick mop of curly hair and skin pitted by acne scars. He was heavyset and wore black glasses—definitely not Stephen Bening.

"Also no record of him attending or getting an MBA from Harvard," she added dryly. "He must have figured out a way to get into certain databases to make it appear as though he did."

"So is this what it takes to be rich? You lie about your past?"

"And your present. Check this out." On the monitor, she put up a photograph of a young woman in a black velvet evening grown. "Last year, Richard Ingram's wife—they own El Mirasol—filed for divorce on the grounds that he was having multiple affairs. The judge awarded her nine hundred twenty-five million."

"Nearly a billion-dollar divorce settlement."

"But while they all have secrets, I don't see how any of this gets us closer to figuring out who Robin Hood is."

I studied the photos of the wealthy victims. "Why don't we ask *them*?"

She shook her head. "These are powerful people, Kate. You confront them about their dirty laundry, and they'll have their lawyers make your life a living hell. *If* you can even get hold of them."

"I'm not going to confront them. They're going to help me figure out who Robin Hood is. I think he is someone they know."

Thomas Speyer's assistant told me he was traveling and would call me when he "returned to the States." I got similar responses from three other estate owners, all of whom seemed to be traveling, in board meetings, or away at conferences and inaccessible for weeks. The messages were courteous but delivered with the quiet subtext that they were never going to call me back.

Stephen Bening agreed to meet with me. Sort of. His assistant said he was happy to meet with "Hale Bradley's daughter" and "might" be available to meet me for a whopping twenty minutes if I was willing to come to his Bel Air estate at eight thirty the next morning. Once I agreed to eight thirty, the assistant emailed me ten minutes later, asking if I could do seven thirty at Shutters in Santa Monica instead. Once I agreed to that, the time changed to eight forty-five at his estate. Apparently being a rich entrepreneur meant your schedule was undergoing constant transformation and down-to-the-minute management. It also made you extra cautious around media. "As a condition of the interview, Mr. Bening prohibits cameras or recording equipment."

That didn't go over well with David, who thought I was wasting time on an interview that wouldn't produce any footage. Like me, he was concerned Channel Eleven's journalistic integrity was in question if we let interview subjects call the shots. But after much deliberation, he and Bonnie agreed that another interview with one of the tight-lipped estate owners—with or without cameras—might yield important information.

I arrived a few minutes early and was quickly ushered into the study, this time by a man with a clean-shaven head and a soul patch, the tech version of a butler. The silence in the study, apart from the ticking clock on the fireplace mantel, was deafening, but the room had the same effect on me as before.

At precisely 8:45 a.m., Stephen breezed into the room. "How is your father, Kate? What can I help you with today?" he asked before sitting in the chair across from me.

"Robin Hood is someone you know," I said quietly.

He waved a dismissive hand at me. "It's not a bad theory, but the FBI has been through all that with us. It appears to be a dead end."

"The FBI may think that's a dead end, but hear me out. Despite what he says, Robin Hood is not a man living on the outskirts of society in the slums of poverty. He has access to high-end technology to bypass sophisticated alarm systems. He's a clever leader, making sure no one on his team knows anyone's identities, and he inspires his team by telling them they are changing the world. He is not Russian, but probably American. He is someone on the inside. Someone who's probably been to your house and who would know what luxuries you own and which ones are worth stealing. He is someone you know."

He was silent for a long moment. I couldn't tell if he thought my theory was brilliant or crazy. "Why would someone I know steal from me?"

"The Channel Eleven News team is looking into all of the owners who've been robbed, and some unflattering details are coming to light."

The impatience left his eyes, and in its place was a new expression—wariness. "What are you getting at here?"

"Every victim is one of America's wealthiest one hundred, including you. But in many cases, the victims are earning massive salaries even as they've laid off thousands of people and their stock prices have plummeted."

"That's not true in every case. Certainly not mine."

I didn't look up from my notepad. "And when that's not the case, we find other curious details. Out-of-court settlements, puffed-up biographies, tax evasion, criminal charges, DUIs."

"Where did you get this supposed information?"

"One of our producers is adept at mining the deep web for information that isn't available through normal searching—"

"I *know* what the deep web is."

"What I'm getting at is that perhaps Robin Hood has targeted this elite group because he wants to expose your wrongdoings."

He shrugged. "Do you mean this is some kind of revenge? Blackmail? For what? For laying off people to improve stock performance? Big companies have to constantly evolve and produce shareholder value. CEOs often lay off people to achieve that. The wealthy are easy targets for lawsuits, hence the volume of claims against us. Besides, none of what you've said is true for me. I laid off fewer than ten employees last year, and I don't have any scandals to expose."

I paused, rubbing the back of my neck. "We found some inconsistencies in your bio too. You claim to have graduated from USC, where you'd been the head of the champion debate team in 1996. But there's no record of you graduating from USC, and that year, the captain of the debate team was a man named Esteban Diaz."

He frowned. "You guys really *are* digging for dirt. It's bad enough that we've been robbed of millions, but now we're the targets of what sounds like a smear campaign. If it's any consolation, I didn't lie about being captain of the debate team. Esteban Diaz *is* me. I changed my name after college, anglicized Esteban to Stephen."

I hadn't expected that. "And Bening?"

His face flushed red. "Comes from my American father. He left before I was born, but I adopted his American-sounding last name in my twenties. Far more doors in the tech industry opened to me as Stephen Bening than they ever did for Esteban Diaz."

"But the photo—"

He laughed, showing off expensive cosmetic dentistry. "Doesn't look like me. I know. Once I got my first job at a tech company in Chicago, I lost sixty-five pounds, got my teeth fixed, and started wearing contacts."

Was he telling me the truth? Or spinning a story to paint himself in a better light? "So you're saying you're actually the Esteban Diaz who graduated from USC and Harvard."

The bald man with the goatee walked into the room, and Stephen glanced at his watch. He stood. "Not only would both USC and Harvard confirm that I graduated—and with honors—but that I received what was later called the Wisdom scholarship—a full scholarship given by an anonymous donor to the top student in the LA school district."

~

Stephen was lying. Every instinct told me he wasn't telling the truth about being Esteban Diaz. You didn't get to be one of the top CEOs in the world without having great skills at spinning a story the way you wanted it told. But I couldn't blame him for lying. His image would definitely be ruined by a story claiming he had lied about attending USC and Harvard.

Could that be the missing link? Was it plausible that Robin Hood had chosen the estate owners to rob because he wanted the stories of their shady pasts to come to light? These estate owners certainly had enough sordid stories to keep the media humming for weeks.

Back at the newsroom, I typed "Esteban Diaz" into one of the news department's search engines. The software would search vast archives of newspapers, magazines, and publications around the globe for relevant articles, stretching back decades in some cases.

It turned out Esteban Diaz was a fairly common name, and I found articles about numerous people with that name in professions ranging from foot doctors to performance artists to hard-core criminals. I scanned through the articles, wondering if I'd be better off asking one of the interns to do some research on one of the many public-records search engines.

A headline caught my eye. "Housekeeper Dies in Trousdale Estate." The *Beverly Hills Courier* article was dated August 31, 1991, and read:

"In the early-morning hours of August 30, 1991, paramedics were called to the Dunne estate in the Trousdale section of Beverly Hills. Charles Dunne, producer of recent box office hit *Mortal Enemy*, and his wife,

Darlene, were asleep in their second-floor master suite. But downstairs, Delfina Diaz, the Dunnes' housekeeper, had fallen down the sweeping granite staircase that graces the grand foyer of the Dunne estate and was dying of a head injury. She lay there for at least seven hours until discovered by the Dunnes' cook that morning. Diaz was taken to Cedars-Sinai Medical Center, where she was pronounced dead. She is survived by her son, Esteban Diaz, a junior at Roosevelt High School in East Los Angeles.

"Diaz, who at age fourteen left Guatemala and crossed the border in the trunk of a car, had a nearly twenty-year history of working in Beverly Hills estates for clients who included celebrities, socialites, and fashion mavens. Funeral arrangements are pending."

Next to the article was a grainy photograph of the woman identified as Delfina Diaz. Thick waves of dark-brown hair were pulled back from her face and secured by a black headband. She appeared to be in her early forties, with a regal nose and almond-shaped eyes that bore a striking resemblance to Stephen Bening's.

This woman had to be his mother. Wasn't Stephen's renowned software named Delfina?

I typed "Stephen Bening" and "Delfina" and found an article in *Forbes* magazine:

"The idea for the Delfina software came to Stephen in high school when he saw how his mother, a housekeeper who worked in Beverly Hills homes, had to keep track of all the requirements of her half dozen clients each week. She scribbled notes in a worn notebook, and when she lost it on the bus one day, she no longer had a record of the clients' security-system codes or phone numbers and lost track of their required cleaning routines. Stephen figured if a housekeeper needed help tracking customer information, big companies probably did too. He named the software after his mother, but she died in an accident years before the Delfina software became the leading customer-relationship software used by Fortune 500 companies around the globe."

Stephen was telling the truth.

CHAPTER TWENTY-TWO

I hated sushi. I'd tried it everywhere from the most authentic Japanese restaurants with expensive tasting menus to trendy pop-up sushi restaurants, and there was nothing about the experience that I found enjoyable enough to repeat. When Jake texted me that he had new information he wanted to share over sushi, I should've suggested someplace else. So it was my own fault that we were at Sushi Zo, a restaurant so orthodox that there was nothing cooked on the menu except rice, they took offense if you asked for a fork instead of chopsticks, and the menu declared in several places, "Please refrain from asking for any substitutions or sauces on the side."

Jake arrived dressed for a date. His hair was neatly styled, and he wore a light-gray cotton shirt under a black lambskin coat. It was the first time I'd noticed he was wearing aftershave—woodsy but not overpowering.

We sat in a quiet corner of the crowded restaurant. At least we wouldn't be easily overheard—or even noticed—but the narrow tables and dim lighting made it feel more romantic than I'd hoped.

I'd made a mistake coming here. Knowing how he felt about me made me hyperaware of how I looked at him, wanting to make sure I didn't send mixed signals. The sake the waitress poured upon our arrival wasn't helping either. So after a shot, I vowed to stick with water the rest of the evening.

Still, there was no denying that he was attractive. Was it possible that something real was developing between Jake and me? We had similar interests, including a dogged determination to solve crime mysteries. When we worked on the Suitcase Murder, it was as though we shared the same brain, blurting out similar theories at the same time. I glanced up from my drink and noticed him smiling at me.

"You still heading to the Big Apple next month?" he asked.

"I'm still figuring out what I'm going to do. But they're making it hard to say no."

He smoothed the linen tablecloth with his hand. "And your rescue-captain guy, is he going with you?"

I shook my head. "He can't get a comparable position with the Fire Department of New York."

"And you're still going?"

"I . . . don't know."

"You should go, Kate. This is what you've always said you wanted," he said quietly. Then his expressive blue eyes, glimmering with hope, met mine. "But if I were your fire captain, I'd be going with you."

The warm way he was looking at me made me break my vow about not drinking the sake. I downed the rest of the cup.

As if Eric had a sixth sense, his text flashed up on the screen: *Can you meet me tomorrow morning?*

"Sorry," I said to Jake. "Would you give me a quick sec to reply to this text?"

Jake nodded, and I typed back, *Sure.*

Finally back in LA. Doing some early-morning training in Bear Canyon tomorrow. Can you meet me at 9 tomorrow at Switzer Falls trailhead?

Definitely.

I wasn't sure where Switzer Falls was, but I was glad we were finally going to see each other, no matter where it was.

The waitress arrived and placed a plate of salmon sashimi on the table. "Compliments of the chef." She bowed, then took two steps back.

I looked up at the chef behind the sushi counter in the center of the room, and he waved. "*Irasshaimase*!" he shouted at us, a phrase that sounded like a stern directive but was actually a respectful way to say "Welcome."

Jake dove into the sashimi with his chopsticks. His mood lightened. "Now that I'm at home during the day, I've been watching a lot of the Robin Hood coverage on TV. That, and *The Price Is Right*. I've seen every network's stories, and your reports are the best, of course." He raised his sake cup in a semitoast and downed a shot.

"You're a little biased."

"More than a little," he said softly.

I took a bite of the sashimi and decided that maybe I could grow to like sushi after all.

"So what's this new information you have on Robin Hood?"

Jake leaned forward. "We're stumped," he said. "My friend who's one of the detectives working the case says the chief is white-hot angry because no one can figure this part out."

"What part?"

He lowered his voice. "Robin Hood hacks into the security systems at each estate. All of the estates have internet-based systems, so let's say he's exploiting a flaw in the systems and shutting them down remotely. That's extraordinary in itself, but there are any number of hacker organizations—Anonymous and Lizard Squad being the most famous—who could carry that off. But then what?"

"Once the security system is down, a group of people who don't know each other break in. Getting instructions called out via headset, they carry out a multimillion-dollar heist in under fifteen minutes."

"Except they don't break in. No broken glass, no jimmied doors or windows. They just walk in."

I shook my head. "Police have repeatedly said the thieves broke into the homes. Forced entry, the chief said."

His tone was strained. "That's what we are *saying*, but there is no evidence of any forced entry. Ever."

"Why are police withholding that from the public?"

"Same reason as always."

I nodded. Police generally kept quiet about details only the criminals would know. That way if a suspect seemed to know nonpublic information about a crime, it was likely that he was somehow involved.

He drained his sake. "But what's got us and the FBI totally stumped is *how* the thieves are just walking into some of the most expensive estates in America without breaking and entering."

"Maybe he's got a crackerjack locksmith on the team."

"Takes too long. From start to finish, the heists take under fifteen minutes. There isn't time to pick the lock."

"Maybe the estate staff left the doors unlocked."

He shook his head. "Didn't happen. We verified that the doors were locked before the heists. But here's what's got all of us scratching our heads. They were *still locked* when police arrived."

"The thieves locked the doors *after* they left?" I said. "How?"

"Exactly. Where did they get the keys? You've got this high-tech heist, but all of these homes still have low-tech dead bolts that require traditional keys."

"They paid off the staff at each estate? Maybe the security guards?"

"After dozens of interviews, there's no evidence—or suspicion—that any of the estate help was in on this."

"How would he be doing it, then? How would he have keys to every estate?"

He shrugged. "It's like Robin Hood is a ghost, walking through walls."

Switzer Falls was a trail in the San Gabriel Mountains about thirty minutes' drive from my apartment. I wasn't much of a hiker, but I did own a pair of expensive hiking boots I'd bought from REI after my friend Teri convinced me to go on a nighttime hike in Griffith Park with the Sierra Club. She ended up bailing on the hike because of the flu, and the pristine boots ended up in the back of my closet. Until today.

Once I passed through the graffiti-marred entrance to Switzer Falls in the Angeles National Forest, I was transported to a place I hadn't known existed in LA. A light mist floated in the air from the streams that crisscrossed the trail, rare moisture in normally arid LA. Even the noise from the busy freeway a few miles away was hushed by the sound of rushing and bubbling water.

Eric was waiting for me at the trailhead wearing jeans and a blue plaid shirt and carrying a small pack on his back. There was an awkward tension between us as he hugged me. "Do you want to start walking?"

"No," I said quietly. "I want to know about Carrie."

He rubbed the back of his neck. "I'm sorry about how that went down. Really, I am. I swear nothing happened between us. She was in LA because her father was injured. Her mother just died, and she's going through a divorce. I was trying to help her out."

I felt a braid of tension growing in my chest. "Are you in love with her?"

The question seemed to surprise him. "No. And she knew it. Even when I was helping her and her dad, she'd tell me, 'Your mind is somewhere else.' And she was right. I was thinking about you."

"*Were* you ever in love with her?"

"What we had was casual. And it's in the past."

"Why didn't you tell me about her? Why did you keep it a secret?"

He was silent for a long moment, looking down at his hands and then back at me. "I don't have a good answer for that, Kate. I've been going through a lot, settling Brian's estate and . . ."

Like any good reporter, I wanted to press for a better answer. But there was something about the gentle way he spoke and the way his brown eyes met mine that made me stop asking questions. For now.

The canyon walls, big-cone Douglas firs, and California black oaks at Switzer Falls were so towering that I couldn't help but feel small and insignificant as we walked along the leaf-carpeted forest floor. A few yards down the path, the trail ended abruptly, and we reached a rock-strewn stream swollen with rainwater. It would definitely require some boulder hopping to make it across the twenty-foot span.

I was a city girl with great skills at navigating traffic snarls, but I didn't have much experience balancing on slippery rocks and fording a rushing stream. The sun wasn't helping either. It was hiding behind gray clouds, making the whole setting look even more foreboding. And while I was slowly making my peace with water after my near drowning a few months ago, I still didn't trust it. Especially when it was studded with sharp rocks.

I considered suggesting that we head back. But just as I was about to say something, Eric took my hand. "You can do this."

The first softball-size rocks were in shallow water and close together—relatively easy to navigate. I steadied myself on each one of them by holding on to his hand. But as we reached the middle of the stream, the water became deep, and the rocks spread farther out.

"You okay?" he said, looking back at me.

"I'd be okay if we headed back," I said, my ankles wobbling.

He scanned the stream behind me. "We're too far in to go backward from here," he said. "It's easier if you hop quickly."

He let go of my hand, and I watched him hop the next three boulders swiftly, as if he were a gazelle in the wild. In three graceful jumps, he was now fifteen feet away from me onshore. Then he turned to me, his arms outstretched, beckoning me to follow. "You won't fall in," he said, his voice muffled by the sound of the rushing water.

I wished I had the confidence that he had in me, because I was pretty sure my next step would land me straight in the water. The distance to the next rock was too great. And while the whitecaps on the fast-moving water looked like something from a *National Geographic* photograph, I knew the danger that lurked beneath. I stood there a long moment, knowing that I couldn't go back and yet terrified of taking the next leap.

As I teetered on the rocks in the middle of the swollen stream, I imagined the worst—falling in, sinking underwater, hitting my head on a rock, going unconscious. A fat raindrop splattered on my cheek, and a ragged gust of moist wind rushed up and whipped at my hair. Great. Now I was going to be stuck in a river—okay, a deep stream—in a rainstorm.

Then, seemingly brought by the wind, I felt the courage rise in me, and in an unexpected and somewhat graceful set of moves, I leaped from boulder to boulder until I found myself on the shore. Dry.

Eric squeezed my hand. "You were like a water ninja out there."

Anyone else saying those words might have sounded patronizing, but after all we'd been through with water, I knew his pride was genuine.

We continued on the narrow trail, which opened up suddenly to a majestic rock formation hugged by tall, gnarly trees that looked like they'd been there forever. He sat on a fallen tree trunk and motioned for me to sit beside him. He opened up his pack and peeled an orange.

"I used to hike here with Brian. Wish you could've met him. He could make even an ordinary hike like this feel like we were embarking on a once-in-a-lifetime adventure." His voice drifted off. His eyes expressed more than he said in words. "Carrie remembered what it was like when he was alive. She remembered the small stuff and the big stuff—I didn't know then how important those moments would be to me now. That's what it was all about when I was with her. Remembering what we did with Brian."

I hadn't understood the depths of grief that still hung over him after Brian's death. I had always assumed that once we'd found happiness together, his grief had somehow faded away. But grief is a journey without a clear ending.

"I think that's why I didn't tell you about her," he said. "I didn't want to admit that I was stuck in the past. Stuck remembering when Brian was still alive. Losing him has been harder than anything I've ever had to do. I've seen people die, watched them die in front of me, after hours of trying to save them. But Brian's death still hits me in a way that . . . I can't describe."

I was ashamed at my selfishness. All this time, I had been seeing Carrie as someone who had stolen his heart away, when in reality she was Eric's portal to the past, a time when Brian was alive and the world felt warm and unending. I'd been focused on the choices ahead of me and failed to realize that Eric was still grieving, choosing instead to see him how I wanted to see him: a strong and courageous firefighter who risked his life to save others. But even brave men like Eric couldn't survive long on a pedestal.

"Now I'm the one who's sorry," I said, leaning my head on his shoulder. "I didn't realize how much you were still hurting."

I could see his grief coiled in his chest, as though pain were something visible. "There's one thing I've learned from grief, and that's how enormous and how powerful love can be. I love you, Kate."

I hadn't expected that. But the look in his eyes left no doubt that he meant it. As the rain began to fall, he cupped my face in his hands and eased into a long, lazy kiss. He laced his fingers through my hair and deepened the kiss until the heaviness inside me lifted. I'd missed him.

We held each other for a long time, listening to the gentle rain tapping on the leaves above us. It felt good to be with him again, his arms wrapped around me. But as I breathed in his familiar clean scent and felt his heart beating through his light jacket, I knew something was wrong.

He brushed a lock of damp hair from my face. He smiled at me with tears in his eyes. "I've lost Brian, and now I'm about to lose you. It's killing me that you are going to New York and I can't go with you."

I closed my eyes, wishing the words away. Something deep inside me ached.

A tear escaped my eye and rolled down my cheek. I brushed it away. "We can make this work long distance," I whispered. "I know we can."

"We can try. But it won't be enough. To build a life together, we have to be in the same place."

CHAPTER TWENTY-THREE

Later that day, as my agent, Sharon, rattled off the remaining fine points of the deal with ANC, I felt a buzzing sensation in my arms and head as though my body had an alarm system that had been tripped. But there was no off switch.

"At what point would it be too late to back out?" I asked.

Her tone was clipped, impatient. "We're beyond that point. You received the agreements I sent, didn't you?"

I stared at the documents, neatly bound with black binder clips and studded with bright-yellow "Sign Here" flags. Then I remembered the way Eric held my hand as he pointed out the constellations in the night sky over a rolling surf at Zuma Beach. I thought about the time we stayed up until four in the morning watching scary Halloween movies, his arms wrapped around me, making me feel safe. How would I survive being away from him for days and weeks—into forever?

"Everyone gets cold feet when they get to a finish line on a deal this big," she said. "Sign the papers this morning, and send them back to me. Then you can celebrate with some bubbly."

I couldn't imagine celebrating. Instead I scrawled my signature on all the agreements. Then I sat at my desk in the newsroom, staring at the blur of reporters making last-minute, hurried phone calls and producers rushing to assemble the noon cast, certain I was making all the wrong decisions.

~

"I've arranged for you to meet—well, interview—three of the estate owners . . . three of the robbery victims," my father was saying.

As I raced into the newsroom the next morning, cell phone pressed to my ear, I was sure I had misheard him. "What are you saying?"

"They've agreed to speak with you . . . together . . . on camera."

He was extending an olive branch. That could be the only reason for his tone, soft and punctuated with uncomfortable laughs. My dad was never at a loss for words, but he was stumbling all over them that morning.

I set my purse on my desk. "Which estate owners, and what are their conditions?"

"The owners of El Mirasol, La Villa de la Paz, and Château du Soleil. And as far as I know, there are no conditions."

I leaned my head against the wall. "Are they your friends? Campaign supporters?"

The soft lilt in his voice was a sign he was relaxing. "I know Stephen Bening, of course. And so do you. I have well-placed friends who know the others."

I slid into the empty conference room across the hall and closed the door. "Why, though. Why are they agreeing to do an interview?"

"Does it really matter? Ask whatever questions you want."

"They want to strike back at Robin Hood. Through the media. That can be the only reason they'd let me interview them."

"All I know is that they want to tell their side of the Robin Hood story. And I told them you were the best reporter to interview them."

I leaned back in the chair and stared at the ceiling. It was an odd feeling, one that was entirely new for me. I didn't trust my own father. "What's this really about, Dad?"

His voice was heavy. "I'm trying to help you, Katie."

Anger flashed through me. "Now you're trying to help me? How many times did you demand that I stop reporting on this story? And don't forget you disinvited me to the luncheon with the First Lady."

He cleared his throat. "Definitely not my finest hour. And after our conversation there, I started thinking about your mother."

He was quiet for a beat, which made me nervous, so I jumped in to fill the silence. "My mother?"

"There was an antique store next to where I had lunch last week. They had an entire window display of Depression glass. Royal Lace cobalt blue, just like she collected."

"My mother collected Depression glass?"

"Whenever we traveled, we had to stop by antique stores to see what treasures they had. She always said she loved four things most of all. You, of course. Me, most of the time. Her work in the mayor's office. And that Depression glass." I could hear his smile through the phone. "And it occurred to me that if she were around today, she'd tell me that no matter what pressure I was under, I shouldn't put my political problems ahead of your happiness."

"Dad, I—"

"We would've argued about whether I was actually doing that, of course. We were both stubborn that way. But you get your idealism from her and your stubbornness from both of us, unfortunately."

"I don't think I'm stubborn—"

"And she would've been right, Kate. I'm trying to find a way to make up for what I put you through on this story."

I felt a pang of remorse for having questioned his motives. And more than a little daunted by the prospect of an interview with three of the heist victims. As much as the interview was an enormous win for

Channel Eleven, I didn't think it would stir up much sympathy from viewers who were enthralled by whatever daily event Robin Hood held to help the poor and needy.

I worried, too, about how it would appear if viewers knew a US senator had arranged the interview. Would it look like I was simply my father's mouthpiece, as Russ had accused me of being?

And just how forthcoming would any of the owners be? Stephen Bening had been curt and efficient in dismissing Robin Hood's tactics and unwilling to go much beyond his carefully scripted thoughts. I expected the others would be the same. Worse, the interview probably wouldn't put me any closer to figuring out who Robin Hood was.

"Thank you. I wasn't expecting—"

"Thanks for letting me do this," he said and then brightened. "Now, I warned all three of them that you wouldn't go easy on them. Go and prove me right."

The interview was set to be recorded on the patio at Stephen Bening's Château du Soleil. The billionaires had asked to be interviewed in Channel Eleven's news studios, but there was a calculated feeling to an interview in a studio space, and I preferred to have it in a more informal setting. Plus, I figured an outdoor setting at one of the residences would put the billionaires at ease and hopefully get them away from the carefully prepared answers they'd surely rehearsed.

The estate's patio was set on an acre of lush, manicured grounds, with sculpted hedges, picture-perfect palm trees, and the cobalt-blue Pacific Ocean as a backdrop. Josh had lit the patio for a prime-time special, using lights and scrims I'd seen used for Anderson Cooper–level interviews. The interview was set for three p.m., when the afternoon sunlight would add to the effect, giving the Château du Soleil a dreamy, fairy-tale quality.

To prep for the interview, I'd read everything Hannah put in front of me about the three billionaires. I'd even made it most of the way through Stephen Bening's book, marking key points with purple Post-it notes. I arrived early, hoping to calm my nerves and go over the questions Hannah and I had written—and rewritten—the night before. We'd chosen the words carefully so that I appeared as objective as possible, even though I wasn't. All I needed to do was to absorb the questions to the point where they felt natural so I could ask them without referring to my notes.

When I arrived, Josh and Christopher were in the midst of repositioning the lights, and the frown on Josh's face was so stiff that I knew better than to stand around watching. None of the interview subjects had arrived yet, so I started pacing the lush green lawn. Then, seeing how that was making Josh more nervous, I headed toward the orchard at the back of the property.

Under the cool canopy of the olive trees, a lone sparrow called out its song. Suddenly I was remembering, reliving the night with Eric here. The orchard came alive for me—running with him through the trees on that moonlit night. The feel of his skin against mine. The smell of his aftershave drifting in the wind. Midnight whispers beneath silvery leaves.

The loneliness swept through me, stealing my breath. Where I'd felt warm and loved the night I was here with Eric, a chill ran through me. My eyes blurred with unexpected tears, and I began walking briskly, trying to halt their progress.

Then I realized I'd walked all the way to the back of the grove, where the weathered cabin stood. In the daylight, I noticed its thatched roof was sagging and the front stoop was missing several floorboards—a far cry from the mystical place it had seemed to be with Eric. Its front door was slightly ajar, so I knocked gently.

"Hello?" I called out.

My heart raced as I pushed the door open and took a step inside. The interior was as weathered as the outside, with water-stained wood floors and faded gray paint peeling around the windows. The place smelled of old papers—even though there was no evidence of any—and a metallic whiff of electronics. On the back wall were tall racks of sleek black computers and equipment. A single glass table studded with several monitors and a trio of keyboards sat in the center of the room. The combination of serious computing power and the crumbling shack surprised me.

"What are you doing here?" A voice startled me.

I whirled around to find a man in black slacks and a T-shirt standing inches behind me. He was built like a fireplug, and an eagle's wing tattoo ran the length of his left arm.

"I'm Kate Bradley," I said, extending my hand. He ignored it. "Channel Eleven."

"You need to step outside. Now."

I did as he said. He closed the door behind me and jiggled the handle to be sure it was locked.

"Guests are not allowed here." I recognized a hint of a Chicago accent. "How did you get in there?"

"The door was open."

He took off his wraparound sunglasses and peered at me. "And you walked inside? Would you want someone to do that to you if you left your door open?"

"Sorry, I didn't think it was a big deal." I motioned toward the cabin, making small talk. "This cabin must be over a hundred years old. What's with the thatched roof?"

He pulled a notebook from his back pocket. "Owner had it moved from Guatemala."

"Why?"

"His family grew up in it or something. What'd you say your name was?"

"Why do you want to know?"

He double-checked that the door was locked. "I'm going to have to report that you were here. That's why."

"I'm about to interview Stephen, so maybe I should tell him myself. But I bet he won't like hearing that his security is so lax that I was able to walk right into his family's hundred-year-old cabin."

He shoved his notebook into his back pocket. "Yeah. How about we forget this ever happened. But if you're the one doin' the interview, they're looking everywhere for you."

The billionaires came prepared for the interview. Any hopes that this would be a freewheeling discussion were quickly dashed by Richard Ingram's response to my first question, "What do you think Robin Hood is accomplishing?"

"I have the advantage of both genetics and upbringing. My good fortune was not due to superior personal character or initiative so much as it was to dumb luck," he said, as though I had asked a different question. "As I look around at those who did not have these advantages, it is clear to me that I have an obligation to direct my resources to help right that balance."

Of the three of them, Richard, dressed simply in brown slacks and a checkered shirt, was the most unassuming. His accent, a gentler version of a Texas twang, and his light-blond hair and naturally wrinkle-free face—even though he was well into his sixties—made him look like he could be your next-door neighbor. Except Richard Ingram was one of the giants of the energy business and worth over $8 billion.

As if they had planned it beforehand—and I knew they had—Stephen added, "We believe that giving is primarily a private matter, but we also understand that our actions set a public example. That's why the three of us have pledged to donate twenty million dollars—each—to what we're calling the Mayday Foundation. We're going to take a page from Robin Hood, but without stealing from others to accomplish our goals."

That was a bombshell. Instead of coming off like whiny billionaires complaining about their losses or pointing fingers at police, they had craftily shifted the talking points to how they were going to be *more like* Robin Hood.

"What are your plans for sixty million in giving?"

"First," Stephen said, "we're going to be a lot more effective than Robin Hood. The funds I'm putting in are to disrupt the generational cycle of poverty, especially for at-risk children and their families. Programs like prenatal health care and early learning and development."

Donna Chase piped up. "My funding will focus on helping the homeless find employment, and teaching and supplying families in poor areas of the country with equipment to grow their own vegetables."

Donna had the most harried look of the three. Even though her designer dress looked like it cost upward of $5,000 and she had the coiffed elegance of a billionaire, she had thick, worried bags under intense hazel eyes that seemed to be working on another problem even as she spoke to me. She was restless, too, shifting in her chair as though ready to leap up as soon as the interview was over.

Richard added, "My funding will address urgent threats that imperil humanity. Things like conservation and water scarcity. These are all issues that could bring us to our knees if we don't tackle them now."

"Clearly you were inspired to start this level of giving by Robin Hood," I said. "Even your foundation is named after the May Day celebrations that are associated with Robin Hood."

The three glanced at each other, making it clear to me that they hadn't rehearsed an answer to this question even though everything up until now was parsed, spun, and carefully positioned.

"Our *announcement* was spurred by Robin Hood," Stephen said, eyes narrowed. "But we have always recognized that giving generously is important. While it cannot repair all of the social injustice in our country or the world, it can inspire goodwill, spark innovation, and provide leadership. And we named the foundation Mayday after the international signal asking for help—not any celebration of Robin Hood."

"But would you have given so generously and established this foundation if Robin Hood hadn't brought attention to the disparity between the superwealthy and the poor and made it newsworthy and popular to be giving generously?"

"Without a doubt," Donna said, but not convincingly.

"We were already giving generously long before Robin Hood came along," Richard added with a thin laugh. "And now we've established a sixty-million-dollar fund to help finance important social initiatives, and we're recruiting others to join us. This is only the beginning."

After the interview, Donna Chase and Richard Ingram dispersed like quicksilver, and Stephen disappeared back into his house to avoid having to answer any questions that might spoil their carefully scripted interview.

Josh and Christopher rushed back to the station so the team could edit the interview, and I headed to Stephen's front door. I wouldn't normally track down an interview subject to say thank you, but Stephen wasn't only an interview subject. He was one of my father's biggest donors and friends.

The butler with the soul patch opened the front door, but he was unwilling to disturb Stephen. "Mr. Bening is on a very important telephone call," he said. "I cannot disturb him."

"I need to relay something from my father. Senator Hale Bradley."

Those appeared to be the magic words, as he then ushered me down the labyrinth of hallways back to the study. He flung open the two wooden doors with a flourish, and even though I'd experienced it once before, I got a similar thrill, as though I had stepped into a grand movie.

The library in the study was smaller than the formal library in the rotunda but still impressive, with beautifully bound books arranged in categories on dark oak shelves. One shelf housed science-fiction masterpieces by Arthur C. Clarke, Ursula Le Guin, and others. Another was devoted to biographies of great people such as Madame Curie, Benjamin Franklin, and Stephen Hawking. The bottom shelves were lined with various editions of children's classics—*Treasure Island*, *Robinson Crusoe*, and about a dozen different versions of the story of Robin Hood. I pulled a worn volume off the shelf and carefully turned its brittle, dog-eared pages; it recounted the exploits of Robin Hood and his merry men in nineteenth-century prose, illustrated with exquisite watercolors of Sherwood Forest. Faded handwritten notes were scrawled in some of the margins, and several passages were underlined.

As I leafed through the book, Stephen stepped into the room still engrossed in a call, his smartphone pressed to his ear. When he saw me, he quickly told the caller he'd call back.

"Everything okay?" he said.

My footsteps echoed on the marble floors as I walked across the room to shake his hand. "My father would never forgive me if I didn't thank you for allowing us to record the interview at your home."

"Not a problem." His gaze fell on the book in my hand. "Give your father my regards."

"Whose idea was it really to set up this sixty-million-dollar fund?"

"As we said, we all came up with it together."

"It wasn't my father's idea? A way to paint all of you in a more positive light?"

"Your father is brilliant, but this one isn't his idea," he said. "Why is it so hard to believe that we would like to bring light and hope into this troubled world?"

I stared at him then. Not just because they were the words Robin Hood had spoken. It was the cadence in his voice. Familiar, like a flash of déjà vu.

Then I glanced down at the Robin Hood book still open in my hands. The notes in the margins started swimming before my eyes. Prickly heat raced up my spine.

"It's you," I said, my voice barely audible.

"Excuse me?" His smartphone beeped, and he glanced at it.

I stood there for a long moment, firmly planted in one place, my mouth open but no words coming out.

"Are you okay?" he said, looking up from his phone.

The words finally came out like thick molasses. "What better way to plan a heist than to rob yourself first?"

"I don't know what—"

"Because you've been robbed, that immediately takes you off the suspect list."

"I'm not sure where you're going . . ."

I set my purse on the stone table and ran my fingers through my hair, realizing I was in too far to back down. I glanced at the door and considered running toward it, but my feet felt bolted to the floor. My voice, when I finally found it, was reedy and thin. "You have the technical skills to hack into security systems and take them down. You wrote at least two papers about how security systems are far too vulnerable to attack."

He laughed. "Are you suggesting that *I'm* that Robin Hood character?"

My hands were clammy. "You're a natural leader. That's why you were named CEO of the Year and given dozens of other accolades. That's how you were able to lead a group of strangers to commit these heists."

He rolled up his left sleeve. "A lot of people have leadership skills. But you know what I'm lacking? A reason to rob estates."

The facts hurtled through my mind. It was an odd sensation, a feeling of knowing answers that hadn't yet coalesced enough that I could form sentences or speak them aloud. "What Robin Hood needed was access. Which you have. You know some of the victims and have attended fund-raising events at their homes. You are well known enough that you could walk freely around their homes at these events and get an idea of where they kept their jewelry, their luxury items, the keys to their expensive cars. No one would suspect you were casing the joint."

He looked at me as though I might be wearing a tinfoil hat. "You're making no sense." His expression turned to one of concern. "Can I get you something? Water, maybe? Perhaps you're dehydrated from the afternoon sun."

I paced the floor, trying to work out how he'd done it. "You use your access to case the joint and find out where all the good stuff is. But once you disable the alarm system, how do you get inside without any sign of forced entry?"

He handed me the water. "Exactly. You think someone like me—or anyone, for that matter—can break into highly guarded estates?"

I thought about it a moment. "You don't need to. Break in, that is. You only need access to the keys."

"Clearly something I don't have."

I unscrewed the cap and took a long swig of water. "But the valet has them. When I came to your fund-raising event—and again today—your valet took my car keys and my name. Many people leave their house keys on the same key ring, so it would be easy for the valet to copy the key and match it with a particular last name."

He went to the fireplace and opened the glass doors. When he turned a metal key on the side, blue gas flames sprung up. His tone was mocking. "So Robin Hood's entire plan hinges on some minimum wage valet finding a locksmith and copying house keys—without getting caught—while wealthy patrons are at a fund-raising event."

I stepped over to the fireplace and remembered the story about key apps Conan had pitched a few weeks ago. "Now you're patronizing me, Stephen. Because in your line of work, I'm sure you know this already. There are apps that allow you to take a picture of a key with your phone and have the key made and delivered to you. All you have to do—all the valet has to do—is take a picture with a smartphone. You used those same keys to have your team lock the doors *after* the robberies."

He relaxed into a leather armchair by the fireplace. Anyone looking at him would think he was calm, as though we were discussing the weather. But I suspected that confidence had been honed by years on the debate team and in the boardroom. "You've thought of everything. Except you're missing the big picture. *Why* would I ever rob other rich people? I have enough money of my own. In some cases, more than some of those who were robbed."

It was a solid argument, one I couldn't argue with. "That's exactly why no one would suspect you. And exactly why the stolen goods never turned up on the black market. You're wealthy enough that you didn't *need* to sell the stolen goods in order to finance your Robin Hood events." I withdrew a copy of his book from my purse and flipped to one of my many purple Post-it notes. "And you know why you did all this? Because you want to change the world. You say so in your book. 'Economic inequality is our biggest social challenge. It has reached a tipping point where eighty of the world's richest people control more than half of the world's wealth. The only way to encourage global economic growth and the survival of our companies is to ensure the welfare of the poor.'"

He leaned back in his chair and stretched his arms above his head. "Plenty of people agree with that statement. But that doesn't make them Robin Hood either."

I nodded and took a huge gulp of water, hoping it would steady the muscles that were pulsing on the back of my neck. It didn't.

"Do you *understand* you are accusing one of your father's biggest donors of being a thief? A felon?"

My stomach sank to the floor and stayed there. As I gazed at him in his dress shirt and expensive slacks, looking everything like the lord of the manor in this impressive setting, I had the sudden feeling that I was making a complete fool of myself. That I was completely wrong about him being Robin Hood, and because of his friendship with my father, he was allowing me to babble on until I reached the same conclusion. At the same time, he actually seemed to be enjoying the sparring, which made me think that perhaps I wasn't far off the mark.

"You knew the news media would be all over the heist story because it hits all of our hot buttons," I said. "Theft. Greed. And you knew that the events you planned—the event to give away scholarships, building housing for the homeless, the food backpack giveaway—would be on such big scales that they'd bring major media attention to your message."

"But here's the flaw in your thinking," he continued. "Why would I risk my entire fortune, my career, and my life to do that when I could write a twenty-five-million-dollar check to charity?"

"Again, exactly why no one else will suspect you. But I have a theory. Do you want to hear it?"

He shook his head. "Honestly? No. I've humored you long enough."

"Hear me out," I said, taking another slug of water. "Esteban Diaz comes from a life of poverty. His mother crosses the border into the United States illegally in the trunk of a car. An American man promises to marry her but vanishes when she tells him she's pregnant. Then she's a single mother with a sixth-grade education working two jobs to keep food on the table and raising a son in gang-riddled East LA."

He stood. "This is my story, true. But just because someone grew up poor, that doesn't mean he automatically chooses a life of crime. That's offensive. And more than a bit elitist. We all can't be senators' daughters."

I wanted to shout at him. But if he knew he was getting under my skin, he'd take it as a sign of weakness, and that would make him even more confident. "I'm saying you grew up in a world where your mother—Delfina—worked in estates like these. You saw firsthand that these people had everything while you had nothing. You tell a story in your book about how your mother had to pay for breaking an expensive vase and you went without Christmas presents that year."

He shot me a smug smile. "You know how many people had single mothers and grew up in East LA? They don't all grow up to be Robin Hood."

"They don't all grow up to be the CEO and founder of SalesInsight or be worth five billion either. But here's what makes you different. How did your mother die?"

He pressed his lips in a tight line. "Now you've crossed the line."

"Delfina died after falling down a flight of stairs at the estate where she was cleaning homes. Your mother worked there for twelve years, on that estate worth ten million dollars, and the owner never paid a penny for her funeral or even paid out her back wages. You were left with nothing and had to sue for the back pay."

He withdrew a black pack of cigarettes from his jacket pocket, then crossed the room to pick up a box of matches on the carved stone mantel. "What's the point of telling me my own history?"

I stepped toward the mantel. "Your mother died before you graduated high school. She never got to see you get into USC or become the founder of SalesInsight. She never saw you become a billionaire. She was gone too soon. That's why Robin Hood gives money to housekeepers making their way from the Beverly Hills bus stop to the homes they're going to clean. This is your way of making sure no one else's mother has to toil as yours did."

For the first time, a smile swept across his face. "I can see why you're a reporter. You're a weaver of stories."

"Your mother grew up in Guatemala, right?"

"Yes, what's your point?"

"You had the house she grew up in brought here from Guatemala and placed in the orchard. That's where you 'summoned the champions,' where you led the burglaries, speaking to your team via headset and watching their every move from a bank of monitors hooked up to the GoPro cameras they wore."

He lit the match and pressed it to the cigarette until it glowed red, then inhaled sharply, infusing the air with its pungent smell. He looked at the cigarette. "I named my software after my mother. Surely that's enough of a dedication to her. You think I'd rob and steal in her name?"

He looked out the window, his eyes distant. For a moment, I felt bad for bringing up his mother. But then I realized there was a reason he was captain of a winning debate team in college. He was good at controlling the discussion. I sensed the gaze out the window was a stall tactic, a way for him to make me feel bad and allow him to gather his thoughts. But it wasn't going to work.

"The reason why you—why Robin Hood—came forward and did the interview with me was to explain and apologize for injuring the housekeeper during the Palazzo de Bella Vista heist. It must have been hard on you when a housekeeper—someone like your own mother—was seriously injured in your own heist."

He turned away from the window and looked at me. Anger flickered briefly in his eyes, then disappeared. "You're grasping at straws."

"With your mother gone, how did you get to attend USC? You told me an anonymous donor gave you a scholarship. So you already knew firsthand the benefit of receiving anonymous generosity from others. The power it has to lift you up from sheer poverty and loss to becoming one of the world's great innovators."

"It is a good story. But it's a fairy tale with a false ending."

"I never expected you to confess to being Robin Hood, of course. How could you when it would land you straight in jail?"

He fixed a hard gaze on me. "I'm not the Robin Hood you're looking for, Kate."

"Your entire book is about changing the world. You're telling me that it's a coincidence that Robin Hood also leads his forces by telling them they're changing the world?"

"Lots of people want to change the world. They don't rob the wealthy to do it." He riffled through the pages of the book and then looked up at me. "You know, as a favor to your father, I went out on a limb and did *two* interviews with you. And here you are—accusing me of being a criminal."

His words hit me like a slap across the face. For a moment, I considered apologizing, then realized that was exactly what he wanted me to do. "You planned our first interview together at the height of the fever about Robin Hood—even placed the interview in this extravagant room—knowing full well that it would make the superwealthy look out of touch and unsympathetic. Anyone else would think that was proof you *weren't* Robin Hood. But in my book that's called strategic losing."

His expression remained grim, but I thought I saw something briefly light up in his eyes. "What do you do from here?"

I hadn't thought that far.

He blew a cloud of smoke. "Air your half-baked theories in a news report? My lawyers will sue for slander before your report finishes airing. Maybe instead, you'll talk to the police. But who in the police department is going to pursue this theory when there isn't a shred of evidence?"

"You've thought of everything."

He stood. "You actually hoped I'd confess to your crazy story so you could score the news story of the year. But all you've succeeded in doing is wasting my time."

CHAPTER TWENTY-FOUR

I was still shaking when I drove back to the station from Stephen's estate. I knew with blinding certainty that he was Robin Hood.

Yet there was no evidence that would prove any of my theory. Zero.

As I inched down the jammed 405, I called Jake on my cell phone. After I spelled everything out, there was a long pause on the line.

"Are you okay, Kate? You don't sound so good . . ."

"I confronted him, Jake. I told Stephen my theory that he was Robin Hood. It didn't go over well."

"No doubt," he said dryly. "You just accused him of grand larceny. Just because he had a copy of *Robin Hood* in his home library. I see where you're going with this, but—how can I say this?—we've got nothing to go on."

"But you could question him, right?"

"Maybe," he said, drawing the word out. "We can't just accuse a robbery victim of perpetrating the crime, especially a deep-pockets one with a very high profile who's already suing the police department over our botched handling of the evidence at the crime scene."

"But you'll do it, right? You'll question him?"

His voice sounded small on the car speakers. "I can't. My hearing to get off suspension isn't for a few more weeks."

I honked my horn at the Lexus driver who cut in front of me. "You're not convinced. Are you?"

"I am, but . . ."

"I hear it in your voice, Jake. Give it to me straight."

"Your theory is interesting but impossible to prove. There's nothing but a story—a good one, though—that links Bening to these crimes. Besides, the public isn't demanding that we find Robin Hood, so there's no pressure on police to go out on a limb to accuse anyone. In fact, I think the public would be fine if we just let Robin Hood keep on doing what he's doing."

"So what you're saying is that no one wants to catch or convict Robin Hood, because he's doing so much good?"

He sighed. "Kate, the mastermind you say is behind it all is not only one of the victims but also someone with a stellar reputation who's already giving millions to help the poor. Why would anyone accuse him of being Robin Hood when there isn't a single shred of evidence to link him to it?"

I drew a deep breath. "He robs the rich and gives to the poor. Then gets the media everywhere to show the over-the-top and excessive wealth the billionaires are enjoying and convinces the *victims* that the only way to salvage their image is to give hundreds of millions more to the poor."

"Right," he said softly. "Everyone wins."

After I hung up with Jake, I pulled off the freeway and sat in the car, lit only by the glow of the dashboard, realizing the magnitude of what Robin Hood had done. Millions of dollars stolen but no real victims. No evidence. No one wanted to find the criminal. The suspect was not only a robbery victim but also a high-profile philanthropist with no motive. It *was* the perfect crime.

My dad was waiting in the conference room when I returned to the station. The receptionist said he'd arrived fifteen minutes earlier and she'd ushered him into the conference room instead of asking him to wait in the lobby. She was concerned that other visitors and station employees might insist on taking photos with him or buttonhole him about some issue they wanted him to address. I was more worried about my father's reason for being there.

My breath was high in my throat as I headed to the conference room. Stephen must have called him and told him about my accusation. I knew my dad would be furious at me for putting one of his major donors through that. The fact that he had come to the station instead of calling me told me that what he had to say wasn't going to be easy to hear.

I stood outside the conference room, my hand resting on the smooth metal handle, slowing my ragged breathing and fighting the urge to flee. I closed my eyes, trying to drum up a strategy to deal with my dad's anger and defend my theory about Robin Hood, but any ideas I might have had were extinguished by my rising anxiety.

When I opened the door, my dad was sitting at the long conference table holding a bouquet of flowers. Not the kind you picked up at a grocery store but an extravagant explosion of yellow, pink, and red flowers.

"Congratulations," he said, rising and embracing me in a hug.

My dad rarely hugged for more than a moment or two, and this hug must've gone on for at least three seconds. "What for?"

"Stephen called me," he said, handing me the flowers.

I took the flowers from him, breathed in the sweet scent of hyacinth and honeysuckle. Still, my pulse raced.

"He was very happy with the interview," he continued, taking a seat in the conference chair at the head of the table. "You asked some tough questions—as he expected—but he and the others thought it went very well."

I stared at him. "That's *all* he said?"

"Your interview is a great way to go out at Channel Eleven and begin your new career at ANC."

I sank into the swivel chair next to his. "That's what Stephen said about the interview?"

He shot me a look of concern. "Yes. Weren't you happy with it?"

"Sure," I said weakly.

"Andrew Wright says you're starting at ANC in two weeks. Are you ready for the move?"

I tried to wrap my head around what he was saying, because I couldn't believe Stephen called him and didn't say a word about my accusations.

"I signed the contract, but I've changed my mind about going," I said, trying to keep my voice steady. "I know what I'm good at, Dad. Train derailments, car wrecks. Disaster. Los Angeles. *This* is where I belong."

He was silent for a long moment, then placed his hand on mine. "Katie," he said quietly. "Ever since you saw all the reports about your mother's accident in high school, you've wanted to be the reporter who investigates from the scene, uncovering what happened, who did it, and why. But you're not going to find your mother by continuing to report on car wrecks and tragedy. You're not going to understand her better."

"I'm not looking for my mother." My voice sounded strange to me, as though it were not even my own. "I'm looking for the good. For the glimmer of hope in all the tragedy."

"I know," he said softly. "Don't you see those were all the things we looked for after her accident too? Reporters talked endlessly about the three anonymous Good Samaritans who came to her rescue and pulled her out of the blazing wreckage."

I'd never considered that my search for good stemmed in any way from my mother's death. But for weeks after her death, police and journalists searched for the identities of the people who had rescued my mother. None of them ever came forward. Instead of basking in the nationwide admiration that would have been showered upon them if they'd taken credit for their good deeds, these three rescuers remained quietly anonymous.

"Then there was endless coverage of the two firefighters who gave her CPR for over half an hour," my dad said.

I'd read about the firefighters too. Their photos were plastered throughout numerous newspaper stories, and they were interviewed on TV. One was a young firefighter who had just finished his year as a "probie," a firefighter in training. The other was an experienced firefighter who had recently won the Medal of Valor for rescuing a two-year-old boy from a three-alarm fire.

"I know you memorized every detail of that night from the reporters' stories. But you're not going to find *her* in stories if you keep reporting on car wrecks and tragedy. She's already in you. The way you think. The way you see the world."

Tears clouded my eyes, and my body began to gently shake. I couldn't answer for a long while. I'd never had such an intimate conversation with my father, and my emotions were still raw from the confrontation with Stephen. "Do you think so?"

His tone lightened, and then I heard a soft joy ring out in his voice that I hadn't heard in a long time. "Truth is, she'd love your Robin Hood story as much as you do."

Another swell of tears came, and I felt them roll down my cheeks. I hadn't considered how I might be similar to my mother in any way. How could that be when she died before I was old enough to have formed any memories of her?

"She'd be proud of you, Kate."

The next morning James Russell was on ANC, yelling, "Police conspiracy! Are Los Angeles police officers behind the Robin Hood heists? Is that why they withheld key evidence at the crime scene?"

Meanwhile nearly every news channel was still chewing over the billionaires' announcement about the Mayday Foundation, whose purse had already expanded to over $170 million. "It's self-serving," one of the pundits on our network said in the morning-news magazine. "In order for there to be a global market that will further enrich these billionaires, the rest of the population must at least be able to afford housing and food. Otherwise, if no one can buy, there's nothing to sell. The super-wealthy want all the accolades for helping the poor—but it's something that ultimately benefits them in the end."

While wall-to-wall coverage of the latest development in the Robin Hood story flashed on every monitor in the newsroom, I tried to get hold of Stephen Bening. I left a message on his cell phone, called his assistant every hour, and emailed him. No response. I wanted to ask why he didn't tell my father I'd accused him of being Robin Hood. And after a night's sleep, I had more questions.

By lunchtime I was frustrated, and Stephen's assistant knew it. "Look, I can't tell you what to do," she said. "But he's probably not going to call you back."

"Did he say that?"

She hesitated. "Not exactly. But I can say that you're wasting your time if you keep calling."

She hung up.

"You look like you could use this." I turned to find Eric standing behind me, dressed in his navy-blue firefighter uniform. He handed me a cup of coffee.

"How did you get in here?"

"Security guard waved me through."

I gave him a teasing smile. "Security sure is getting very lax around here."

"I'm on my way to La Jolla for a training session. Do you have a minute?"

I glanced around the newsroom and saw several reporters watching us. Even Hannah had stopped what she was doing and set her headphones aside to get a closer look. Non–news personnel were seldom allowed in the newsroom. A firefighter in uniform was even rarer.

"Let's go somewhere less noisy," I said, then led him into the small conference room. I slid the door closed, shutting out the din of the newsroom.

"I've missed you," he said, taking my hand in his.

I drew a shaky breath. Seeing him, his brown eyes alight with excitement, was making my heart race. "I've missed you too."

"I've been thinking, and . . . I'm a complete idiot for letting you go."

"I'm the one who's a complete idiot for signing the contract in the first place."

He smiled and stroked my cheek with his hand. "You say that. And I believe you. But I also know that working at someplace like ANC is something you've always dreamed about."

"Maybe some dreams aren't all that important after all."

He met my statement with a reassuring smile. "This one is."

"Then what if we try this long distance?"

He thought about that for a moment. "I want more than that with you," he said, his eyes pleading. "I don't want to just hear on the phone about your day. I want to be a part of it."

"Where does that leave us, then?"

He opened his arms, and I moved into his embrace. Then he leaned in and kissed me long and hard. But when he pulled away, he looked even more troubled than before.

He reached out to stroke my hair. "I don't know how to make this work. I only know that I want to."

There was a swift knock at the door, and Hannah peeked her head in. "Sorry to interrupt. But the network wants a report about the Mayday Foundation. David needs you in editing now . . ."

I wasn't ready for this moment to end. "I'll be there in a few minutes."

Hannah didn't move. "He said to tell you they need you now."

Eric had a faraway look in his eyes, and I wondered what he was thinking. "I'll call you as soon as I get to La Jolla."

~

We finished the interview package and uploaded it to the network with only a few minutes to spare. Back at my desk, I sank into my chair and watched the piece air on the network news feed for the East Coast. Normally I would've been excited about having a report airing on the network, but any joy I might have felt was dampened by the ache of leaving Eric. A longing that deepened as the afternoon wore on.

Hannah sat next to me and watched the last minute of the report with me. "If this is inappropriate, tell me. But *who* was that firefighter?"

"He's the guy I'm leaving behind to go to ANC."

"You're kidding, right?" I turned to look at her. "I mean, the way he . . . well, he seems like a keeper. And the way he looks at you . . ." Her cheeks flushed bright red. "I'm shutting up now because I've definitely said way too much."

My thoughts were spinning. One moment happy at seeing him again and full of hope. The next moment feeling wiped out at the thought of leaving him.

"Okay. Seriously trying to focus now," she said. "What's next on the Robin Hood story?"

I glanced at my scribbled notes detailing my repeated attempts to contact Stephen. "I need to get Stephen Bening on the phone, but I've tried all morning, and his assistant says he's not going to call me back."

"Why do you want to talk to him?"

I wasn't ready to explain my theory about Robin Hood. "To follow up on the Mayday Foundation interview."

She thought about it for a moment. "Can you arrange it so you run into him?"

"A guy worth north of five billion dollars doesn't exactly run in the same circles as I do."

"But he's one of your father's friends. One of his biggest donors, right?"

I frowned. "I can't ask my father where Stephen Bening is."

"Yeah, probably not. But maybe he's on your father's calendar."

~

My dad's assistant, Lisa, was sharp—she could smell manipulation miles away—so I planned out every word I was going to say to her. Wrote it out like a script for a report.

"My dad wants me to stop by when he's meeting with Stephen Bening, but I've forgotten what date that is," I said to her on the phone.

"Oh, he didn't say anything about that."

"Hmm," I said. "Want me to email him for the details?"

"No, no. Let's see . . . your father is going back to DC on Thursday, so Stephen's coming in tomorrow at two thirty. I'll put you on the calendar."

"It's supposed to be a surprise. Stephen is a rare-book collector—he's got quite a library—and my dad asked me to pick up a copy of a first edition of a Raymond Chandler novel for him."

"He could've asked me to pick up the book." She sounded like her feelings were hurt.

"He only asked me because he knows how I like to haunt antique bookstores." It wasn't the least bit true, but I doubted she knew that.

She sounded distracted, which probably meant another call was coming in. "See you tomorrow at two thirty."

~

My dad ran his meetings like clockwork. Most visitors were lucky to get thirty minutes, and even though Stephen was a big donor, I suspected the meeting wouldn't last much longer than the prescribed twenty-eight minutes. I arrived at my father's office at 2:55 p.m., hoping that they were winding up the meeting so my arrival would seem spontaneous.

I carried a book in a gift bag, in case Lisa asked about it, but she was too busy coordinating some other guests and waved at me as I sped by her desk. I opened my father's office door and stepped inside, swiftly closing the door behind me.

My dad's office was furnished very conservatively. United States and California flags flanked the room, and dominating the back wall was a painting of the California hillsides back in the late 1800s. Absent from the office was any sign of technology—no laptop, no tablet, not even a TV set. My dad and Stephen were seated around a small glass-topped table. They looked up at me, startled.

"I didn't know you were meeting with anyone," I said. I'd rehearsed the line several times on the way over to make sure I could say it with some authenticity.

My dad smiled, but I could see he was confused. I'd rarely shown up at his Los Angeles office unscheduled. Not even on his birthday.

"I brought you a treat." I placed a bag from Café Luxe on the table, my heart beating so fast I thought he might be able to hear it as I leaned over.

My dad's expression went from surprise to delight. He wasn't one to indulge in pastries, but if one was placed before him . . .

"You two know each other, of course," he said. "Stephen, do you mind if Kate sits in with us for a minute or two?"

Stephen looked straight at me, his dark eyes boring a hole through me. "I think we're about done anyway, Hale." He closed a notebook on the table.

My dad didn't seem to register the tension in the room, and if he did, he was ignoring it. "That interview you all did is getting a lot of attention around the Beltway," he said. "How much has your Mayday Foundation raised so far?"

I detected a slight tremor in Stephen's voice. Was he worried I was going to accuse him of being Robin Hood in front of my father? "Nearly two hundred million. And my phone is still ringing."

"And still no solid leads on who Robin Hood is."

Stephen opened his mouth to reply, but Lisa poked her head in the office, interrupting anything he was going to say. "Your three o'clock is here, Hale. All five of them. They're pacing the floor in the conference room."

My father stood and swung on his suit jacket. Stephen stood as well, poised to leave.

"Sorry to step out," my dad said. "But I've got some disgruntled union officials down the hall, and they're not very good at waiting. I know you both can find your way out. See you in DC next month, Stephen."

He gave me a quick hug and hurried out the door. Stephen tried to follow behind him, but I stepped in his path.

"Why didn't you tell my father I accused you of being Robin Hood?" I said quietly, making sure my father was out of earshot.

"This is a clever way to get my attention. But after our last meeting I don't know what more we have to say to each other."

I closed the door slowly so as to not draw Lisa's attention. "You didn't answer the question."

He rubbed his jaw. "Your father and I are friends. What would I have to gain from embarrassing you by telling him your outrageous theory?"

I shrugged. "Perhaps to pressure me *not* to file a report about you being Robin Hood?"

"I'm not Robin Hood, Kate, but I'm flattered that you thought I was. Because off the record, even though I was robbed, I've come to admire him."

I took a step back. "*You* admire him?"

He pushed the hair out of his face. "When I first started SalesInsight, we were operating out of a converted warehouse in downtown LA, just on the edge of Skid Row. No matter how many times I walked through the area, I couldn't believe I was in a civilized society, in the richest nation in the world. I always expected someone would show up and say, *I've got to change this*. Then Robin Hood did."

I leaned on the edge of my father's oak desk. "But as you said in your first interview with me, stealing is always wrong."

"It is. But I think what he did was brilliant. If we could get ten of the one hundred richest Americans to give a small fraction of their wealth, we could solve Skid Row. We could solve childhood hunger in this country."

"You didn't say any of that in our interview. You called it theft. A felony."

"It was theft. But have you considered that sometimes theft can be used for good? Everyone benefited. The wealthy lost nothing—insurance will replace what Robin Hood stole—and he inspired many of us to think differently about our wealth and how we can use it to change lives."

"Sounds like something Robin Hood might say."

He shifted his weight to the other leg. "Who were the victims, Kate?"

"There were at least two. Your team member is still in a coma after being trapped in the fire. And a housekeeper was seriously injured."

He adjusted the sleeve on his gray sport coat. "I'm sure Robin Hood regrets both of those. But think about a firefighter. If one of them loses a life or is injured in the pursuit of helping another, no one says firefighters shouldn't be saving people in disasters. We accept that loss as the price of doing good. The Robin Hood team member was doing good. It's a tragic loss, but he's helping change the world."

"Again, sounds like something Robin Hood would say."

"If we're pointing fingers, you could say that you played a pretty big part in Robin Hood's plan."

I raised an eyebrow. "*I* did?"

"Robin Hood's mission would've been impossible if the public didn't know about it. When police were covering up evidence, Robin Hood needed someone to make the connection between the coins found at the crime scenes and at the large-scale giving events. He needed you to tell the story in a way that people would understand what's at stake. Whoever Robin Hood is, he needs someone exactly like you."

"Exactly like *me*."

"A reporter who understands that things are not always what they seem. Who's looking for good in the midst of the crime and tragedy. Wasn't it you who broke the story about Good Sam a few months ago? Maybe that story showed Robin Hood that one person could change the world." He strode to the door and opened it. "As much as you needed Robin Hood to get the Story of the Year, Robin Hood needed you."

"You say need*ed*. As though it's over . . ."

"I'm willing to bet your Robin Hood is finished with robbing estates. I'm sure he regrets that two people were injured in the robberies. And now that he's started a movement for shared prosperity and even the billionaires themselves are giving to the cause—I can't see why he needs the heists to continue."

"You're done with the heists?" My eyes met his, but he said nothing. "Will you just admit that *you* are Robin Hood?"

"Who is Robin Hood? That's what you want to know, isn't it? To me, Robin Hood is anyone who fights the system that permits politicians or wealthy individuals to amass too much power and control over our world. Robin Hood is anyone who works hard to help others."

"And if you were this Robin Hood?" I asked quietly. "Would you tell me?"

He paused for a moment, drumming his fingers on the edge of the door. "Robin Hood would never confess to anyone."

CHAPTER TWENTY-FIVE

I had the Story of the Year.

As I raced back to the newsroom, I knew that my discovery of Robin Hood's identity would make headlines and catapult my report into the national spotlight for weeks. Every news outlet was talking about him, seemingly nonstop—Robin Hood was donating homes to the homeless, giving cars to the working poor, distributing thousands of food baskets, and funding hundreds of college scholarships. Viewers, inspired by Robin Hood, were joining in. There were stories of people painting their elderly neighbors' homes, of car dealers donating vans to disabled veterans, and single-mom waitresses receiving 200 percent tips.

"The legend of Robin Hood is that he's an outlaw living on the outskirts of society," I could say in my report. "But the Robin Hood behind the sophisticated, high-tech heists of the one hundred wealthiest Americans' estates—is one of the richest men in America."

Yes, I had no evidence. No proof. I had absolutely nothing a reporter usually relied upon. But I had a story that would touch viewers' hearts. A story about a poor boy from Guatemala who became a multibillionaire and dreamed up a perfect crime to give to the poor, the sick, and the homeless; to challenge the superwealthy to put their unused wealth to work changing lives for the better; and to inspire others to join in his mission to bring light and hope into the world.

But as I sat at my computer back in the newsroom, my heart pounding with the thrill of finally getting to reveal Robin Hood's identity, my fingers froze at the keyboard.

What *good* would it do to expose Stephen as Robin Hood? Especially now that he had disclosed—without admitting to being Robin Hood—that he had ended the heists.

The truth is all that matters. Since the moment I set foot in my first journalism class, every professor and every news director I had worked for since had repeated the same mantra: reporters must hold tight to rigorous reporting of the truth.

I had believed that.

But Robin Hood was changing the world for the better—a world where thousands of people would not have to worry about a meal tonight, where hardworking, smart kids could afford to go to college, and homeless shelters had beds and meals so families could get off the streets.

Exposing Robin Hood's identity would end all that.

"What're you going to do, Kate?"

I swung around to see David heading my way, a Dr Pepper in his hand.

My face flushed. Did he know that I'd figured out who Robin Hood was? I stood. "What do you mean?"

"I mean, what are you going to do for your last report on Channel Eleven tomorrow?"

"I'm planning to reveal Robin Hood's identity."

He laughed. "Well, that would be a helluva way to go out. With the biggest story of the year."

I was about to launch into the details and then decided not to. I'd become a reporter to find the silver lining. To make a difference. And in that moment I realized that the best way—the only way—to do that was to keep silent about Robin Hood's identity.

"Of course I'm kidding," I added with a little too much enthusiasm.

"You had me going there for a second. But seriously, you can choose your own assignment on your last day. Anything you want to cover."

"Anything? So I could do a story on a hunch no one else has, with no witnesses on tape and no evidence?"

"Yeah, probably not that." He smiled, a twinkle in his eye. "I'm gonna miss you. And in case I don't get to say anything later . . . good luck at ANC. You deserve it."

"Thank you," I said, hugging him.

He patted me on the back like a coach might do. "And if you hate it there—and you probably will—don't think you can come back and get another reporting gig at Channel Eleven."

It was my turn to stare at him.

"Now I'm the one pulling your leg," he said, grinning. "Go there and kick some butt."

He hugged me again. And as he let go, he looked at me with moist eyes. "Show them how it's done."

The sweet scent of honeysuckle hung in the air as I stood outside the gates of Stephen's estate and filed my last report for Channel Eleven. His Château du Soleil was drenched in sunshine this afternoon, glittering in the warm afternoon light like a beacon of hope.

I'd already had a goodbye lunch back at the station, and when I was asked to say a few words, I tried to sound lighthearted about my departure and new adventure. But as I spoke and glanced over the room, I felt tears gathering in my eyelashes. I was going to miss Hannah as my producer and researcher most. Maybe I could convince ANC to bring her aboard too? I was even going to miss David and his lectures. And I couldn't imagine covering stories with any cameraman but Josh. Who would ever put up with me like he did?

My knees shook as Josh trained his camera on me for the last time. "Is it possible to commit a perfectly good crime?" I started. "Could you plan and carry out crimes of massive proportions—tens of millions of dollars—where there were few victims, and yet the proceeds from the crimes provided college scholarships to hundreds of poor students, thousands of backpacks filled with food for the struggling poor, housing for the homeless and working poor, and more?

"If you were Robin Hood, why would you risk everything to commit such a perfectly good crime? First, you'd have a consuming passion to change the world. A passion shaped by your own experiences with crushing poverty, perhaps, or observing others living in squalor in places like Skid Row. A passion so powerful you could convince good people to knowingly commit a crime. Second, you'd have an entrepreneurial spirit and experience that makes you believe that you have the power to change the world. Third, you'd also have to believe that by taking this risk, you'd be bringing global attention to the plight of the poor, inspiring others to join in changing the world, and ultimately convincing the wealthy victims themselves to join in your crusade. And last, you'd need a willing news media to pause from wall-to-wall coverage of crime, tragedy, and violence to trumpet the good you're doing.

"The Robin Hood story lives—like most important stories—in the murky shades of gray between what's good and what's not. Yet there *is* such a thing as a perfectly good crime. And that's why this reporter—who also suspects that the heists are now over—has stopped trying to uncover Robin Hood's identity and is focusing instead on the light and hope he's bringing into the world."

My report opened the six o'clock newscast. A half hour later, the air had a surreal feel to it as I watched Josh put the equipment away in the news van. It seemed impossible that I had just filed my last report for Channel Eleven and that my next report would be from New York, a city I'd visited but had never lived in.

When I unlocked the passenger door to the news van, I spotted a manila envelope on the front seat. Josh always locked the van, so I was puzzled by how it got there. *Kate Bradley*, it read.

"Did you put this envelope in here?" I called out to Josh, feeling the envelope's contents. Whatever was inside was thicker than paper. Clothing, maybe.

"What envelope?" he asked.

I tore it open. Inside was a green felt hat with a red feather. Exactly like the one Jake had shown me—off the record—that was found at the estate crime scenes. As I lifted the hat, a note fluttered to the floor.

"Saw your report, Kate. Thank you for helping change the world. Esteban."

CHAPTER TWENTY-SIX

Traffic was surprisingly light as I headed home late that evening. In fact, it was so light on a long stretch of the 101 that I began to wonder if Super Bowl Sunday had come around or aliens had abducted thousands of Angelenos' cars. I was seriously considering both theories when traffic came to a sudden crawl.

My cell phone rang, and Eric's photo flashed on the screen. I put him on speaker.

"Hey," he said, his warm baritone soothing my traffic-frazzled nerves. "I'm in La Jolla now. I've been doing a lot of thinking since we talked in the newsroom."

"Me too."

I heard the roll of the ocean waves behind him.

"Where are you?"

"At the beach. I came here to think. There's something here that you have to see. Something . . . that makes everything clear."

My breath hitched. I was desperate for everything to be clear. "What is it?"

"I can't describe it in words. Would you come here and see it with me?"

His words, gentle and warm, floated in the air. La Jolla was over a hundred miles south of Los Angeles. Two hours in traffic. But I would have crossed mountains and time zones and rivers to see him.

"Everything will be clear," he said.

I pressed hard on the accelerator and smiled, my heart dancing at the possibility.

~

By the time I reached the beach in La Jolla, a seaside community on the Pacific Ocean, the sun had already set. I felt a rush of anticipation as I parked my car on a side street and, following Eric's instructions, started toward a narrow sandy path that led to La Jolla Cove, a beach tucked between towering sandstone cliffs.

The moon was hidden by a thick blanket of clouds, turning the grayish night skies black. I heard the sounds of the waves lapping onshore, but a bluff blocked my view of the ocean. A few steps along the dark path, I spotted Eric waiting for me. He was dressed in shorts and a gray T-shirt, and his feet were bare. He smiled like a kid with a surprise.

"Close your eyes," he said. Then he stepped behind me and placed his hands over my eyes. "You can't see through my fingers, can you?"

"Nope. Where are we going?"

"Ten more steps and you'll see."

I walked in front of him along the sandy path, and after he counted off ten steps, he lifted his hands from my eyes.

What I saw took my breath away. The water was lit up by an eerie light, like molten blue metal rippling through the waves. Onshore, the view was even more astounding, as billions of tiny neon-blue dots on the sand made it look like twinkling stars had washed ashore.

"I knew you'd love it," he said.

"What is it?" I whispered, afraid to break whatever spell had been cast on the ocean. And on me.

"It's bioluminescent phytoplankton. It's only found a few places in the world. Sometimes it lasts for a week. Sometimes only a few days."

We stood there a long while, watching the waves roll in and lap the shore, then bubble on the sand—a few white stars twinkling overhead, blue glow on the sands, and dazzling patterns at the water's edge.

"Remember chasing fireflies in the orchard?" he asked quietly.

My eyes scanned the beach. "This is like those fireflies a million times over."

He scooped some wet sand and showed me the glowing blue specks. "When we caught a few fireflies, you said it was like capturing a tiny star. Then I knew. That's when I knew you were the one, Kate."

He turned toward me, and the look in his eyes left no doubt he meant it.

I blinked back tears, feeling like the neon waves slipping onto the beach, one moment certain of my direction, and then realizing I was being pulled in another. I gazed at the ocean, at the neon-blue lights carving the shadows and lighting up the waves, certain they were flashing me a message. *Stay here. This is where you belong.*

Eric took my hand in his. "One of the things I love about you is that you have big dreams. Important dreams. I could see it the night you interviewed the billionaires about their Mayday Foundation. And I realized it again when you told me you wanted to tell stories to change the world. You have to follow your dreams to New York, Kate."

"You want me to go?"

"Your dreams are as important to me as they are to you. If your dreams are taking you to New York, that's where I want to be too."

I stared at the sliver of the moon peeking out from the clouds, luminous over the blue ocean. "But you *can't* go with me."

"After we talked yesterday, I asked the fire chief to put in a good word for me high up in the chain of command of New York's fire department. It'll take a long time to get trained and certified there, but in the meantime, there might be work for me training their fire teams in swift-water rescue."

"*Might* be work?"

"That's good enough for me right now."

A warm sea breeze ruffled my hair as I leaned into him, feeling the heat between us, his arms around me. "What about *your* dreams?"

"Don't you see?" he whispered. "Because of you, all my dreams have changed. Now, everything I have ever wanted, everything I dreamed about, only matters if you're with me."

My throat ached. "You can't—you shouldn't—give up everything for me."

He reached out and touched my cheek. "When I saw this glow-in-the-dark beach last night, all I could think of was you and how much you would love it. Then I realized that even this rare, mysterious, glowing liquid fire meant nothing if I couldn't share it with you. A firefly in an orchard is just an insect. Lights in the dark. But when I'm with you, they're tiny stars in your hands, lights swirling around our heads." He cupped my face in his hands. "I *want* to do this, Kate. This is me starting on a new adventure, a new chapter. With you."

Our eyes met for a long moment. A warm shiver radiated through me as I grasped the depths of his feelings for me. The realization both overwhelmed and soothed me, and the moment took on the heightened fullness of a powerful dream.

I fell in love with him all over again. The first kiss was fast, too heady, taking me by surprise as his mouth moved hungrily on mine. But the next kiss was slower, generous. Heat rushed from my center, and my breath caught high in my throat. Even with the brilliant neon-blue light show playing in the waves behind us, there was nothing else in the world but him.

For the first time, I knew where I was headed and exactly where I belonged.

ACKNOWLEDGMENTS

I cannot tell you the exact moment the story line for *Perfectly Good Crime* crystallized enough for me to begin writing it. Ideas had swirled and danced around me for months, sometimes monopolizing my dreams. I had captured them in notebooks but had not yet begun to put them into a story. Then the first novel in the Kate Bradley Mystery series—*Good Sam*—came out, and I started hearing from hundreds of readers. Like me, they were seeking good in the world—some shared stories of real-life Good Samaritans, while others told me of their own acts of kindness for strangers. I was inspired by their posts, their stories, their letters. And their questions. "What will it take to bring worldwide attention to helping those who are less fortunate?" a reader in Michigan wrote. From these connections with readers came a desire—an obsession, really—to write another mystery about the search for good, with Kate Bradley and Eric Hayes at the center.

Perfectly Good Crime would not be possible without help from many readers of early drafts. Thanks to author and friend Kes Trester, who was certain I could write a sequel to *Good Sam* and gave many constructive notes; reporter and producer Barbara Schroeder, who helped me work through Kate's dilemmas as a journalist; authors Lori Costew, Lisa Wainland, and Darlene Quinn, who read drafts with an eye for consistency; and screenwriters Joan Singleton, Catherine Vanden Berge, and Debrah Neal, who helped me keep the story twists in line.

I was also fortunate to have guidance from Larry Collins, a battalion chief of the Los Angeles County Fire Department, who advised on fire department procedures. Thanks also to Los Angeles Police Department senior lead officer Julie Nony for help with police department details. My knowledge of online games is limited, so I had help from my son, Jake, who steered me through that story line. And perhaps no one knows this manuscript better than my daughter, Lauren, a budding writer herself, who listened as I read the manuscript aloud at various stages.

Bringing this novel into your hands required the talented work and vision of Lake Union editor Christopher Werner and editor Angela Brown along with the attention to detail of copy editors Riam Griswold and Susan Stokes.

I'm truly grateful for all of their support—and to you for choosing to read *Perfectly Good Crime*.

ABOUT THE AUTHOR

Like her heroine Kate Bradley, award-winning and bestselling author Dete Meserve is always looking for people who are doing extraordinary good for others. Instead of tracking a killer or kidnapper, Meserve's mysteries seek to uncover the helpers, the rescuers, and the people who inspire us with selfless acts of kindness. *Good Sam* is the first Kate Bradley Mystery, followed by *Perfectly Good Crime*. Kate also plays a pivotal role in Dete's stand-alone novel *The Space Between*, helping protagonist Sarah Mayfield solve the mystery behind her husband's disappearance. The film adaptation of *Good Sam* will premiere on Netflix in spring 2019.

When she's not writing, Meserve is a film and television producer and a partner in Wind Dancer Films. She lives in Los Angeles with her husband and three children—and a very good cat that rules them all. For more on the author and her work, visit www.detemeserve.com, or connect with her on Twitter @DeteMeserve and on Facebook at Facebook.com/GoodSamBook.